Praise for

The Road to Etheral

Book Three of the Imperealisity Series

I am ready for that next book! Impressive! I'm looking forward
to seeing what those next adventures are going to be! Mr. Wayne
has made me wish I was there with Marty and his friends...
Stephen Pacios, Kennewick Washington

I enjoy the read of Marty, Bailey, and Steve as they continue
to surprise the readers in this series with all of the new
adventures and events. I have been able to unwind in this
mysterious world of magic and excitement as they travel and
find they have new powers and new ways to use them.
I am looking forward to reading the next books in this series.
Jan Altergott, Kennewick, Wash.

The Road to Etheral

Book Three of the Imperealisity Series

Gary Wayne

To order additional copies of this book, contact:
Xlibris
1-888-795-4274
www.Xlibris.com
Orders@Xlibris.com
789088

CONTENTS

DEDICATION

I hope all of you who read my books enjoy them as much as I enjoy writing them. To find a story you like to read is always a step in your learning process, from your very first book as a child to your favorite books in your teens and adulthood. As you travel on your adventures in life, you will find it has always been reading that gives you the real facts, the true way to gain knowledge about everything happening around you and in the world.

It is you I dedicate this book to as you will be among the voices to be heard in the years to come. I wish you the very best in your education, and I hope you will never stop reading all the books you love.

Gary Wayne

ACKNOWLEDGMENTS

I have found over the years that no matter what I write, someone else needs to proofread it for me. In that manner, I won't look like a massive waste of mismatched words and unfound punctuation. I have always enjoyed writing, producing articles for independent news media across our nation, and creating commentaries for Facebook and Twitter.

Having produced a storyline of this magnitude with over eighty thousand words, it is my intention to make sure you can understand all my thoughts, all the ideas and feelings I have placed in the pages you read.

So I wish to say thank you to a couple of very wonderful people who took the time out of their busy lives to check this work.

Marilyn Taylor of Berkeley, California, and Kennewick, Washington
Karen Ramage of Tacoma and Pasco, Washington

As I write, I simply hit the keys and then have to return and reread it all, but these ladies are the ones who make me look professional. They are the ones who make sure all the *t*'s are crossed and *i*'s are dotted.

They place the punctuation where it belongs to make sure everything I have written explains a story that has come from my mind.

INTRODUCTION

Suddenly there was what sounded like someone pounding on one of those huge church bells about five times some distance away from us. I thought, "What the hell is that?"

Then Steve said the same thing I had been thinking aloud, "What the hell is that?"

The Elders split up then some headed our way and the one left with Steve, said, "All of you must get inside to be safe."

Everyone looked around as all the guards ran to separate locations near those huge crossbows and the King and Queen were escorted inside. The Elders came over to us and said, "It looks like we will soon be under attack so, all of you must go inside now for protection."

"What do you mean for protection, we need to see what this is," I said.

All of us were looking at the sky. I still felt something but at that moment whatever it was just seemed to be calm as it did not seem to present a threat. It still felt like a bird, and it seemed to be just flying. It was a good distance from us.

I asked, "Where is this attack happening?"

"Our outer towers have rung the alarm bells so now everyone in our city and around it must get inside."

"So, you're telling me it's not near us now correct?"

"Yes, that is correct."

"I feel something, but it's a huge bird. I don't feel anger, hate or hostility, but it is coming our way." I told the Elder.

"That is probably what will attack us." He said.

As it got closer, I told everyone to get ready in case we must protect the people. Most of the team were in different areas. Sophia pulled out five arrows and stuck them in the ground near her.

We waited, as the King, Queen, was inside looking out and I notice many of those who waited on us standing next to them. Some of the Elders were brave enough to stay just outside of the building but close enough to get inside if need be. The guards were set up by the huge crossbows ready for whatever it could be that would attack us.

I was looking around to see where everyone was and out of the side of my eye, suddenly, I noticed something huge then that feeling I had of a calm flying big bird turned into the thoughts and feelings of food along with hunger.

CHAPTER 1

Travels on a New Road

Well, there have been several events in as many days. We had fought a beast, seen amazing birds and weird animals, and even saved a god.

Yes, a real god. We had freed people from slavery and found many new friends.

We ran into little people who were called Denarians, and they gave serious thought to robbing us of a wagon and horses. They had traveled many weeks, lost their way, their horses, their wagon and never located what they were seeking. They realized they had a long walk ahead of them to return home. All of them felt they had let down the elders, and an invisible creature was still destroying the lands they loved.

Before meeting all of us, they wished to find a way to return and help others battle that invisible foe in their homelands. It has been said that whatever was destroying the property and people started in the western regions. They had stopped to find out if it would be easy to take a wagon and horses from us. As things progressed, they found retrieving those items would be more of a challenge than they were ready to face. Some of the events that took place allowed us to help them change their minds on what they would do next. I was sure what we did to assist them in locating what it was they came looking for, permitted them to make a wise decision to become part of our adventurous team.

Now two wagons are leaving Mike and Marilyn's place. One wagon is heading north. The other wagon with our group is headed south. Our team has decided to find out if we could help the Denarians with the problem they have in the region where they live.

It seems our base camp will be located high on a hill just above Mike and Marilyn's property. We now have a good number of people we saved joining us, as they wished to create new lives helping on the land we just received. All of them will be building new homes and helping one another in any manner they can. It's not close to our entrance into this world, but the land encompassess all the eye can see. Where we are leaving from at this time is about a five-day walk from our home, which just happens to be in another world.

We have managed a great deal over this past week, finding that it just gets more exciting with every mile we travel.

The wagon headed north is journeying back to a farm near the entrance to this world. George and his wife April own farmlands near that area and are headed home with a new member of our team. Riding along with them in case they run into trouble, is one of the Denarians who recently joined us to save this planet and the people on it. High above them fly two dragons, Sky and Jasmin, who were sent to protect all of us. All of them will soon meet with my mom and grandmother and Steve's and Bailey's mothers. It will take them three to four days to travel that distance as they will be in the wagon.

George and his wife have been ready to travel home for some time. They have been worrying about their property and home after seeing their neighbors missing. They will be happy to see their farm and, of course, now our mothers and Gram. They have been, I guess you could say, babysitting the farm to protect it in case of problems.

Some of the people we freed from slave labor wished to build new lives and homes for themselves and others, along with farming to grow and raise more products to sell. Some of them know how to make toys, things like bows and musical instruments similar to what Mike creates. They have said they will make more of them to sell. They will also be collected and stored in a new building. In that manner, anytime people must travel to town, they can have things to barter with or merely sell.

They will also be creating our new base camp and running a legal lumber mill operation. A couple of the Denarians have stayed to engineer some of the building projects and create them. Oscar is a building designer. Ruther is a master woodworker. Another, who goes by the name of Magic, has found her place in life, it seems, as a cook. We also have a new protector for our camp, who is called Winterish. Between her and her companion, which just happens to be a huge bear, I don't think there will be any problems with outsiders.

It seems our base camp is going to grow since we have found out all that land on the hill is being turned over to Steve, Bailey, and me by Constable Warren Mc Daniels. He was the one who told us we had helped round up a group that had cost them lots of scriptable over the past few years. I know it sounds weird to call money scriptable, but I was thinking about that after I had heard what they call cash and remember reading about places back home that used the word *script* as money. So maybe that is one more connection between worlds other than our entrance.

I've been told in this world, it is not your age that makes you a leader but your wisdom and desire along with strength. I have found the three of us can do amazing things, things we could never do at home, but I still feel like myself. One thing is for sure it seems we have gained a lot of new knowledge over here. Our wizard says in this world, it is because Mother Earth is teaching us new things every day.

Our wagon heading south is going to be on the road, traveling about 150 miles. All of us know what that last wagon ride was like from the entrance of this world to Marilyn and Mike's place. So this time, we put a few more bales of straw in the back of both wagons to ride on. Tasha, Datilina, and Bailey, holding Tabby, were riding up front.

In the rear of the wagon was Jack, our wizard or, as many in this world wish to call him, "the wise one." Burdock, who is the leader of the Denarians, is seated next to him. Both are settled with their

3

backs to the front of the wagon bed, their backs pressed against all our packs and a few other bags. It was as if they were looking behind us. The rest of us found places along the sides of the wagon. So, all of us stretched out and had plenty of room.

I must say I am pleased we have a good-sized wagon as it's longer and broader than a standard wagon, I have been told. I guess I am comparing it to the U-Haul trailers my dad used from time to time back home. This wagon was wide and we could lie across the width, stretch out, and sleep comfortably. George said it was designed for larger loads.

George and April's daughters, Heather and Krystle, were sitting next to me. They have their pets with them, as I have Ziggy with me. Yes, in case you don't know it, Ziggy is my ferocious, cute little furball monster masher.

Steve and his ferret, Max, were sitting across from me with Vanessa, he on one side of her and her pet pig, Agatha, on the other side. All of us have our packs set in the front of the wagon, but our sleeping bags have been placed behind us for pillows.

I mentally asked Steve, *what do you think of our adventures so far?*

Marty, I was never expecting anything like what we have been involved in. I know when I spoke to my mother, she could not believe any of what we have done so far.

Well, we now have a long way to travel in this wagon, and it could be a four- or five-day trip, I replied.

I know, but we did toss a few more bales of straw in the back this time, Steve mentioned.

Speaking out, I commented, "We all might as well get comfortable and enjoy the ride." After a few hours of traveling, we noticed a few other farms with corn and animals, so I asked Vanessa, "This is the way to town. Is that correct?"

"Yes, it is, Marty. There are two towns on this road. Of course, it depends on which turn we take at what they call the crossroads. I don't know why they call them that because they really don't cross each other. They just split. One path goes somewhat to the right. The other one goes a little bit to the left. It generally takes about a full day to get to each of the towns."

Heather said, "Dad stops and trades with many of the other farmers along the way. Then he shops when we get to town."

Steve asked, "What does he customarily take to trade?"

Krystle commented, "Dad takes some of the things he makes and some of the produce we grow about twice a month and about once a year. He gathers up chickens with produce to trade. Most of the things we need, we can trade for. Dad loves just visiting all the people."

Vanessa commented, "Dad said your parents loved to travel to town with him and our mother. They enjoyed getting to know all the shop owners and some of those who owned farms along the way."

"Burdock, what can we expect to see around your area? I mean, mountains, rivers, storms—and how many people?" I asked.

"Marty, a part of the country is covered with mountains, much of them covered in trees. Of course, like here, there are large areas of open fields and crops. Many of the people make homes on the sides of the cliffs, but we have homes like you will see in the town before us as well. In my hometown of Etheral, you will see a huge mountain where most of the townspeople live. The king and queen, along with the elders, reside there as well."

"I have always heard of homes located on or near cliffs. However, I have never seen them, so that will be cool."

He asked, "Cool? What do you mean, 'cool'?"

I replied, "Homes made on the cliffs of mountains are always cool."

"It's routinely warm in our area, and the homes on the cliffs have a moderate temperature all year round," he said.

"Cool is just a way of saying 'neat,' 'great,' 'awesome,' or 'good.'"

"Oh, I see. So, cliff homes are cool," he replied.

"Yes, they are."

"Most of our people live quiet lives and raise small families. We are like most who live off the land, as we do all we can to make sure and protect Mother Earth. Many people in our homeland are craftsmen and create wonderful things," he continued.

5

I suddenly got a thought from Jasmin saying, *We are following George and April up to their farm. April says those who are waiting for all of us will be so happy to see Mom and me.*

I replied, *I am sure they will as Mom and Gram will be excited like all get out to see both of you.*

Well, it's going to be a few days, it seems, so we will just follow and camp near them and make sure they are safe, Jasmin said.

Thank you. I know they will feel much better having both of you there. Keep in touch and let me know if there are any problems. If you run into trouble, I will send a small 747 your way.

A what? she asked.

You know, when Max changes into a huge eagle, I stated.

Oh yes. Okay, all of you, stay safe.

We will, and see you both again soon, I replied. I sent a thought to my mom and said, *Mom, hello. This is your awesome, excellent, and perfect son.*

She said, *Marty, I can tell you have been over here too long.*

I just mentally had a conversation with a dragon, and she is traveling with her mother and watching over George and April on their way back. So, you and all the others will soon have a chance to see real dragons. That's two real dragons.

That is so great, Marty. You know your grandmother will have a heart attack when she sees them.

Mom, I sure hope not. It will be a few days before they get there, so you can warn her ahead of time. I bet our fathers would love to see them as well. You might want to give them a heads-up and let them know.

I will send a message to them. Then they can come over in about two or three days if that is about the time they should arrive, she said.

That might be a wonderful thing for all of you to see. Anything happening on the farm?

No. Everything is just fine as far as we can tell.

George was concerned because we had stopped at his neighbor's about half a day away from their place and found no one around.

From what he was saying, they never leave their farm without someone there. He figured the entire family is missing.

That's why he was concerned? she asked.

Yes. Let the others know it might be best if they keep their eyes open.

We will. So, you're not returning with George and April? she inquired.

No. There is a new team member with them by the name of Meesha who is protecting them and, of course, two dragons flying overhead. The rest of us are traveling a good distance south to see if we can stop something that is destroying the lives and homes of Denarians. Sounds like they have an interesting problem.

Will you be able to help them? she probed.

We are not sure as we are not even sure what the problem is. But I hear whatever has been destroying the Denarian lands is invisible.

Invisible? she asked.

Yes. That is what they have said, but of course, we won't know until we get there.

Marty, are you kids ready for that kind of stuff?

Mom, I think from all I have heard, it is the three of us who will save those people. We have already done some amazing things. Everything we have been told about their prophecy says we are here to protect what they call Mother Earth.

Well, I wish your fathers could be with you because I know they could help you just as we could.

I know, Mom, but we are kind of stuck with all of you there, and our fathers are working. The only way all of you could help us is if George found someone else to watch the farm.

I know, and when George gets here, we will be having a discussion. All of us have a feeling you will need our help soon.

Mom, let's just hope things go all right. Tell the others I said hello and that everyone here is doing well.

Okay, son. Hope to see you soon.

You will, I replied.

Steve asked, "How long have we been traveling?"

Vanessa said, "Not sure, but it has been a suitable number of hours. I can tell you that."

Tasha must have heard all of us moving around and talking. As most of us were wondering if we were stopping soon, she yelled back, "Any of you ready for a break?"

Of course, everyone said, "Yes," "You bet," "Let's do it," "I'm game," and "Yes, I am ready."

So Tasha found an open location near a field and pulled over. Then we all climbed out of the back of the wagon. I pulled out the ramp. Then the animals descended to join us. It was nice to be walking about instead of just sitting. Soon, all of us were chatting about something to eat.

CHAPTER 2

First Lunch Break on the Trip

"Vanessa, what do we have for lunch?" I asked.

"We have lots of water and our orange drink, as you call it, and we have a lot of Mom's homemade bread along with her soup."

Bailey said, "That sounds great to me."

Burdock and Jack were both ready for some of that soup, and Jack commented, "Vanessa, your mother is one great cook, and her homemade bread is about as good as I have ever had."

"I agree with that. I am just pleased that she took the time while she was at Marilyn's to bake up more loaves of bread," I said.

Vanessa commented, "Mom told me you asked about how we keep things cold, and she informed you we use plants. She said I should show you how we do it. We will be picking more plants as we go along so we can show you how that's done. The next time I need to make some up, we can sit down, and I will show you and the others how easy it is to create the cold."

"It will be good to see how you do that just in case any of us ever have a need to keep any food cold."

"I will show you how to find the plants first. We need to locate a place that has a sizable number of them. We will mix them with soil and water, then squeeze them out into patties so they can remain cold," Krystle replied.

Heather said, "Marty, it really is easy."

Tasha spoke up, saying, "Let's all grab something to eat."

Everyone walked to the back of the wagon, where Vanessa set up the baskets and jugs of water. She passed out bowls and cups. Next, everyone helped themselves to stew and slices of April's homemade bread.

I mentally asked, *Ziggy, how are you doing? You sure have been quiet over the past few hours. Are you sick or something?*

No. Just enjoying the ride this time as the last time was very rough. I'm not sick.

I am pleased to hear that. I would hate to see my little Amazon beast bouncer getting sick.

She replied, *You know, I kind of like being a bouncer. You know, a little smash here and a little smash there.*

I bet you do. You know, you can change anytime you like back to your warrior garb. That way, you could look more dangerous as a real bouncer.

Well, Agatha and I have said we will stay as we are until we are needed. It kind of makes others think there is less to worry about.

True. The element of surprise, I said.

Yes, and you have taught me well, Marty.

Burdock asked, "Marty, what's it like where you come from?"

"That's kind of difficult to describe in a way as we have cars and trucks instead of wagons. Those are like fancy wagons without horses. You can sit inside of them with a roof over your head. They have doors and comfortable seats, and we don't have paths. We have paved roads."

"Wow, that sounds like the future."

"Well, I guess it is for everyone here, but you know, simplicity in life is a lot better than the rush, rush, rush of a future filled with all sorts of technology."

"Tech what? What is that?" he asked.

"The word is *technology,* and it's the future when it comes to inventions. It's what an inventor creates as he produces new ideas and makes a product. I guess you can say technology is all the science, math, and education a person has in his or her life that brings about a different approach to making anything happen. It would be like, you want to build a fire. How would you do that?"

"I would gather small pieces of brush and twigs and find larger dried branches. Then I would use a match and start the fire."

"What if you never had a match but knew you could make one?"

"I have never considered that before. I suppose I would gather some pine and make several small sticks about two inches in length and very thin. Then I would have to soak them in sulfur or something like that, from what I understand."

"You have never had to make any before, have you?" I asked.

"No. I have never had to do that because when I go to town, I can get small boxes of matches."

"Well, the people who invented those matches were creating a new kind of technology."

"So what I think you're saying is when you invent something, you're using technology to do that—in other words, what you have in your brain."

"I think that is probably a good way to put it."

"I need to think about that for a bit and see if I can create some new technology," he said.

I was eating April's homemade bread, thinking, *This is really getting habit forming.* I was enjoying every mouthful as it just seems to have a quality that is delicious and very filling.

Jack asked, "What was that thing you talked about that you could sit in?"

"You mean cars and trucks?" I asked.

"Yes, I think that was what you were talking about," Jack replied.

I stated, "About a hundred years ago, many people used wagons to travel, and then people started coming up with new ideas of how to make a wagon move without horses. Last year in school, we studied the period of the 1800s in Earth years. Someone came up with a steam-powered engine that was used to move a wagon without horses."

"Wow! A way to move a wagon with no horses?" he asked.

"Yes, but that was only the start of many things to come. You see, Jack, things in this world are much simpler in my mind. This is greater than all the new industry or inventions you could ever find in our world. People here seem to have less stress and fewer problems than those at home. I mean, just trying to fall asleep at home is sometimes a real challenge because of all the things you are thinking about that will have to be done the next day."

"Marty, I get so tired at times, I can't sleep. Isn't that about the same thing?" he asked.

"Jack, from all I have seen so far over here, life is simple. It's quiet, calm, and laid back. In our world, you get stressed out just trying to make it across the street."

"Seems like you live in a real future world."

"Well, I guess one might say that as we used to think that things in the future could never be seen or ever invented. But many of those things we dreamed of a hundred years ago are a reality today. To be honest with you, I am pleased to be in your world, and I really love the way people live here. Of course, I am not sure about running into any kind of gas storm that I have heard about."

We laughed at that one.

Tasha said, "Okay, let's wrap it up and get back on the road."

I helped Vanessa move the water jugs, and Steve hopped up in the wagon, took the basket, and then set it up front, with the packs placed on top of it. The ramp had been down all this time for the animals, and now they headed back up the ramp to find a nice cozy place to settle in.

Steve came to the back of the wagon and asked Vanessa if she needed a hand to get up in the cart, and she looked at him for a few seconds and then said, "Yes, I would like that." Soon, the two of them were sitting together with their pets, and Krystle and Heather were sitting across from them with Sam and Snowball.

Jack and Burdock hopped up front with Tasha. Bailey was in front of me as we climbed into the back of the wagon. Then Datilina climbed up, joining all of us.

When she got into the back, I moved over to allow her to have a place to sit, and she said, "Thank you."

"You're very welcome," I replied.

So here I am, sitting next to my girlfriend. Well, I can't call her that as we are not going together, but she is my best friend, and she is a girl. Bailey and I feel the two of us will always be part of each other, and on the other side of me is a girl who just happens to be a bit shorter than others, looks like she works out a lot, and is hot.

Ziggy was getting situated in my lap and looked like she was comfortable and cozy. Datilina spread her legs, then placed two big hammers between them. They are like the one Ziggy has when she needs it. You know, the "Thor Thunder God Hammer."

"So, this is your pet," she said.

"Yes, this is my cute little furball monster bouncer."

"A monster bouncer?" she asked.

"Well, she and Agatha kicked the butt of a Targus."

She spun around and viewed me with a questioning look, then looked at Ziggy and asked, "Did you just say this little furry animal kicked a Targus's butt?"

"I did. You know that little female Amazon warrior you saw earlier?"

"Yes. That was Vanessa's pet pig that turned into that."

"Well, you're sitting next to one more just like her."

"You're kidding, right?" she questioned.

"No. I don't have to kid about that."

"Wow, so it's true about how you three came to this world with pets that can change. Is it also true that the people who join you will become part of the legendary group that will bring hope to all those in our world?"

As I spoke, I mentioned, "I have never read the papers on the legend, so I really cannot tell you. Our families have been able to travel here for many years, and I'm not sure why suddenly, it is the three of us who will save your world."

"It is said you will bring together the people for better lives in our world."

"I am not sure about your prophecy or things like that as I am just me, and I am Marty."

"Well, Just Marty, all of us can sure feel the energy from you that has not been felt for, what some say, centuries. I know your friend on the other side of you has power, and so does Steve, and what they have for power is stronger than most of the rest of us. But you know when you whipped up that sword?"

I inquired, "What about it?"

"You saw the glow on it. Correct?"

"Yes, I did, and I felt the power in it as well."

"Okay, now look at that sword as if it is us looking at you."

"You mean I glow?" I asked.

"Well, in a sense, you do. When we came to the camp, we felt power or energy, but Burdock thought it must be the wise one because they do have powers. At least, that is what he was saying. You see, Burdock told us, 'I have never felt a wise one with that amount of power, but years ago, many wise ones had powers that were strong enough to help the giants.' He was telling us even the giants had wizards and sorcerers, and it is said that at one time, all the giants used to live in our lands."

"So why did they leave?" I asked.

Datilina said, "I am not sure because it was a long time ago. Since that time, Denarians have taken the lands and created new homes and many towns. It has been ages since the giants lived where we are today. Most of the giants live near the mountains, where the dragons and wise ones live. I have always thought it was a kind of protection thing for the three groups."

"Maybe it was for protection or just a truce between all of them."

"As we walked up to your camp, Burdock said, 'Some wise ones do have lots of power, but what I felt was something I had never felt before.' I had never met a wise one, so I just took it as if that is what they feel like when you're around them.

"Burdock told us we don't have scriptable to pay for any horses or a wagon, so we are forced to steal them. Then we will be gone and heading back home. That is what we all planned, and then you stepped out from behind Jack, and all of us knew where that power came from. We knew then there was something special about you.

"As Burdock was heading toward you and you suddenly had a sword in your hand, we all watched him stop dead in his tracks. It was Burdock who figured it out first, I think, as he has never put his sword down for anything or any person. When he did that, all of us suddenly knew there was more going on than just a powerful wise one."

"So, all of you traveled north for what reason?"

"We were told by our elders that an event was going to take place in the north that Denarians would be part of. They said it has been foretold for centuries. They told us those with wisdom have been watching events for as long as they have been alive as it was written that off-landers would come and save the realm and people's lives."

I said, "So you did not find what it was that you were looking for and started to return home?"

"We were going home because we got the feeling whatever the event was, it had taken place up north and was already gone. We felt it was time to return. Then we saw you on the path, tried to catch you and take your wagon. Burdock said he felt your power as we did, but he just felt there was a good reason for it, and when we walked into your camp, he said it was the wise one—or at least, he thought it was."

"Do all of you feel our power and think we're your prophecy?"

"Yes. All of us finally realized that at Mike and Marilyn's farm. Winterish and Healer were with us, and suddenly, it just seemed like it was time. Does that make sense?" Datilina asked.

I replied, "I must agree because all things happen with time, and correct timing is of the utmost importance in all events. I am sure things would have been different if we had all clashed on the path to Mike and Marilyn's."

Datilina asked me, "So do you really think all the things that happened in the manner that they did are the way it was supposed to be?"

"Bailey has always told me things happen at a proper time, at a proper place, and with all players to make sure all events work the way they should."

"If we had gotten together on the path, maybe Winterish and Healer might not have been there at that time," she said.

"That could very well be true because she was a good distance behind all of you. But she showed up at the camp after all of you had been there a long time, and now she is protecting our home base."

"Well, I am pleased we have joined you. I am sorry we were so depressed that we planned on stealing your equipment to get us home."

"I have no idea about the prophecy or things that have been leading up to our being here, but I do know that since we have arrived, we have been able to make things happen, to help others, and as far as I am concerned, we will do all we can to help all of you."

Chapter 3

Fire in the Sky

Everyone was loaded up in the wagon, and we were on the path, heading down the road again.

I asked Krystle, "How long does it take to get to town?"

"It seems we are moving faster than what Dad normally does, so we may be able to be there late this evening."

"That would be good, correct?"

"As far as I know, I would have to say yes."

Heather said, "Most of the time, when Dad is heading to town, he takes his time, and we make several stops and then end up spending the night, waking up early, and entering the town in the morning."

"What do you have to do to buy things if you need them? I mean, we don't have any money, or I guess you call it script or something like that."

"Don't worry. We have a scroll at a few of the shops if we have a need for something."

"A scroll? Is that like a tab or credit where you can pay for it later?"

"Yes, that is what scroll means."

"Okay, one more thing to put on the list," Bailey added.

As we traveled, we watched the clouds, and everyone was making things out of the shapes. There was a house, a goat, a dog, and a chicken, then someone said, "Look at that bird."

I asked, "Where do you see a bird in the shape of those clouds?"

"Oh, not in the shape of the clouds, Marty. Over here." And she pointed to a bird that looked to me like a dove, but it was red.

"I have never seen a bird that red," Vanessa said.

I was thinking, *Neither have I.* As that thought passed through my mind, others in the wagon said, "It's such a bright red."

Steve asked, "What is it doing?"

"It looks like another bird is attacking it," Vanessa replied.

A more significant bird was diving on the red bird. The smaller bird was dodging its attacks very well. As we watched that big bird attacking the red one, it was climbing, turning, and then making a dive-bomber kind of attack on the smaller bird, but suddenly, the small one vanished into thin air.

It was as if it just burned up and was gone. I mean, it looked like it caught fire, turned into flames, and vanished. The other bird was circling around in search of it but only viewed as much as we did.

I looked at Vanessa and said, "I must say, that's a new one on me, but then so many things in your world are new to me."

Bailey declared, "That's for sure."

Steve replied, "I can't believe that bird burned up and just vanished into all that open space."

We were all still looking for the red bird as the attacking bird flew off.

"How did that bird do that?" Heather asked everyone.

Bailey replied, "I have never seen anything like that before. I never saw something like that in our world."

After the bird that attacked had been gone for some time, Krystle said, "Hey, look up there," as she pointed to a spot in the sky that looked like a blur of some kind.

We kept looking at that fuzzy-looking blur. Suddenly, it became that red bird again.

I said, "That is amazing as it must be a method of camouflage."

We kept watching it as it was high above us. It seemed to be traveling in the same direction as we were. Everyone in the back of the wagon watched it as we moved. High up in the air above, we noticed two more birds like that first one that attacked it. Maybe it was the one that struck and it brought back a friend to help it search.

The girls started yelling, "Look up, look up, look up!" and that little bird seemed to understand them like other birds we have seen.

As the larger birds attacked the red bird, it dodged and moved out of the way. The girls all cheered and clapped their hands. Soon, however, the larger birds returned for a new run. Tasha stopped the wagon, and all of us watched the events unfold.

The girls all yelled and said, "They're back! Look up, look up!"

That little red-feathered escape artist turned and stopped in midair in front of those other birds. It was as if it was daring them to strike. It moved out of the way of their attack just as they were about to lay waste to it. It flew over our way, with both birds following it, and suddenly, the girls jumped down out of the wagon, grabbed some rocks, and just as they flew over us, the girls pelted them good. It seemed they were caught off guard, not paying attention to who or what was on the ground, winding up to smack them with surprises.

They fluttered about for a bit as if disoriented as the red bird soared above them. It was as if the prey was watching and saying, "Take that, you bullies."

Soon, they recovered and were flapping their wings, looking around and shooting to the clouds, ready for another run at our little red friend. As they approached, it just turned and flew straight at them and then burst into flames and was gone again.

As we traveled, we hoped we would see it again. As the miles passed, that bird was nowhere in sight. I must admit it was an attention-grabbing situation.

I said, "Hey, Steve, that would be a good one for Max to learn."

Steve answered, "Yes, it would be."

We came to a fork in the road. Actually it was more like a V, and Tasha asked, "Vanessa, which way?"

"We need to go to the town, which will take us south, and I think that will be the one on the right."

"So there are two towns. Correct?"

"Yes, there are two of them, and they are both about the same distance, but one of them has a better road, and it's heading south, from what I remember Dad saying. I think we must follow that path on the right."

"Okay, well, I guess we take the path on the right," Tasha said.

Steve yelled out, "Hey, can we just stop for a minute? I need to relieve some pressure, if you know what I mean."

Tasha said, "We can do that, and if anyone else wishes a break, this is probably a good place to do that."

A few of us all climbed out of the wagon and found places to pee. What? It's a part of life, and if you are someone who never pees, then I guess you may have some serious problems.

As everyone was talking and getting ready to get back in the wagon, I noticed a tree with fruit on it and asked Vanessa, "Are those good to eat?"

"Yes, they are, Marty. I didn't even notice them. Do you want us to gather some up?"

"That might be a good idea if they are something we can eat. I just thought I should ask before I tried one," I said as I walked over and grabbed what looked like a pear, but the blue color made me ask the question. I took a bite, and if it wasn't a pear, it sure tasted like it. I asked all the others, "Do any of you want a pear?"

A few others wandered over and picked some and enjoyed them as it was a new taste to all of them. Vanessa and her sisters ran over to the tree and chose a good number of them to take with us.

Suddenly, that red bird we had viewed earlier flew down and landed on a branch of the tree.

Heather said, "Marty, look!" and she pointed to it.

It was as if it was studying all of us, tipping its head one way and then another. I stood there, looking at its beauty as all the others gathered around. I noticed it didn't seem to be afraid of us. All of us started talking about how fantastic it looked and asking questions, and one of them was "How can he disappear like he does?"

Suddenly, a small voice was heard, and we all looked around and then back at the bird as it said, "It's something some of you must learn in your travels in our world as it will help you along the way."

All of us looked at that bird. It was our turn to tip our heads one way and then another after hearing it speak.

I said, "Learning something like that may not be something we can do."

"All of you who came from afar to help all of this world can do amazing things, as you will see as time goes by." Then suddenly, it flew off, broke into flames, and was gone.

CHAPTER 4

A Fisherman of Birds

After traveling a few more hours, we figured we were probably about an hour to an hour and a half from town. We had been on the road most of the day and seen many kinds of animals and waterfalls along with beautiful forests.

As we started to travel around a vast lake, I asked Bailey, "What do you think of this place?"

Bailey, sitting next to me, mentioned, "That is a nice lake."

I said, "It is, but it looks like there is someone on the other side."

She said, "I see something, but I am not sure what it is."

I asked Vanessa and her sisters, "Can you tell what that is on the other side of the lake?"

Heather said, "I am not sure, but it looks like a person."

"I kind of thought so myself," I replied.

Bailey asked, "What is he doing over there?"

As he looked around, Steve said, "Looks like he is fly-fishing,"

"Kind of looks like it, but he's not casting in the water," I said.

Krystle said, "What he is doing is catching birds."

Steve exclaimed, "Max just told me he could cure him of that fast!"

"I'm not sure I want to know how. Is Max talking about turning into an elephant and squishing the guy?"

"No, he is thinking of turning into a little bird. Then, after he gets caught, turning into a huge bird and giving him a flying lesson."

We all laughed.

"Oh, look at that bird he just caught. It's a beautiful bluebird," Datilina said.

Suddenly, Max turned into a hawk. Everyone just looked in amazement.

Tasha stopped the wagon and said, "I don't believe he just changed from a ferret to a hawk."

Burdock looked and said, "You people really amaze me."

Datilina, sitting next to me, jumped and asked, "Did he just change?"

"Yes, he did."

Max the hawk was in the air and circling the guy across the lake, but now he was a small bluebird, and the guy cast his line, and Max took it. He started to fly, and he made sure the line was tight, and the guy was hanging on for dear life. Suddenly, that little bluebird turned into a massive eagle and picked him off the ground so fast, he could not think of letting go.

Max was flying around with this man hanging on that line, and I asked Steve. "Would you have him bring our fisherman over here and set him down?"

Soon, a huge eagle was flying over us with a scruffy older man hanging on tightly to his fishing pole. Max slowly brought him down near us, then allowed him to place his feet on the dusty path we had been traveling on. As soon as he had his feet on the ground, Max let him go. The man stood there looking up at Max, flying around over us. Max was shrinking in size into a smaller eagle. Then he landed.

I got out of the wagon and spoke up, saying, "I think you upset my friend by capturing birds."

The man spoke, saying, "He was a little bluebird."

He looked at all of us and at Max, and I said, "Max, how about a hawk?"

23

Max instantly turned into a hawk, and the guy jumped about two feet off the ground and asked, "What kind of creature is that thing?"

I started to walk over to him, and he said, "Stop."

I said, "What?"

He said, "Please stop where you are."

"Would you care to tell me why?"

"I feel it's bad enough that creature can change, but you feel different to me. I can feel something about you that is very disturbing. Are you even real?"

"Of course, I'm real. Tell me why you are catching birds."

"I study them, draw them, learn all I can about them, and set them free again."

"So you are not harming the birds?"

"Oh no, I would never do that. I love birds unless they pick me up and fly me around so high, I don't dare jump."

Steve said, "Max says he is sorry. He thought you were harming them."

"Please tell him I would never do that. If you wish to see what I do, we can ride over to my place as it's about ten minutes in that direction."

He pointed in the direction we were already heading, so I looked at the others, and everyone nodded, and I said, "I think we would all love to see your work."

"I need to go back and pick up the two birds I have caught and take them with us."

"Go and get them as we wait," I said.

Soon, all of us were watching him return with his two new captured birds.

He asked, "May I join you in the wagon?"

"You may. Climb up here and get a comfortable seat. I'm Marty."

The guy was still nervous about getting close to me, but he told us, "My name is Emmitt Bastion."

Emmitt climbed up into the back of the wagon, keeping his distance. I was sitting on the opposite side in the back. Max waited for

Emmitt to climb on board, and then he flew up to Steve and turned into a ferret again.

"Okay, Tasha, let's rock and roll."

"What?" she asked.

"Oh, that just means let us get a move on."

"Okay," she said, "Let's rock and roll."

Emmitt asked, "See that path to the right up ahead?"

Tasha replied, "I see it. Do you want me to turn on to it?"

"Please, if you would. Then when you get past the trees, you will see my research area."

Soon, all of us were looking at a beautiful old house. There was a big barn, but it had windows in the roof areas, something I have never seen before. It also had lots of little doors on the outside of the building about five feet off the ground and about four feet apart.

I commented, "You have windows up on top."

"I wanted to make sure all the birds have sunlight and were not just left in the dark."

"I see," I said.

We pulled up in front of his home, and Steve and I jumped down and pulled out the ramp, and I said, "That's for our animals so they can get out and stretch and remove all the bumps and dents they received today."

Everyone climbed down from the wagon, and Emmitt said, "If you come with me, I will show you where I place my birds."

He picked up his small cage with the two birds. Then we all walked over to a set of large doors on the front of his barn. He opened a small door that was located in one of the full-sized doors so we could walk inside without opening both the main doors.

Steve uttered, "That's cool. A door inside of a door."

Emmitt replied, "That allows me to enter, and if a few of them have gotten loose, they won't just fly away until I learn about them."

We entered a huge room that had drawings and information all over the walls. On large tables were what looked like enormous books. They had heavy covers, and I noticed four holes went through the thick covers and the pages inside. Twine was used for binding the pages and covers together. Emmitt opened one of the books, and we saw drawings and information about each type of bird. He had illustrations of the wings, feet, heads, and beaks and even had a feather from each bird.

"Wow," I said. "You have a lot of time invested here, Emmitt, and I am impressed."

Jack came over and looked at the books along with all the rest of us, and everyone was amazed at the way he set all the information up on every page.

Max turned into a hawk, flew up, and landed on the table to see as well, and he said to me in my mind, *I'm sure glad I never harmed this guy.*

I mentally said back, *I'm glad as well.* I declared, "Max is impressed, Emmitt."

Emmitt said to Max, "Thank you."

Suddenly, Max became a ferret again and looked at all the pictures of the birds.

Steve said, "I think he is studying so he can find one he can turn into if needed."

As he said that, we all laughed.

I mentioned, "We noticed an extraordinary bird today on our way up here as it was red and being attacked by a bigger bird, and it looked like it burst into flames and vanished."

"Oh yes, those are a fascinating and rare species of bird as that is how they hide from those who would kill them or if they just want to be unnoticed."

"I figured it was a way to do that but have never seen anything like that before in my life."

"Well, as you can guess, I have never caught one either."

"I can understand why," I said.

Emmitt said, "Come with me."

He picked up his small cage, and we followed him to an open cage door. He placed the two birds in it with feed and water and closed the door.

He then declared, "Let me show you the birds I have been studying lately," as he walked to a cage with a nest inside of it and a couple of birds. "I have both the male and the female here, and they have just produced new life."

I said, "That is amazing. So, what do you do next?"

"Well, you notice these cages are along the walls, and if you look inside of the cage, you will see those doors I have made on the wall of the barn."

"Oh yes, I noticed those little doors all along the outside of the building when we rode up," I answered.

"When they are large enough to fly with Mom and Dad, I open the outside doors to the cages, and they can simply leave the cages through those outside doors. I have saved and seen over eight hundred different kinds of birds mate and produce, and all of them fly away."

"You need to share this information with all those in your entire world. People of this world need to be educated in all of what you have learned."

He looked at me as if to ask a question, turned his head just a bit, and then asked, "That's it, isn't it?"

"What's it?" I inquired.

"You're not from this world, are you?"

"No. Steve, Bailey, and I, along with our pets, come from a place called Earth."

"I knew there was something about you that was different and powerful. I just did not know why I was feeling it so strongly. I mean, you scared me completely. Now I understand."

"Glad you do because I'm not sure I do," I said.

"For centuries, people have told of the coming of a leader and his friends who gather others and build our world and help the people of all realms. The stories tell of how they have powers or can change. He and his friends have pets that can become more than they seem to be. Max here has proved he can do that, hasn't he?"

"Yes, he has," I said.

Bailey asked, "How come this legend even exists?"

"What do you mean?" he asked.

"I mean, when did this legend even start?" Bailey asked.

"I am not sure because it has always been that three young people from another world would enter ours and help the people and create better lives for all, making Mother Earth safe. It is said a great war had ended, and peace was now upon the lands, but the time of trouble and discontent would rise again. As that time begins to rise one more time, the three would enter our world," Emmitt replied.

Steve asked, "When did that prophecy start, and who started that legend? Is there a way to find out where it came from?"

Emmitt said, "You have a wise one traveling with you, and if anyone should know, it might be him."

Jack spoke up and replied, "Even I don't know when or where it started, but I do know that I was told to be up in this part of the region the other day at one specific location to see and feel something extraordinary. I must say I have seen him and felt his power and witnessed what Marty and his friends are capable of. I have seen all those so far who will follow him. It was foretold that a chosen wise one would travel with the three and gather warriors, Denarians, dragons, sorcerers, healers, scholars, and even giants to help along the way. This is all I know."

"It is said that along the way, people who would do harm will change, and those who would destroy will stop, and people will follow the three," Emmitt commented.

Jack remarked, "Over the centuries, different books have been created now and again to remind all of us about the writings of these three teenagers and a few special pets. Every so often, a new book comes to light to remind our world they will come in our time of need."

"Well, Jack, I am not a scholar, but if I can ever help, I will do whatever I can."

I spoke up and asked Emmitt, "Do you teach others about your birds?"

"Oh no, Marty, I would have to be classed as a man of educated wealth first."

"Do they have schools around here to teach children about birds?"

"Not that I know of, but most children learn facts and information from Mother Earth. Our children are some of the most intelligent in the country."

"So they don't really have schools here?" Bailey asked.

"Not like they have in the big cities, and those are so far away or in other regions. Most children from here already know what is needed in those schools."

"So it's Mother Earth who has been teaching us as well since we have been here. But she does not teach kids about birds. Is that correct?"

"It would seem so if you feel smarter and have more knowledge, and I don't think kids learn about birds."

Steve asked, "So what if you created a school so you could teach others about all your birds?"

"What do you mean?" Emmitt inquired.

"Well, Emmitt, it would mean you could teach everyone about your birds. I think it would be great to set up a school and have you as a teacher for students who wish to learn about your feathered friends. Could you do that if we could help create that kind of school?" I asked.

"I'm not sure that can be done, but it sounds like what you're talking about, I would love as I would really enjoy teaching everyone about birds. That would be a dream come true."

"Well, you seem to have more knowledge than anyone else about birds, so that would make you what they call teachers at home, professors," Bailey remarked.

"To me, it sounds like you are a man of educated wealth," I said.

"I have spent my entire life learning about them, and I would enjoy having the chance of sharing my knowledge with the rest of our world."

"Well, my friend, maybe there is a way to make that a dream come true for you. I'm not saying we have the means to make it happen, but I can imagine it becoming a reality," I stated.

"Jack, do you have any ideas of how we can make that happen?" Steve asked.

29

"I'm not sure, but I do know many of the wise ones, and maybe they have some good ideas as to how we can make that materialize."

"Well, I know that back home, many states are controlled by people who prefer to keep people downright dumb. You see, that way, they keep getting into office and keep stealing from those who pay their wages. Most states that have good education are controlled by liberals who understand education brings children out of poverty and raises them to earn better wages and live better lives," Steve said.

"That is why education is so important, and if we can create good education here, we will be helping Mother Earth and working wonders," I said.

"Back home, they try to cut funding and create corporations that gain profits for what they call stockholders, board members, and the guy at the top who makes millions every year. That guy at the top is called a CEO. That stands for chief executive officer," Bailey explained.

"Education in our world is in the bigger cities and is paid for by taxes, but of course, you realize it does not cost much for our schools because people take a great interest in our children's educations," Emmitt pronounced.

"Real education is funded by our government in our world and paid for by taxes as well. Public education creates minds that ask questions and then reaches for facts, learning about better lives," Steve said.

"Public education has produced some of the greatest minds that anyone could ever have. So I hope we can find ways to help Mother Earth teach others here," Bailey said.

CHAPTER 5

Getting Ready for the First Night

Tasha said, "Well, it's getting late, my friends, so we need to do something. We either move on or ask Emmitt if we can camp here tonight."

Emmitt said, "Oh, please join me as I never have such fine guests, and I would really love to have the company."

"All right, I need a couple of people to unhitch the team with me, then water and feed them, and brush them down. We need a good place to keep them safe, and we need to make sure and find the right places for the bedrolls."

Steve said, "I will help with the horses. Vanessa, would you like to help?"

As he said that, Vanessa said, "I can help."

"Vanessa, is that you?" Emmitt asked.

They both looked at each other and gave each other a great big smile.

Then Vanessa said, "Yes, and my sisters are here too. I thought your place looked familiar."

"Well, it's been a long time. You run off now and help with the horses, and we can catch up later."

Steve said, "I could not ask for better help," and they both walked out to the wagon.

Heather and Krystle walked up, and Heather asked, "Emmitt, how have you been?"

"Good. You girls have grown."

Krystle said, "It's been a long time since we traveled to town with Mom and Dad as we normally stay at Mike and Marilyn's place. Other times, it just seems we ride straight through to get to the shops. Right now, we are going to look and see what kinds of plants you have that we can collect."

As she said that, both turned and ran out of the door.

"Well, Bailey, looks like it's Jack, Burdock, you, and me. So, what do you want to do?"

"I want to see some of these birds, Marty," she said, and she started walking around, looking at all of them.

"There sure are a lot of them," I said.

"These are so very beautiful. I have never seen anything like some of these," Bailey remarked.

"Emmitt, where did you find these?" I asked.

"I have traveled across our country, always learning about them and hoping to protect them all."

Vanessa walked back in and said, "Marty, the girls and I are planning on spreading out sleeping bags and setting up a place to sleep for later. I figure we should eat dinner in the next few hours, and hopefully, we can get to sleep early and wake up and be in town in the morning."

Emmitt said, "As you know, the town is only about an hour away from here. If you leave in the morning, you will be there when the shops open and not have a lot of people to deal with. If some of you wish to sleep inside of my house, you can, and when it comes to fixing dinner, I have a big slab of Raniango on the firepit cooking away."

"What is that?" I asked.

"It's an invader that looks as big as a horse but has horns, lots of hair, and red eyes and spits out juice that burns and melts flesh. Oh, and it has a bad temper. Since they destroy most of what we have as they run through our crops, chase people, and kill them, it is now okay to use them for food."

"I see. Can they be tamed or treated differently so they can be peaceful?" I inquired.

"I don't know how, Marty, as many have tried."

"Well, I guess we shall try some Ringo. Is that what you called it?"

"Well, it's really called Raniango, but if that's what you wish to call it, that's fine with me."

Vanessa spoke out and said, "We had a few of them up near our place. Dad had to get rid of them in the same manner. They are just so wild and crazy. They destroy anything that moves."

Jack said, "I guess I will go check on that firepit and make sure the meat has not burned."

"I will go with you," Burdock said, and both headed outside.

I yelled at Bailey and asked, "Are we sleeping in the wagon tonight?"

"That's fine with me, Marty, as it should be nice and soft."

I mentally asked Ziggy, *Is sleeping in the wagon good for you?*

Marty, you always know what is right for you is good for me. Wherever you go, I go as well. Wherever or however you wish to sleep works for me.

Well, I thought we should sleep on a bed of nails that have sharp points on them.

You mean like the nails you used on my Ziggy house?

Yes. They pound them through a board, and after they have about a hundred of those nails, with the points about an inch through on the other side, they turn it over, and people sleep on them.

Ziggy was standing right beside me. She turned her head to look up at me and then sent me a thought, *Marty, maybe sleeping in the same manner as you will not be what will give me the best night's sleep. I know you're kidding though.*

Yes, I am, my little friend. I would not put you through anything like that. I just figure I will open the sleeping bag, and we can sleep on that as it should be fine with all the straw we have in that wagon, I replied.

Bailey yelled and asked, "What's up?"

"We were just discussing sleeping on a bed of nails or in the wagon," I said.

She looked over to where Ziggy was and mentally asked, *Ziggy, did you like the idea of a bed of nails?*

Not me, she replied.

"Sounds like Ziggy and I have a different idea of comfort, Marty. I will take the straw in the wagon," she said.

"I think we all agree straw is really what we need tonight," I said.

"Let's go see about this thing Emmitt killed for dinner. Jack and Burdock have already headed that way."

"Emmitt, we are going to check on your firepit," I stated.

He was standing near his desk and not paying attention to the fact that Bailey had joined us. "Okay. As soon as Bailey gets done wandering around, looking at the birds, I will close this up, and I will join you."

"Oh, I'm done, and I am impressed," she said as she was already standing next to us with her kitten in her hands. "These are so beautiful, Emmitt."

"Thank you. It's always nice to know others love the beauty and lives of our little friends."

Soon, all of us were walking toward the firepit, and whatever was cooking smelled great to all of us. Everyone seemed to have followed the smell. As we got close, I noticed Jack was just doing that chef thing where he sampled the meat with his hand under the fork so he wouldn't drip on anything. I was not sure why he was so worried about dripping on the dirt, but it looked like something a good cook would do.

The girls had been gathering plants, and Krystle came up to me and said, "These are the plants we need to make things cold."

"Are there many of those around here, and if you pull them up, will they be good to use in a week or a month?" I questioned.

"Oh yes, there are lots of them here for some reason, and when you pick them, you put them in a small pouch. Then they will be good to use for many months. I know Mom has kept them longer because once they are dried, they probably last forever," Krystle declared.

"Wow, that's cool. Can you please show us where you found those?"

As I asked that question, she started walking toward a place around the big barn and said, "This place has a good number of plants."

I looked at Bailey and mentally said, *Join me*. Ziggy, of course, was already at my side.

Bailey was keeping step with all of us. Tabby was jumping over rocks and weeds so she could follow, so Bailey stopped and pick her up and carried her.

As we followed the girls, we viewed what she said were a good number of plants. I looked at them, then said, "They just look like weeds to me."

She said, "Well, Marty, that's because you're not a plant expert like me." Then she laughed.

Bailey asked, "So these are what your mom uses to keep things cold?"

"Yes, but you must pick them at the right time. You see those little yellow flowers are about halfway up the stem, and that is when you must pick them because if they rise further up the stem, which they will do, they lose what is needed to create cold."

Bailey said, "I am sure pleased you are with us on this trip. I have a feeling we will need some of those plants. Did you get enough to last for a good long time?"

"I have plenty as I picked some for Mom as well."

Ziggy asked me mentally, *Are they good to eat?*

"Can you eat those, Krystle?" I asked.

"I suppose you can, but I would think they would taste bitter. I've never tried any before."

"Well, let's get back to the others and get something to eat that's not bitter," Bailey said.

"I am for that as I am a bit hungry, and I know my sisters are too," Vanessa said.

All of us were handed plates. Emmitt handed out knives and forks, and all of us were enjoying a delicious meal.

I asked Emmitt, "If this animal spits out acid that can melt a person, how did you make sure and get the meat away from that?"

"It has a pocket inside of its mouth, and the rest of the body does not have any acid in it. It seems to be created inside of that pocket in its mouth somehow."

"I see. That should give you food for some time then, if that's the case."

"It should, and most of the time, I dry the meat, and it lasts me for several months. I will make sure you have some to take with you. I have some that I have already dried."

Bailey inquired, "Do you have many of these creatures around here?"

"Very seldom do we ever see one in this area. I found this one about a four-day ride from here as I was looking for a special kind of bird. Never found the bird, but came home with a wagon loaded with meat."

Everyone was saying how great dinner was, and I had to agree, even if I did not know what it really was. The flavor was excellent.

Bailey commented, "Emmitt, thank you for sharing your food with us, and now I must say I am getting tired and need some sleep."

I asked, "Have all of you figured out where you are sleeping?"

Jack said, "Emmitt told us we could sleep in the house."

Burdock commented, "To us, that sounded pretty good."

"Well, I can understand that coming from you two as it seems you have not had a real roof over your heads for some time," I asked. "Vanessa, what about you and your sisters?"

"We thought of sleeping in the wagon, and hopefully, others will too."

"Bailey and I, along with our pets, will be there, and I have a feeling Steve will be there as well."

"Did I hear my name?" Steve asked.

"Yes, you did. Are you sleeping in the wagon with the rest of us?"

Steve looked at Vanessa, and she looked at him and nodded, and he turned back to me and said, "Yes, I am."

"Tasha, what about you and Datilina?"

36

"George told us of a way to sleep on the seat and in the footway of the wagon before he headed home, so we thought we would try that out."

"It works great," Steve said, "as George and I did that on the way to Mike and Marilyn's. I got a good night's sleep too. You need to get a good blanket or maybe a good amount of straw to sleep on though."

"Okay, let's all head to the wagon and get some sleep."

I turned to Jack, Burdock, and Emmitt and said, "Hey, you guys, see you in the morning."

They all replied, "In the morning."

Soon, everyone was loaded into the back of the wagon, and sleeping bags were spread out, and everyone looked like they were ready for a good night's sleep. Bailey and I figured to get up in the front of the wagon bed just behind the seat and get comfy there.

As I was moving about and getting ready to lean back, I found a huge bag that was lumpy and asked, "What is this?"

Vanessa said, "Mike put that there. He told me we may need what he had made for barter along the way."

"What is it?" As I asked, I started to open the bag, and inside were flutes, tambourines, and drumsticks. "These things are very nice," I said.

She said, "He makes those kinds of things and takes them to different towns to exchange them for food and other supplies. In some of the towns, he sells them to shops and returns looking very happy. He said we will probably need them since most of us have no way to pay for anything."

"I must admit that is one thing I never really thought of and should have. Well, is everyone comfortable?" I asked.

Steve was next to Vanessa, with Max resting nearby, and said, "This is great."

Heather and Krystle said, "We are good, and so are our pets."

Ziggy was curling up in my lap, getting ready to fall asleep. I noticed Agatha was still a pig, and she was falling asleep on one side of Vanessa. Bailey was next to me, and we had Tabby snuggling up to both of us. "Have I ever told you how much I really love being

37

next to . . . Oh yes, I guess I have as she is my favorite blonde in blue jeans."

Datilina and Tasha were bedding down in the seat of the wagon and on the floorboard up front. Both of them were flipping out blankets on top of some straw where they would be sleeping to create a soft bed.

I looked around and did a head count to make sure we had everyone and then made sure I was not feeling anything strange. Everything looked and felt right to me, so now it was time to get a good night's sleep. We would be heading into town in the morning after breakfast.

Soon, it was just the sound of silence with a small amount of snoring, mostly from Steve and Datilina. I got in position between Ziggy and Bailey. Then I turned out the lights. No, there are no light switches here. I was just letting you know I fell asleep, and so did everyone else.

CHAPTER 6

Back at the Base Camp

Things seemed to be moving along rather well back at our main camp.

Ruther and Oscar, both being older, were moving very well for their age. After we had left, they rounded up a few of the people who wished to travel back up the hill. When they all reached the top, they noticed the buildings were deserted. Lots of logs had ended up in the pond. Of course, the pond was much smaller now and was not the lake they had before.

Oscar spoke up and asked, "One of you worked in sawmills before. Is that correct?"

"Yes, I did. My name is Gaspard, Mathew Gaspard."

"Well, I hope you don't mind me calling you Mat."

"That is fine with me. Most of my friends call me that. Sometimes I get called a lot worse, but it sure seems we are among friends."

Oscar asked, "Would you please grab one more person and join me as we search to make sure all the parts and equipment are ready to be used?"

As they moved off to make sure the mill was ready to start back up, Ruther said, "Okay, we need a few of you to see if you can get some of those logs lined up alongside one another on the shore. We need a couple of logs ready for that skid next to the saws."

One of the people standing near Ruther said to some of the others, "To be honest with you, I think this is a great location. What I mean to say is we have heard this land belongs to Marty now, and he said we could start building our homes up here. To build up here gives all of us a better view for miles in each direction. If we can start cutting lumber, we can create more houses next to those that are already here. Marty said he wants this to be the base camp. So, we will make that happen."

Oscar walked up and spoke out, saying, "Mat just told me the mill is in good operation, and we can start it up whenever we are ready. After we get it started, we can place lumber in piles here. Then we can also haul some of the lumber down by wagon and start building that new storage area Mike was talking about."

Ruther asked, "Oscar, can we start up the mill and start cutting logs and stacking lumber?"

"Yes, we can," he replied.

Ruther commented, "We have so many logs here, we could build a city. So we can stack it and cover it and move some down the hill. A few of the people down there can start the building process while we continue to work up here."

"Okay, so let's make sure the others agree," Oscar answered.

"Mat, what do you think? Are we ready?"

"I think we have all the workings for a good legal sawmill. We have found several blades and chains and all the railings we will need in that storage building over on the side of the mill."

Oscar spoke up and asked, "Would all of you please come over here? I want your thoughts on what we should do when it comes to designing the layout of the homes."

As all the other men and women gathered around to listen, Ruther announced, "If we set up shop in that building in the back, we can design the layout of how we will place the homes. We can create a few different plans for new homes, keeping our ideas and drawings in that building."

One of the other people asked, "It seems a good number of logs are still pouring down that stream into the pond. My question is, how soon do we start production of cutting the logs?"

Mat spoke up and said, "I think we need to kick this mill into gear and start working. If we wish to continue the operation and sell the lumber, we can get permits needed in the forest next to the stream and sell the lumber across the country to make some scriptable. That way, we can put more food on the table and maybe even create pay for everyone."

Ruther said, "I must agree with Mat, and it seems Oscar likes that idea as well, so let's just have a show of hands to see who is ready to get to work. Remember, now you're working for your own lives and homes."

Oscar said, "Well, I guess that settles that since all hands have been raised. Okay, I need one man or woman to run down the hill and gather up more people to start working. We need to let them know we can move into the houses up here for the time being. You may bring a wagon and let them all ride up here if that is better. Just let Mike know what we are doing."

Ruther said, "I would like a few of you to come with me. We need to look around this property and get an idea of how to set up homes and things for the best protection if need be. Then I will make some designs for the houses, but I need to get some paper and pencils. Then you can look at my ideas and make comments on changes in the layout and structure if need be. Mat, you're in charge of setting up the operations for the mill, and you will run that."

Mat stated, "I need two with me to kick this baby in gear. It seems we have people already rounding up those logs."

Oscar found an open area and started speaking to a few others about how he would want to cut the lumber. He noted that it all had to be stacked in different locations and covered. He was telling them the process of building would be easier if they had a plan and stuck to it.

The day was progressing well on the top of the hill, and Marilyn and Magic were enjoying each other's company in the kitchen area. Winterish and her bear helped in the camp below, at the barn area, and also on the hill to make sure it was set up for sleeping. She worked with Mike on using some of the unused space in barn areas to set up bunks and then traveled up to the mill area to set up the old bunkhouse.

As she walked in the door of that bunkhouse, she said, "This will never do. I need a few others to help me tear out some of these areas and set them up so people can have privacy."

Soon, she had a half dozen others helping her. Everyone seemed to be enjoying the idea of freely working and supporting all the others. So as the day was being experienced at home base, meals were being created, and people would soon be eating, with work getting done.

Marilyn walked out into the yard near the house. As she looked around and viewed people on the hill, she realized the water was not being dammed up anymore as it had been when the entire illegal operation had been there before.

Mike walked over to her and said, "I think our lives have recently changed."

Marilyn looked at him and said, "I think you're right, and it looks like we have new friends who are working and going to be hungry soon. I'm going to help Magic fix meals for all those hungry people."

One of the men had walked down the hill, approached Mike, and said, "We have voted to start the mill. We can create the lumber for the new homes as logs are still floating into the lake, and the entire operation is ready to run. If we cut the lumber and wagon some of it down here, we can start working on a new storage area. But for right now, they seem to want to build mostly on the hill. They wish to create that base camp the three spoke of. One thing great about it is it has an unobstructed view of all the eye can see."

Mike replied, "I know Marty said if it's his land now, he wants to make it a base of operations. I would imagine having buildings up there for people to live in would be a good idea."

"Oscar asked me to come down, gather more people, and use a wagon to bring them up there as it will make going back and forth easier. He also said some of us can actually live in those buildings up there since they are set up with rooms."

"That is an excellent idea since the rooms are already there. Well, let's get a wagon ready then," Mike said.

After hitching up the team, they rounded up others who were wandering around, gathering firewood, and clearing places for sleeping and said, "Okay, they need some of you up on the hill as they are about to start up that mill again. Some of you may be able to live in the buildings up there."

One man said, "Makes me think of what we just went through."

Mike said, "Well, it's not. It will be where Marty and the others stay when they are here, and that area will also have homes for all of you who wish to live up there. It's not going to be the same because this time, you are working for a better life and a new home. No one is keeping you here, and no one is turning you into slaves."

The man spoke up again and said, "Well, let's go see if we can cut up some logs and build some homes."

Soon, the wagon was headed up the hill with twenty people and Mike at the lead.

CHAPTER 7

The Wagon Heading North

April said, "George, you know we have people on the farm, so if we have time, we should stop at Bogart's and see if we missed something. I mean, I would sure feel bad if something happened and we could have stopped it."

"I know, hon. I think we will stop and see what happened when we get there."

Meesha asked, "What was wrong at that farm?"

George said, "When we came by it last time, there was no one there, and I have never seen them leave without one of them on the farm."

April commented, "It's rare they would just up and leave with everything unlocked and windows open, things like that."

"How far are we from their farm?"

"We have another full day at least before we reach them. What would be nice is if Marie or one or two of the women could meet us there. Then they could just ride back with us."

"I am not so sure they will want to walk for half a day just to meet us there," George stated.

"It was just a thought, George. Just a thought."

"I know, and I also know the kids want to have their moms with them on some of these adventures."

Meesha asked, "Do you have another wagon on your farm?"

"Oh yes, we have two more, but they are seldom used, and we do have four more horses, so I mean we could hitch up one of the other wagons, and then it's just a matter of who goes back and if we can get Fred and the others to come over to babysit the farm," George stated.

"Oh, George, you know Fred would rather be on an adventure than babysit our farm."

"I guess I know that."

"You know, if we get there and they want to return to the base camp and you have to stay and take care of the farm, I can always bring them back if that will help," Meesha said.

George replied, "Well, that is an idea as we do have several things that still should be done before we get a change in the weather."

"Well, if you would like me to help in that manner, just let me know. I am here to help you any way I can and make sure you're safe," Meesha commented.

Jasmin, are you with us? April mentally asked.

Yes, we are, April. We are just flying and watching and making sure you have no surprises.

Thank you. Please tell your mom I said hello.

I will, and don't worry. We are making wide circles around you as you go so we can see movement if it happens.

Just stay safe. None of us want anything to happen to either of you.

We are fine, and we are watching, but keep in touch.

Thank you again, Jasmin.

You're very welcome.

April said, "Jasmin just told me there is nothing around us and the coast is clear."

"Jasmin?" Meesha asked.

"The young dragon," April replied.

"Oh, you know I forgot they were even around. I mean, you can't see them. I love it that I have had the chance to see a real dragon in my lifetime."

"Well, we feel the very same way. George and I have never seen any before, either. I have a feeling a lot of things we are experiencing are due to Marty, Bailey, and Steve being over here in our world."

"What is their world like?"

"Well, it's a kind of fast-paced life and, from my point of view, very much the future. Everyone is in a hurry and having something to do and places to be all the time. Marty was saying that the technology is growing so fast that people are losing jobs. Then if they lose jobs, they lose incomes and then lose homes and find they have disrupted families."

"Yuck, that sounds awful and not a world I would want to be in, that's for sure. I mean, we have our problems here, but I think Marty and them can fix many of those problems. Their world sounds like a place that would be terrible to live in."

"Well, all worlds are different, and if you stay with Marty, you may find yourself in some of those other worlds, helping them out."

"I guess that part would be interesting, visiting other worlds and helping people."

"Yes, and I think as a team, all of you will be doing that together."

"Do you think Denarians will fit in as we enter those other worlds?"

"I have a feeling that if you're with Marty and the other two, no one would ever say anything negative about anyone on that team, and that includes Denarians. On top of that, why would anyone figure you won't fit in?"

"We are different, you know."

"Different? Meesha, some of you may be shorter, but you are people. Everyone is different in one way or another. Some are tall. Some are short. Many have different colors and have different looks, but that does not make them bad or dishonest. It does not mean they have no feelings. People need to understand one thing, and I heard Marty say this the other day. No matter who you are, when you're born, you become part of the collective of lives in every world. He said where they come from, it's called humanity."

"Well, that makes sense. It would be called humanity here as well then. Correct?"

"I don't see why it wouldn't as all people here are part of a collective of lives as well. We are called the primary race, but in Marty's world, they are called the human race. They both mean the same thing. Meesha, you are part of a big family now, and we all love you, so never in any way think you're not accepted."

"Well, I do appreciate that."

"So, what is it like to be a farmer up in this area?"

"What do you mean?" George asked.

"I mean, where I come from, the ground is rocky and hard to grow things."

"Well, we have good land with lots of good soil. There are some rocks but not very big ones. Tilling up the fields is relatively easy if that is what you mean," George stated.

"Yes, that is what I am wondering because, at home, I know my mom and dad sometimes must bring in big huge bulls to move some of the rocks. In that manner, they had clear fields to plant."

"Your father had to use bulls to remove the rocks?" April asked.

"My dad would go out there with ropes and the bulls, and he would wrap those ropes around the rocks and have two bulls pulling on some of them to remove them, then drag them out of the fields. Even with Mother Nature, it can sometimes be challenging."

"That is unbelievable as those rocks must be huge," George stated.

"Sometimes it would take my dad most of the months leading up to the growing period just to clear a new field. It seems what you have up here for soil is a lot better than what we have down where we are and a lot fewer rocks."

"Well, I must admit we don't have the rocks like you saw back at my brother Mike's place. I think the more you go south, the more rocks you find."

"I think the most massive thing George had to remove from our field was an old tree stump over the past couple of weeks," April mentioned.

"Yes, and it was a long-rooted thing, but with some digging and the help of strong hands and Mother Nature, it was removed."

"What do you farm in your place?"

"We raise wheat, charros, topo, squash, varies kinds of melons, and things like that, along with chickens, pigs, and cows."

"Marty's grandmother used to visit us often, and she said, what we call charros are potatoes, and topo is called corn where they are from. She said that many things are the same in both worlds."

"That is kind of weird, isn't it?" Meesha asked.

"In a way, it is. If all worlds grow in the same manner, there will be similarities. George also creates things from branches and limbs that have fallen from trees. He trades those things for lumber and fittings to create wagons and sell them. Soon, you will see where we farm."

Chapter 8

Morning of the Second Day

I rolled over and ended up putting my arm around Bailey, and she just snuggled up to me as if that was how we should be sleeping. Then it seemed we both became aware of our position. I opened my eyes a little as Bailey turned her head back toward me, and we looked at each other.

She said, "This is kind of sweet."

I said, "No, Bailey, it's not sweet. It's excellent."

Tabby crawled up on top of both of us, and she was now finding a lovely little space between us and falling asleep. Suddenly, there was movement from my backside, and I had a small furball pulling up close behind me.

I heard Ziggy say in my mind, *Oh, you are nice and warm.*

I was thinking about how lucky I was to be in the position I was in as I fell back to sleep. A few hours later, the sun started to rise, and it must have hit Steve in the face first as he started opening his eyes and looking around. No, no one really hit Steve in the face. It was just sunlight. Steve looked over at Bailey and me as both of us were wrapped in each other's arms.

Steve nudged Vanessa and said, "Look at that."

Vanessa opened her eyes and said, "What?"

"Look over there." And he pointed to the four of us.

Vanessa said, "That is nice as it does keep you warmer, you know."

"Really?" Steve asked. "Well, maybe we should try to keep warm the next time we fall asleep."

She looked up at him, turned her head a little bit, and said, "Well, Steve, if it gets cold, that would be a proper thing to do, but you climbed into your sleeping bag."

"Oh yeah, I forgot about that."

"It's okay. Sometimes you must do what comes naturally, Steve," Vanessa said.

Heather and Krystle were stirring about and setting up and said, "We need to take our pets out for a walk," and they jumped down and grabbed their cats, put them on the ground, and went for a walk.

Ziggy woke up saying, *Oh, I need to get down from here.*

Okay. Do I need to move or something? I asked.

No, don't worry. You're fine. I will just change and jump down.

Bailey started to come to, and she kind of wiggled around a bit and snuggled up close to me and said, "I could sleep like this for a long time."

I said, "I am sorry, Bailey, but we all need to wake up no matter how great this feels."

"I know, Marty, but I just enjoy being close to you."

"I understand that, and I have always liked being close to you as well. But then you already know that, don't you?"

"I do," she replied.

"But then you know how I feel most of the time, don't you?" I asked.

"I do, so can we snuggle a little bit longer?"

"Well, I must admit it is nice to have you close to me—I mean to keep each other warm, of course."

"Oh, of course."

"Come here and let me hold you close," I said.

She just snuggled up and started making a sound like she was purring.

I asked, "Did you become a cat?"

"Not yet," she said.

"Well, are you going to soon?"

"I might if there is a reason for it."

"Lately, you have not been telling us about things to come, so why is that?"

"Marty, I never used to tell you everything I found out about before. You know I can't tell you everything because it may change things to come."

I said, "I know, but you used to give us hints about things now and again but not lately."

"Well, I can tell you a few things I've seen. I'm not sure where all of us will be traveling at the time of the events. One thing I have seen is someplace with a good number of people looking over a railing at water about sixty feet below. It looked like some kind of canal with a walk on both sides. One other thing I viewed was you standing next to a sword that was almost as tall as you."

"You're not afraid that will change things to come?"

"I don't think it will."

CHAPTER 9

Let's Get Breakfast

Ziggy came back to the wagon and mentally said to me, *Well, I guess you two are the last ones to get out of the wagon.*

Steve walked up and said, "Hey, come on. This isn't just your room." Then he laughed.

It seemed as if everyone else had been up walking around and getting breakfast ready. Both Ziggy and Agatha were in their pet forms and wandered around, smelling things.

I jumped down, and Bailey handed me Tabby. Then she jumped down next to me and said, "Wow, do you smell that?

I said, "Yes, I do, and it must be coming from the house."

Tasha and Datilina were saying, "That sure smells like someone knows how to cook, that's for sure."

Vanessa and Steve were standing close to us, and Steve said, "That smells awesome."

The two of them headed to the house, and Bailey and I were walking just behind them. As we entered the house, we heard Jack, Burdock, and Emmitt in the kitchen, talking about the town we would soon be visiting.

Emmitt was saying, "There is a nice place to eat about halfway through town on the right-hand side called Bobbles Burrow."

I looked at Bailey and said, "They sure have some weird names for places here, don't they?"

She said, "I think it's just that we are not used to their way of life yet."

Steve said, "Well, I don't know about you two, but I am hungry, and that food smells great."

"Oh, we're hungry, all right," I said.

Burdock said, "Grab a plate and get in line."

We did, and as we walked past the three of them, they just started putting food on our plates and said, "Find a good place to sit and eat."

"Wow, this really looks like a good breakfast," Heather said as she was getting her plate loaded up.

Vanessa said to Krystle, "This is like home."

Krystle said, "Well, yes, but it's not us cooking."

All the protectors and pets were getting fed. Ziggy came up and bumped into my leg and sent me a thought saying, *I have a feeling there will be lots of scraps for all of us pets.* Then she turned to Agatha and said, *I could really get used to this.*

Agatha replied, *I could too.*

Everyone had a full plate, and then our three cooks loaded up their plates, and we all sat and enjoyed a good breakfast. Emmitt was telling us about a small place in town where we could barter items for supplies and about a café that served good lunches if we would still be there at that time.

Bailey asked, "Do you mean Bobbles Burrow?"

"Have you heard of that place already?" Emmitt asked.

"We heard the three of you talking as we entered the kitchen."

"Well, they have a good lunch menu."

"Not sure how long we will be in town as we have a lot of distance to cover," I commented.

Emmitt replied, "Well, take your time. If you get in a big rush, you may forget things and mess up, as I have done before many times."

"I understand getting in a rush does create problems as I have done it myself at home," I responded.

"What's it like where you are from, Marty?"

"Emmitt, it's not a lot different from here if you were to see our world about one hundred years ago. I am sure you would love to check out our birds as well."

"That would be nice. Especially if I could do that and learn about them."

"Most of our world is a big rush to do this or rush to do that kind of thing. People never spending enough time with their kids and always having to work because the wealthy basically control all we do. My friend George was saying the wealthy tried to control everyone here at one time. I guess he and his wife, April, love what they have now."

"George and April Roberts?" Emmitt asked.

"Yes, that's right. I heard you know the girls. So, I guess you must know their parents."

"Of course. They normally stop by on their way to town every now and again. I noticed Vanessa along with her sisters here last night after all of us arrived. But the last time I saw them, they were a lot younger, and I sure didn't recognize them at first," he said.

The girls heard us talking about them, and Vanessa said, "Emmitt, we will have to tell Mom and Dad we stopped by and had the chance to see you again."

"It's been so long since I have seen you, girls. Your parents have been by over the past years as I have found notes now and again from them, but I must be out looking for birds."

"Normally, we stay at Mike and Marilyn's because by the time we reach their place, we are all wagoned out, if you know what I mean. We join Mom and Dad every now and again because we know some of the shop owners and their wives. Often we just sit around and talk with them as we don't have people around our home to speak with most of the time."

Emmitt said, "Well, I am glad to have had the chance to see you three again. And yes, tell your mother and father I said hello. Maybe the next time they pass by, all of you will stop and I will be here, and we can catch up on all the things that have been happening."

I said, "I had the chance to meet George and April the first time I stepped into this world."

"Amazing," he said. "Can you believe this, Marty? You know their family and now all of us here. This is so very special to me."

"Small world, isn't it?" I asked.

"Yes, I guess it is, Marty."

Everyone was having a conversation about the birds, Emmitt's farm, or what we would see next. We finished breakfast, and everyone pitched in and helped clean dishes and tidy the place up a bit before we walked out to get the wagon set up for travel.

Chapter 10

Load Up the Wagon

"Here is some extra dried meat to take with you, and you may need some of this in your travels," Emmitt said.

"What's that?" I asked.

"It's called scriptable, and you will need it."

"I can't take your money."

"You can. And you will. I am able to help you, so please believe me when I say I can afford to do this."

"You know, you can always join us if you like as we have the room, and who knows what kinds of birds we will see?"

"I know, and I would love to go. But now I have two that recently produced, and I wish to make sure they survive and fly."

"Emmitt, I don't know what to say. But thank you."

"You're very welcome, my friend. You get in touch with me if you ever need my help."

"You have already helped us out a lot, and again, I wish to say thanks."

Everyone standing around said, "Thank you," at different times.

We started loading the wagon, fluffing up the straw, and moving bedrolls around for more comfort. Tasha, Steve, and Vanessa harnessed up the horses and hitched up the wagon for the trip. I handed the dried meat to Krystle, who was already in the back of the wagon arranging things. She placed the meat in the basket with the rest of our food. Heather handed up Snowball and Sam, and Krystle found a comfortable spot for them to settle down.

Tasha asked, "Who is up front this time?"

Burdock said, "I guess I can climb up front for about an hour."

Steve said, "I will too."

They both moved up into the seat next to Tasha. Then everyone else scrambled up in the back. Vanessa sat next to Agatha. Ziggy was next to me on one side and Bailey on the other with her fearless kitten in her lap. Datilina seemed to be good riding up toward the front of the wagon.

Jack was the last one to climb up into the back, and he sat at the front as well. He said, "Sometimes it's better to see where you have been rather than where you're going."

"I guess we are all on board and ready to rock and roll. Steve, do we have everything?" I asked.

"As far as I know. I have Max, and I can see Bailey and her pet are not running down the path after us."

We just laughed at that one.

I looked at Bailey and said, "I would not leave you, Tabby, or Ziggy behind."

"Okay, let's get this show on the road. Emmitt, thank you again for all your hospitality and help. I hope to see you again soon."

"You're all very welcome, and be safe, and remember, if I can help in any way, get in touch with me. Send that big eagle to find me," he said.

We had to laugh at that one as well as Steve said, "If you ever want to fly again, I will have Max pick you up."

I asked, "I'm looking forward to seeing this town up the road. Vanessa, how large is it?"

"Marty, it's small."

"So what is the name of this town we are going to pass through?"

"It's called Molumphy, and you can't just pass through it as you will have to turn around and come back to the main road and then continue south again."

"Interesting name," I said.

"I think the family that has lived there for years and years founded it and, of course, used their own name," Heather commented.

"Seems like you told me the name of a different town the other day, or your dad did, and I don't remember that name."

Vanessa declared, "At this moment, I can't think of the other town's name either."

"Well, I guess it's not important," I said. Looking at Datilina, I asked, "Are there certain things we will need when it comes to your area?"

"Not as far as I know. The temperature is about like this, so we won't need heavy clothing, but if we can round up food and water for us and the animals, we may want to do that."

"Did you all have horses or wagons when you started out?" Bailey asked.

Datilina said, "We had a wagon when we started out, but about a week before we saw you the first time, the horses must have eaten something, and they got sick. We could not help them, and soon, they both died, so we started walking back."

"This would have been a long walk home," Ziggy commented.

"Yes, I think it would have been, and that is why we needed to get a wagon and at least one horse."

"Not nice, you know," I said.

"I know, Marty, and we discussed it among ourselves for some time because it was not something we wanted to do. I am sure pleased things worked out the way it did."

"I am too, and all of us have found some excellent friends because of that. It seems like a backward way to join our team," I replied.

"I guess it really was," Datilina said.

"So, what is it like where you're from?" Krystle asked.

"Well, there are forests with trees so large, you can get tired just walking around them and lots of rocky cliffs. There are a few waterfalls that I have always loved. The main town sits high on a mountain, and it is a beautiful sight."

"When was the last time all of you saw your town?" Vanessa asked.

As all of us were speaking, I noticed Burdock had turned and was listening, and Steve and Tasha were as well. As the discussion continued, everyone was paying attention as if learning in a classroom.

Burdock spoke up, saying, "All of us in the group were summoned to meet with the elders. Some of us rode up there. Some walked. But all of us arrived to see what they wanted. We were informed that something special would soon be happening. Of course, little did we know that something special was you. We spent the day speaking about it to some degree as they were telling us to look for three kids and pets. We were getting our wagon ready with help from the guards. They pointed out things we might need and then packed us up and sent us on our way. And that was about three weeks ago."

Datilina stated, "All people can go up the road to the high town, and that is where you find the king and queen of Etheral. The elders live there as well. You see, our cities were built for all to live a good life, and if anything attacked our towns, we could travel up the road to the top of the mountain, and we would all be safe behind high walls and archers. It's set up to be the highest point around."

Tasha cranked her head around and said, "I used to enjoy walking or riding up the hill just to see the view. It was wonderful looking out across the lands."

Datilina commented, "My parents and I would travel up there now and again, but I have always found it to be a long road to go up there. So for the most part, I have not bothered to travel up to the top of the hill. Most of my friends and family are in the lower city. As all of us were summoned to meet the elders before we left, we were very impressed with what we saw. Most of us had never been inside the castle walls."

Tasha said, "Yes, I found it wonderful just to meet them. They set us up with a wagon and supplies. Then we were heading out of the gates on our way north. I did not believe in any prophecy, but they did, and they were in a hurry to find those kids and pets. I thought it was rather strange."

"So do people have the chance to visit that part of the town often, or is it restricted?" Steve asked.

59

"Restricted?" she asked.

"Restricted is when you are not allowed to be someplace without permission," Bailey said.

"Well, I just think the king and queen have guards around them all the time and in the castle. If we wanted to go there at normal times, I guess we would have to have permission. I mean, people don't just walk in and see the royalty and elders, if that's what you mean."

"So what else is up there besides a castle?" Vanessa inquired.

"There is, of course, the castle for the king and queen along with the elders. There are also big houses for those who support all the royalty daily. One for all the guards and any laborers and one for all the staff who work at cleaning and cooking and such. The town of Upper Etheral is huge, with the castle in the center. All the shops and homes are spread out all over the upper part of the mountain," Tasha replied.

"Well, I am looking forward to seeing a real castle as I have never seen one before," I said.

Bailey spoke up. "That makes two of us."

"No, that makes three of us and possibly more," Vanessa stated as she looked at her sisters.

"I look forward to seeing it then, and all of you will be there," I replied.

"I love that idea, Marty," Tasha replied.

As Tasha made her statement, Datilina said the same thing. "I love that idea."

Bailey said, "Great minds think alike."

Burdock and Steve both had comments to add as well, with Burdock saying that place was fantastic. "We didn't have a lot of time to look around when we were there, and it would be nice to spend a good few hours there checking it all out."

Steve spoke out and said, "The more I hear of things around here, the more I feel like we're in Wonderland where Alice visited."

"Alice?" Heather asked.

Bailey remarked, "Steve must be talking about the little girl who fell into a rabbit hole and found all kinds of new adventures."

Krystle commented, "I really don't understand how falling into a hole in the ground could possibly ever be an adventure."

"It was a book of dreams and adventures of a little girl who, at times, could grow taller or smaller depending upon where she was," I replied.

"So that would be like all of you when you grow so tall," she said.

"No, not exactly. That Wonderland was a book created by an outstanding author," Bailey said.

Chapter 11

Arriving at Molumphy

After about an hour, the town came into sight, and all of us in the back of the wagon peeked over the front seat or leaned out over the side of the cart to see what it looked like. We could see a few people wandering around the houses, going into the central part of the town. We passed a few homes on the way, which were a bit different from what we could find back home. Most of these homes were made of rock.

The first house we rode close to looked like it had three floors. It looked like it had a basement and then a first floor, which could have been the main floor. Above that was what looked like the third floor. There was a long set of stairs going up the side of the building to what must have been the front door.

I thought, *I'm sure glad my parents don't have a house like that. I could just picture myself being worn out by the time I reach the top or the bottom of those stairs.*

Looking at the house, I noticed two pipes coming off the roof, which must have been the chimney for the second and top floor. It was a big house, and it made our house at home look small.

We looked at all the houses as we entered the town, and most of them had shutters that could be closed, I figured in case of storms. We passed about six more houses, and then we noticed what the entrance to the town itself was. It was like an entrance to a castle of some kind as there was a wall that looked like it encased the entire village. Oh, and it had a big arched opening. You could see about two feet of a picketed gate hanging on the back side of that arch. It could be dropped to prevent anyone from entering.

I was thinking, *The only thing missing here is a moat and a drawbridge. I guess if they had animals like that one Emmitt found, they could close the gate and keep it out. Or could they? He did say that thing spit out acid of some kind.*

As we passed under the arch and into town, I looked up to view that gate, which must have been at least six inches thick. We rode across a grooved area in the ground made of stone that would have allowed that gate to lock in place when it fell.

We saw shops and houses. There was a big tower just inside the gate that must have been at least thirty feet tall. It had a walkway all around the top part of the tower, kind of like I remembered seeing on a lighthouse on the Oregon Coast, and it had a couple of windows. Maybe they needed a lookout from time to time. As I looked around, I noticed the tops of at least three other towers in other parts of the town.

At any rate, the town seemed nice, and I felt a lot of happiness around me as if people were just pleased to be living here. All the buildings were different colors: white, yellow, green, and blue. It was the same for all the shops as they were all different, as if to tell them apart.

Steve said, "Other than all the different colors, this looks somewhat like what home would have been in the early years, don't you think, Marty?"

I said, "It does in a way without paved streets, crosswalks, fire hydrants, and stop signs. It almost has the look of a small town from the wild, wild West."

The more we advanced into town, the more I noticed that everything was designed around a well on the side of the street, close to the center of all the buildings. It looked like there was a street crossing, this one at the end, but I could not see where it went. For the most part, the town had about twenty significant shops and businesses. There were a lot of homes behind all those shops that we could see as we passed a few streets.

Many of the homes we could view behind the main street buildings reminded me of those that were painted white and had boards running up and down every so often and across to create a design. I think they call them *Tudor* or something like that. The windows looked like they were leaded glass, and some of them had attractive designs in them. They all had what seemed to be bars on the inside and shutters on the outside. The doors on the houses looked like they were thick and very sturdy.

In some places, they had flags on poles near the houses that had swords crossed and streamers flying below them. The roofs did not have shingles, like my father and I put on the Ziggy house. These roofs had something that looked like wood shakes or wooden shingles. It seemed like it might do the same kind of job as the asphalt ones.

Some of the homes had grass on their roofs. *Kind of weird,* I was thinking, *and I would sure not want to mow those lawns as I really hate heights. I could picture myself trimming the grass and falling off.* I was not sure how that kind of roof could stop the rain from getting in. *Maybe they have tarps, tar paper or some kind of rock or concrete under that, but it must work, or they would have changed it, I am sure.*

Tasha asked, "What do you want to do, Steve?"

Steve turned and asked, "Marty, what do you want to do?"

"Steve, that's entirely up to you because you're in the seat next to the driver."

Steve said, "Let's just park this thing someplace safe and look around."

Tasha replied, "Sounds good to me," and she took us to the center of town and found a suitable place to hitch up the horses.

Ziggy said, *I think I am going to remain a small loveable furball while we are here.*

So I pulled out the ramp and allowed all our pets to climb down. After that, everyone else jumped out of the back, took their places by their pets, and started wandering off to explore.

Some of the people from town who were up early gave us happy smiles and waved, but kept doing what they had set out to do. We viewed several shops and small stores. As we watched, people were coming out of homes and heading to those stores to open them up. All of us walked around and viewed some of the construction and designs of the buildings.

"Steve, look at how they support that building by placing those stone blocks and then piling timbers and more stone blocks. It looks like they were doing all they could to keep it from collapsing," I said.

"It does look like it has had one heck of a brace job," Steve said.

The entire building was leaning, but they had braced it to stop it from tipping over. It reminded me of that leaning tower of pizza, peso, or pieta. You know, that big tower that looks like it's about to fall over.

We looked at a few more houses. Then Bailey asked, "Why do they have a door up there on what looks like a third floor, with no walk, railing, or porch? I mean, what if someone opened that door and walked out?"

"Well, they would have a big step to the bottom, that's for sure," I commented.

"That would not be a step I would wish to take," Steve replied.

"Maybe it's a way of loading things into that top floor by driving a wagon under the door at ground level and then using a pulley system to raise things," I remarked.

As we continued to look around, we noticed some houses had ramps and some that didn't. Some had two floors, and a few had three. Down where there was a basement area, we could see a regular door entrance and what looked like a garage door about ten feet away.

Steve said, "I bet they use wood or coal to heat these places, and that is how they get it into the fireplaces or furnaces they might use."

"That could very well be true as that is how they did it, years ago in America," Bailey said.

Jack walked over and asked, "Did you see that well? It's so clear, you can see the bottom."

As I walked over to it, I said, "No, not yet." Then I looked down inside, and the water was about ten feet below the top rim of the well. As I viewed it, I could see down about forty feet to the very bottom. I said, "This is amazing as you can see the bottom so clearly. This water must really be pure."

People started to gather here and there and looked at us as if we were part of a museum. Many of them smiled and waved just like those we had seen earlier, and some said good morning as they walked by. There were a few who seemed to walk past us and then get a distance away and just watch us.

I turned to Bailey and asked, "Am I growing horns or something?"

"No, Marty, you're not. Why would you ask that?"

"It just seems some of those people just like to stand and look at us, and I am wondering if it's something I am doing, or is it because we have such a varied group of people?"

"I think it's a fact we are a varied lot," she replied.

"Yes, I guess you're right," I said.

Steve said, "Nope, buddy, you're growing horns. Big ones at that."

Ziggy sent me a thought, saying, *It could be that power everyone else feels as they get near you. Notice the air is exceedingly clean, and the water is pure, so maybe they feel your powers more easily.*

You could be correct, and I am sure we will find out, I sent back. I said to those around me, "Ziggy thinks because everything here is so clean and clear, our powers can be felt quickly."

Bailey said, "My mother told me we should learn to conceal our powers so people would not know who we are and would not feel our strengths. She was saying people will come out with weapons to protect themselves from us as it grows. On top of that, I have seen that in a vision."

"You saw that in a vision? When were you going to tell us about that?" Steve asked.

"Really, Bailey? When is this supposed to happen?" I asked.

"I am not sure as I saw it as all of us were walking around someplace and people running away and returning with crossbows."

"Well, it sounds like we need to learn how to hide our strengths and powers," I said.

"How can we do that as I am sure that would be beneficial?" Steve asked.

"I am not sure, but if I can bring forth my sword and hide it, maybe we can do the same thing with our powers," I said.

"Well, it may be like our pets hiding the powers they have and what they can become," Bailey said.

Chapter 12

Shopping in Molumphy

Burdock said, "Let's check out the equipment store and see what they have."

I said, "Sounds good to me," and all us guys headed for that store.

All the girls started window-shopping, looking for things like dresses and jeans and other things a girl might wish to have. Datilina and Tasha were looking after the horses, and soon they started browsing stores that made leather goods. Most of our pets just milled around our wagon. Some of them crawled under the wagon and got comfortable.

All of us guys walked into the store, wandered around, and viewed all the tools, ropes, and hooks. For all of us, it was like being in a candy store.

"Look at this, Marty," Steve said. "My dad used to have one of these years ago."

I replied, "I think my dad still has one."

Jack asked, "What's that you're talking about?"

"They call them scythes for cutting down weeds, and I guess in the old days, they used to cut wheat and even hay with them."

The store owner walked up and asked, "In the old days?"

"Well, the old days where we are from," I said.

"Son, they still use these all around here today." He paused a moment, looked at me, looked at Jack, Steve, and Burdock, and said,

"I see you have a wise one with you, and I know he has power and strength, but it seems you have powers as well. That young man in the back has some powers too, it seems."

"I am sorry if that bothers you, sir," I commented.

"No bother, son. It just seems you are very young to be a wise one, but you have the powers of one."

"We have been told that several times since we came over here."

"Came over here from where, son?"

"We are travelers from a great distance and are heading to the Denarian region to help them out with some problems."

"How great a distance might that be that you say you are from?"

"A very-long-ways away."

"I'm Tony Matthews, and this is my store."

"I am Marty, and our wise one is Jack. This is Burdock and my friend Steve."

"Welcome. Now please tell me how I may help you."

Burdock said, "We were just going to look around and see what you have. Then we can figure out if we are going to need any of it."

Tony said, "Well, you be my guest."

"Thank you," I replied.

Tony asked Jack, "Can I speak to you?"

Jack responded, "Of course."

So the two of them walked off to the other end of the store. Steve and I knew what it was they were talking about.

Suddenly, it was as if Tony had become an overjoyed kid happy to find a merry-go-round. He came running back to us and said, "I knew it the moment you entered my store. Wait until the townspeople here about this."

I spoke up and asked Tony, "Please don't tell everyone just yet."

"Of course, but they will all know if they walk past you. Someone came through here yesterday talking about some teenagers with pets that freed a god, and most of us didn't believe the story, but now after feeling your power, I understand it could have very well been true."

"It is true, and we have a trip to make south, about another hundred miles, to help some of our new friends and their families."

"That is the Denarian realm," he said.

"Yes, it is, and Burdock and his friends need our help, and we are going to do what we can."

Burdock spoke up and said, "An invisible monster or demon is destroying our outlands."

"Let me know what you need, and I will do what I can to help you out."

"Thank you very much, sir," Burdock said.

We started looking around, and we found rope, shovels, and tarps.

I walked over to Tony and asked him, "Would you consider bartering for some of the things we need?"

He asked me, "What do you have to offer?"

"Someone gave us some homemade items to barter with, but I am not sure if you would be interested."

"Let's take a look, son, and see what you have to trade."

I said to Jack, "We will be right back as I am going to show Tony the things Mike gave us to barter with."

"Okay. We will set things on the counter and hope we can come to an arrangement."

As we reached the wagon, Tony said, "This is a very nice wagon. It looks like it was made north of here. I know of only one person who makes this kind of wagon, and he is a friend of mine."

"This is George and April's wagon from up north," I responded.

"I have known them for years, young man, and we barter all the time, so whatever you need, we can deal with. Let's not worry about what you have now as you may need that later. George and April have three daughters, and we see them here every few months."

"The girls—Vanessa, Krystle, and Heather—are with us."

"They are?" he asked.

"Yes, they are," I said, and as we were talking, I noticed them walking out of the shop two doors down and yelled, "Vanessa, would you please come over here?"

"Oh my gosh!" Tony said. "Wait until my wife sees them. She will be so excited they are here again. Vanessa how are you, dear?" he asked.

"I am very well, Tony, and how is Becky?"

"She is fine, and you and your sisters should run up to the house and surprise her."

"We can do that."

And off she ran. She yelled at Heather and Krystle, and all three of them ran down one of the side streets, with their pets following behind.

Ziggy was right beside me, and I mentally said, *I guess they were excited.*

She sent back a thought, saying, *It sure seemed so.*

Do you ever wish to find other clothes to wear? I asked her.

I am fine the way I am when I am a person, if that is what you mean, Ziggy replied.

Well, yes, because I think being a cute little furball with a dress on would probably make you look out of place. I just think that you may wish to get some other undergarments and clothes to wear while we have a chance to get them.

Marty, sometimes I wonder about you. I mean, who knows? Maybe I could be a cute little puppy in a dress and look great. It might be a good idea, doing some shopping though, she said.

Well, I think one of these times, we need to consider getting you and Agatha a new wardrobe, I replied.

If you say so. I will send a thought to Agatha to see if she wants to change so we can shop, Ziggy said.

Tony was saying, "My wife and I never had children, and when these girls come to town, it's like getting a visit from children you love and miss. They are so wonderful."

"Well, I hope your wife will be surprised," I commented.

"Let's go see what your friends have found and see what we can do."

We walked back in, and I looked at the counter and said, "Hold on, guys. That will be a lot more than we can afford."

"Let me see what we have here," Tony said. He started looking things over and writing down details and said, "I think we can handle this without any problems."

"That would be great," I replied.

He said, "I wonder when George will be in town again."

"I can ask him if you like."

"Sure, but that will take some time."

"No, not really. Let me see what I can find out."

He looked at me as if he did not understand the mind-meld thing or the calling and hanging up.

So, I walked off to the side a bit and mentally reached April, asking, *When do you and George plan on revisiting Molumphy?*

When we get home and get things squared away, we will probably be bringing your moms back with us to Mike and Marilyn. Why?

So about two weeks? I asked.

Yes, give or take a few days.

Okay. I am dealing with Tony, and I think he wants to make a deal.

She kind of laughed and said, *That, sounds like Tony. Just tell him whatever you need, we will cover with produce and handmade goods.*

Okay, thank you.

Tony was still looking at me, and I said, "April says they will be back over here in about two weeks, give or take a day. I told her you wanted to make a deal, and she laughed and said, 'That sounds like Tony. Just tell him whatever you need, we will trade for produce and handmade goods.'"

"Did you just communicate with her somehow?"

"Yes, I did."

"Really?"

"Yes, sir," I said.

"So you really are from another world?"

"We are, but our world is not so different from yours. It seems that what you have here is the early years of our country around one hundred years ago."

He replied, "I hope sometime we will be able to talk about the differences."

"I am sure we will have time when we get events under control."

"Marty, I guess we are good. I have a list of all the supplies you have here, and if you need more, just let me know. Oh, and please tell April it is great to see the girls again."

"I am sure the girls will tell her, but I will contact her and let her know."

Bailey, Tasha, and Datilina came into the shop, and I looked at Bailey, and she said, "I traded a flute for a new skirt. What do you think of it?"

I looked at it, and it was made of leather and looked great on her as it was about from her waist to her knees and sliced about halfway up all the way around roughly every two inches. Of course, she had shorts on now instead of jeans under that, but it gave her a new world look. She had a new leather top as well and was now starting to look like a warrior, I thought. On top of that, she was just perfect in my mind.

So, I answered her question with a "Bailey, you look hot and sexy in that outfit. But then you have always looked hot and sexy to me."

"How did I know you would say that?" she asked.

I said, "You always know what I will say." Of course, I did not tell her the tennis shoes looked out of place.

"Okay. Did any of the rest of you find things you need?"

Datilina said, "I would love to have a new belt I saw at that one shop, but I don't know if he will trade for it."

Tony asked, "Which shop, hon?"

"The leather shop across the way."

"Let's you and I go have a talk with him and see what he says."

I spoke up and said, "Datilina, this is Tony, and he owns this shop, and, Tony, this is our friend Datilina, and beside her is Bailey and Tasha."

"Well, ladies, let's all go see what we can do."

All three girls looked at one another, and then Datilina asked, "Really?"

He said, "Yes."

I said, "Go with Tony and see what you can do as we have a few things we can trade if need be. Oh, and, girls, you may wish to invest in some good boots along with clothes."

"Wow! Okay."

Then the three girls joined Tony and were off to see the store owner across the street.

Burdock came over, stood next to me, turned his head, looked at me, and said, "It's amazing how people understand you and are just like us, wanting to help."

"I find it interesting myself," I said. "I mean, in our world, I am just a high school student."

"Well, in this world, you are what we need," he said.

"Thank you. I do hope you're correct. Do we have everything we are going to need?"

"We have many things we don't need. However, those items will be good for trade if we need that," Steve commented.

"Okay. Well, let's put all the things we can trade in with the other things Mike gave us in the wagon and then make sure we don't lose it."

The guys walked up, and Steve asked, "Do you think we can find a store that has pants and shirts?"

"I am sure we can, and yes, I agree. Mine are getting crusty as well."

Jack looked at me and said, "I am guessing that means dirty."

"Yes, it does, and we do need to make sure and wash the ones we have as I only brought two pairs of pants and a couple of shirts. Of course, I brought three pairs of underwear, three pairs of socks, and an extra pair of tennis shoes that all need to be cleaned."

Steve said, "I am in the same boat, Marty."

Jack spoke up and said, "I am there as well because I didn't plan on bringing a lot of clothes. This pack carrying my clothes under my robe is starting to give off an odor."

"Burdock, what about you? If so, let's get anything you need while we have a town around us," I said.

"That goes for anyone else who needs to get some clothes. Let's get it done."

"We just need to find a way to wash what is dirty and hang it all out to dry," Jack replied.

"Let's see if there is laundry soap and bar soap and a few towels and add them to the list."

When Tony came back with the girls, Datilina was wearing a new belt along with a new skirt. Tasha had found a skirt and top made of leather. They both looked great. Bailey walked in behind them, and she had new leather pants to go with the rest of the clothes she already got. They were tight fitting and looked great. All the girls had new pairs of boots.

I asked, "What did you trade?"

She said, "Tony talked to the owner, and the next thing we knew, he walked up to us, measured us, walked off, and came back with all this. He said, 'You are part of the team to help us. We will help all of you.'"

"So, Tony, did you tell him five men in black suits would show up and break arms and legs?"

"Five men in black suits?" he asked with a questioning look on his face.

"Just kidding. It used to be in the old days, the kind of thing you find when people strong-arm merchants."

"Oh, I did not have to strong-arm anyone. The people know you're here, and they will soon be gathering to meet all of you."

"Tony, we added a few more items as we needed soap and towels as well."

"No problem, Marty. Let's get you loaded up and get that load covered."

We all walked out. Then Steve and I jumped up in the wagon. We started taking the items and placing them next to all the trade items we already had stacked. By the time we were done with all the wheeling and dealing, we had a three-foot-tall pile all the way across the front of the wagon. We then covered all that with the tarps and used the straw that was in that space to soften more of the other areas.

I kept thinking of how long and wide this wagon was and thought about what Tony had said about George making it. I asked Tony, "You said George made this wagon?"

"Yes, he did. It's a beautiful piece of work. I will have to see if I can get him to build one for me if I get all the materials."

"Well, who knows? Maybe that can be part of that deal. Just don't tell him I suggested that."

We both laughed and tied down the tarp and made sure it was secure.

Some of the townspeople started to wander over to us. Soon, there must have been a hundred people all around us, asking questions about what it was like, where we came from, and whether we were here as the prophecy had said. Some of the people left and then returned with food, water, blankets, and clothes that would fit all of us.

I looked at Steve, and he said, "I guess we don't have to go shopping, do we?"

"I guess not."

Bailey said, "This is beautiful. Do you really wish to give this away?"

The young woman who gave her the blouse said, "It is for you to wear, and if you are wearing it, that means I could contribute to your well-being."

"Thank you. I will wear this with pride," Bailey said.

Ziggy and Agatha had changed because they were going to do some shopping as well, but people walked up handing them dresses, skirts, pants, and lady things.

I said to Ziggy, "I guess we may have some new clothes for you and Agatha as well."

Everyone was getting ready to put things in their packs, and one woman came up and said, "My name is Marta. Why don't all of you grab a clean change of clothes and then take a bath at my place? Gather up all the dirty clothes you have that need washing, and I will make sure they are clean. I would love to do that for all of you. Then all of you will have time to eat lunch before you leave."

Steve said, "A bath is always a good thing, that's for sure."

She said, "I have a bathhouse for people who don't have running hot water, so please come with me."

I asked, "You are willing to wash all our dirty clothes?"

"Yes, all your dirty clothes. So, gather all of them up and come with me and bring a clean change of clothes as well."

As we entered, we noticed there were a lot of different places with doors like we would see at home in restrooms—you know, the stall doors so people couldn't see you.

She said, "I will show you how to fill the tubs, and then you're on your own."

All of us noted how she used the water valves. Then all of us headed to different rooms.

She said, "Just place all your dirty clothes in a pile under the door so I can pick them up. Then all of you enjoy a good bath. It will take about two hours to wash and dry your clothes in this heat."

Steve spoke up and said, "Okay by me."

As we all entered a room, it didn't take long before piles of clothing were stacked under each door. Soon, I saw Marta's legs outside of my bath area. All the dirty clothes I had brought over and placed in a pile were picked up. She placed all our clothes in different baskets. Then as quickly as she had arrived, she disappeared.

I had to admit it was nice to have a good bath. As all of us dried, changed, and walked out of our little rooms, I noticed smiles and could feel happiness from all.

I said to Bailey, "I sure hope she doesn't mix up the underwear."

Bailey turned and poked me in the ribs and said, "Oh, you're just too funny."

Burdock said, "She has a nice little laundry and bathhouse here."

All of us agreed. We asked Marta if we could lend a hand, but her reply was "I have plenty of help. I picked up each pile, which I placed in different baskets. So, if you would write your name on your own pile of clothes, that would be most beneficial."

All of us gathered up pencils and papers, wrote our names down, and set those in our own baskets of clothes.

I asked her, "Are you sure we can't help you launder all this?"

She said, "You go shop and get something to eat. I will take care of this."

We all walked back to the wagon to make sure the load was secure.

Then I said, "I guess we need to find a good place to eat."

Tony walked up as all of us had gathered around the wagon to make sure everything was secure and said, "You won't have to pay for anything today. Everyone in town is pitching in to help every one of you. I told you it would be hard to keep them from finding out."

"Yes, you did say that," I replied.

We made sure everything was ready for the road, and then all of us headed to a place for lunch.

CHAPTER 13

Bobbles Burrow for Lunch

We all entered a place that had a big proud sign that was almost as wide as the building saying Bobbles Burrow. I looked up as I walked under the sign, hoping it would not come unhinged from the wall and fall.

As we entered, we were face to face with a beautiful golden-haired woman wearing a white pearl necklace and a pink blouse. The sleeves came down just past her elbows with small dangling balls all the way around. She was wearing a lovely short black skirt, and it had a pocket with what looked like an order pad in it. She had high cheekbones, blue eyes, a slightly curved-up nose, and superb-looking legs. Of course, I was not really paying a lot of attention to her since I only glanced at her once or twice. Okay, so I appreciate beauty.

She stood there with her hands on her hips and said, "I am sorry, but no animals are allowed in here."

Speaking out, I replied, "Well, let me see if we can change some of that for you." I turned to all those with animals and said, "If you can take human form, please do, and those who can't will have to remain outside."

Suddenly, to my surprise, one by one, every one of them changed. I really did not expect to see all the animals switching to human form. I felt at least two or three would remain as they had been.

I looked at Sam and Snowball, and instead of seeing cats, I now saw a young man and a girl that looked like brother and sister, about the same age as Krystle and Heather. They were both dressed as warriors. The girl was dressed the way I usually saw Agatha and Ziggy.

The boy was dressed in a shirt and pants and had what looked like something women used to wear in the old days. What was that? I think it was called a corset or something like that, but it was leather. He wore black leather pants and had wide leather bands around his wrists. He also had what looked to me to be shoulder pads made from leather. Clutched in one hand was a double-bladed ax like the one Agatha carried. Ziggy and Agatha seemed surprised to see the two of them change as well.

Then I noticed a small girl, thinking someone had allowed their kid to roam in here and join us. I tried not to pay any attention to her as I felt she was just one of the kids from town wanting to learn about what was going on. As I looked at her, she gave me a squinty-eyed look, so I turned my head a bit and gave her that same kind of look.

After I did that, she stomped her foot and yelled, "Stop that!"

I looked around and then asked, "Is she with us?"

Bailey said, "Oh, I guess you really don't know her. Marty, this is my kitten. This is Tabby."

I broke out laughing and said, "I guess I just expected her to be about the same size as all the rest."

"She told me she is a little tired, so she wanted to be a little girl."

I commented, "I see. Well, Tabitha, I am glad you joined us."

"Thank you, Marty. I am too," she replied.

Max had become a kid about our age, with a dull red vest, gray shirt, jeans, and boots that came up between his ankles and knees. The tops of the boots were rolled over. He had a strap over his shoulder with a few pouches on it and gloves that looked big on him. He also had a sword he held in both hands as if he was having difficulty knowing what to do with it.

I said, "Max, now you have shown us just about everything. You have turned into about any kind of animal you can think of, and I guess I have not pictured you as a person."

"Marty, I have often told you, in this world, our mind is our limitation."

I said to Steve, "I guess my grandmother was correct about him as a ferret and being just about anything he can think of."

"Yes, Marty, he is very versatile, but I do think he needs a smaller sword," Steve countered.

Our waitress gave us a jaw-dropping look and started to stumble backward as the changes took place one animal after another. She was trying to grab onto something as she was falling. I caught her in time before she fell over a chair behind her.

I asked, "Are you okay?"

She looked at me and then looked at each of those who had just changed and said, "I am now, I think. Thank you."

We found seats and ordered our meals.

Steve asked, "How old is she?"

I said, "She is probably twenty-two at the most and too old for us."

"Do you think age really matters?" he asked.

I commented, "If people are happy together, age should not be a big factor."

"I think she is older," he replied.

"She is attractive, but it's not me who is concerned about her age. I have all I can handle, and my hands are full with Bailey and my little warrior. You know, Steve, if you never ask questions, you never get answers. Just ask her how old she is. I thought you were into Vanessa."

"Guys don't ask girls their age, and yes, I do like Vanessa."

I said, "So, you're afraid to ask her how old she is?"

"Well, it's just not what is done," he said.

As she walked by me, I said, "Excuse me, how old are you?"

She looked at me strangely and said, "Thirty-one. Why?"

I said, "Wow, I guess I was off as I said you looked like you're twenty-two at the most. However, it was Steve who was wondering about your age and was afraid to ask."

She looked at me, gave me a wink, and said, "Thank you for that."

"You're very welcome."

More people started to gather and were now entering the eatery and gathering around to just see the three from another world, and our waitress walked up and said, "I can get rid of them if you wish."

"Not necessary. I will speak to them." As I said that, I stood up and raised my hand. Soon, it became hushed. Then I spoke. "I am very pleased to see all of you here today, and we will do our best to talk with all of you before we get back on the road. But please allow us to eat. If you step outside and wait, we will be out soon."

Of course, it had only been about four hours since we had breakfast with Emmitt.

As we finished, the waitress walked over to me and said, "All your meals have been paid for. I am pleased I was able to be the one to serve you."

"Well, we could not have asked for a nicer person to take care of us. Thank you. By the way, my name is Marty."

"I know who you and your friends are, and from what I feel and have heard, you're what our prophecy is all about. That prophecy is centuries old. It has been told that since you entered our world, you have done wondrous things already to help others."

"All of us and everyone with us has helped make changes along the way. We are a team."

"Well, my name is Sophia, Sophia Atherton."

As everyone was walking out, I held back to the last and followed them.

As I was getting ready to exit, Sophia said, "If you ever need my help, you let me know because I am a good cook, and you may need one. I also know how to use a bow with complete accuracy."

I said on my way out, "We may have a big need for a good cook at our new base camp, which is about a one-day ride north. We have a lot of people we saved from slavery up there starting new lives, building homes, and they do need a couple of good cooks. As for a woman who can use a bow, that may very well be one thing we will need even now in our travels as it seems we are going to be facing many situations. I will have to find out if we have anyone who can use a bow."

She said, "Look me up on your way back through or ask the others if they feel good about me joining your team now."

"I will ask—but no promises. I hope you have a great afternoon and look forward to seeing you again soon."

As I was leaving, my mind was turning over and over as I thought, *I better be careful here because I better never tick off Bailey by getting too friendly with another woman. Bailey would place my head on a platter.* But then I thought, *she is older, and I am only sixteen. Many feel, age is not important, and others do, even so there will never be a problem. But I can still admire beauty.*

I walked outside to meet a huge group of people that had gathered and was approached by Steve as he walked up and said, "They want to meet you."

"You know, in all my life, I never figured I would really be important to others."

Steve said, "Well, buddy, guess what? In this world, you are important, and Bailey and I are with you all the way."

We walked into the crowd, hearing people asking, "Is this really them?" People could feel my power but still wanted to shake my hand and hug me. One woman hugged me and stepped back and said, "You just cured me of the pain I have had for twenty years with just a hug."

I said, "I am not sure if that was me who did that, but I am pleased you don't have that pain anymore."

Bailey asked me, "Is your grandmother a healer?"

"Yes, she is," I replied.

Bailey took the hand of a man who was having a hard time walking and said, "Please walk with me." He took her hand and then walked with her as she brought him to me and said, "This man needs your help, Marty."

"Bailey, I'm not a healer."

"Try, Marty," she replied.

The man came to me, very slowly put his arms around me, and hugged me. He started to shake, and then suddenly, he said, "Oh, the power you have is so great, and I have never felt that before in my entire life." He stepped back away from me and stood up and said, "You are a healer. You are the one. Thank you for what you have done."

I looked at him, wondering what I had done, and noticed how he walked away and realized he was walking with no problems now. "Bailey, was that real?"

"Yes, Marty, that was real. You have power so great, you can help others."

After touching and hugging people, I found myself ready to climb aboard the wagon and be on the road again. I asked Bailey, "Do we have anyone who can use a bow in our group?"

"Not that I know of. Why?" she asked.

"That waitress said that she's a good cook and can use a bow with complete accuracy. So, I was wondering if we should ask her to join us."

"Oh, I see. So, you just think we should ask that waitress along even though she's hot, do you?"

"Oh, come on. Bailey, you know you're the only girl in my life. On top of that, a good cook might be good, and one who can use a bow could be important to us."

"Yes, yes, sure, Marty," she stated wryly. "Well, let's ask the rest of those with us if they can use a bow. If no one else can, and if all of them agree we should add her to our team, I will try to get over my being jealous of a beautiful, hot-looking girl who seems to take your mind off me. Okay, the question for all of you."

"Listen up," I said, and everyone stopped talking. "We have a question, and we need an answer."

Everyone seemed to just be waiting now for the question.

Bailey asked, "Is there anyone among us who knows how to use a bow?"

We watched and noticed heads shaking and people saying, "Not that I know of" or "I sure can't."

Datilina said, "If we had a person who could use one, that would be a wonderful gift to us all."

I looked at Bailey and said, "It's up to you. Yes, she is hot. Maybe she did take my mind away for a moment, but it's always been you and me, Bailey, and always will be."

"Okay, go see if she wants to join us. Don't worry. If you fall in love with her, I will simply slice your throat."

"Oh, now that is a nice feeling and thought," I squeaked. "Okay, I will go and ask."

I walked back to the eatery and stepped inside, and what I found was a fantastic-looking girl with a bow standing there. Her waitress attire had been changed into a fine-looking leather skirt that hung between her waist and her knees. It was sliced about every two inches all the way around like the one Bailey just got. Under that, she had what looked like skinny jeans that were waist high.

She had boots that looked like they were all leather. She also wore fancy kneepads for protection. She was wearing a top that seemed to allow a young guy's imaginations to go wild. She was holding a bow like those I had only seen in movies as it appeared to have one entire section made from curved wood, and it was wrapped as if to reienforce the entire design. She looked at me and said, "You know you need my help, so I am ready if you are."

I said, "Let's make it happen then."

We both walked out and approached the wagon, and Steve looked at her and said, "Wow."

Then Vanessa smacked his shoulder.

He said, "It was just an expression."

Bailey looked at her and said, "Not only is she a beauty, but also, knows how to look the part of a woman who knows how to use a bow."

"Sophia, you met Bailey earlier," I said.

"Yes, I did, and I am pleased to be able to join you."

"I hope you can use that," Bailey said.

Suddenly, she reached over her back and pulled out an arrow, and looking straight at Bailey, she said, "See the 'O' on that Bobbles Burrow sign behind me?"

Bailey said, "I see it, but it's some distance away now. So what?"

She turned around with fantastic speed and placed an arrow in the center of the "O."

Everyone cheered, and Bailey said, "Okay by me as I think you will make an excellent protector and a great addition to the team."

I said, "It looks like you're part of the team, so go get a bedroll and some clothes."

"Bailey, would you hold my bow please while I get my pack and bedroll?"

Bailey said, "Anytime."

She ran off and, in a few minutes, returned with a pack and bedroll and said, "I am ready anytime all of you are."

Bailey climbed up in the wagon and said, "Hand me your pack and roll. Then I will put it in place with the others."

"Thank you," she said and then climbed aboard herself to join the others.

I heard, "Wow," "You sure know how to shoot," "Glad you're with us," "How long have you been using a bow?" And suddenly, Max spoke and said, "You're awesome."

Sophia spent lots of time answering questions and getting to know her new friends. Everyone was situated on the wagon now except for two of the girls. I walked over to them as they were talking with Tony and Becky, standing in front of their shop.

I said, "Krystle, Heather, we must leave now."

"Tony, thank you for what you and the townspeople have done, and I hope to see you all again soon."

We all shook hands, and then he said, "I see you are getting away with our cook and archer, so now we must replace both."

"Send someone back up to our base camp and find out if there is an archer there. I don't have a clue if there is. You may also find a good cook. We have several good people there. It's about a full day's travel. Just have them ask for Mike and Marilyn."

"Do you mean April's brother and his wife?" Tony asked.

"Yes, that's who I am talking about. We are building our base camp on the hill above their farm."

"I will send a couple of people over there in the morning to see if they have any archers for sure as we never know when we need one."

"I don't mean to take yours away from you."

"You do what you must do to protect our lands and people and come back soon."

"We will sure do our best," I said.

Tony said, "You will have to turn around and leave the way you came in. As you go past the first two houses outside of the wall, there is a road to your left that will take you south."

"Thank you, and we will see you again soon."

We climbed on board, and since everyone was in human form now, no ramp was needed, but once on board, a few of them changed.

Suddenly, a woman came running up to the wagon, yelling, "Don't forget your clothes!"

I said, "Hold up. We almost forgot to pick up all the clothes this lady washed for us."

I jumped down and walked up to her as she said, "I am glad I caught you before you left."

"Well, I think we just about forgot what a great favor you're doing for us by washing everything."

She said, "Come with me. Then I will give you a basket filled with folded clothes. All the clothes are divided by name."

When we reached the basket, I found it to be heavy, yet I felt I could handle it. However, the woman said, "You take one side. Then I will take the other." So, she took one handle, and then I took the other, and off we went.

Back at the wagon, Steve and Bailey both grabbed the basket, and all of us were going to remove the clothes, and the woman said, "Oh no, keep the basket as you will need it later."

I looked at her and gave her a hug, and she started shaking, then looked at me with a surprised look on her face and said, "Thank you.

I am not sure what you just did, but suddenly, I feel less tired and better than I have felt in a long time. Thank you very much."

I said, "No, it is I who thanks you, and I hope you have a great afternoon."

She walked off and looked over her shoulder as she left and waved, and I climbed back on board and said, "It's time, Tasha."

Tasha was upfront with Jack and Datilina, and I heard Tasha say, "It's time to rock and roll."

I gave Tasha the directions Tony had given me, and soon we were rocking and rolling again on our way out of town. We waved at all the townspeople as we were leaving. Some of the kids ran after us for a short period as we were heading out, but shortly we were riding under that arch again, leaving town and heading south.

CHAPTER 14

Leaving Molumphy

Everyone was getting settled in with backpacks and sleeping rolls, and soon I looked over at Burdock, Vanessa, and Stevel. They all seemed to be taking a nap. Ziggy was in my lap now and Tabby in Bailey's. Agatha was next to Vanessa. Everyone who was not napping was talking with our newest team member, Sophia, finding out all about her bow skills. Max was right there with Heather, Krystle, Sam, and Snowball.

Bailey said, "I am glad you invited her along as I had a vision of her teaching the girls how to shoot a bow about two weeks ago. I do have a strong feeling she will be needed."

"You were teasing me and telling me we should take a vote about her joining us, and you already knew she would be with us? So, you had a vision before we came over here that included her?"

"Yes, I did, but I can't tell you all I know, and I feel you understand that," she said.

"Well, I felt it was a good idea to have her with us because I know I sure can't use a bow," I said.

"Let's just say I have a feeling we will all be pleased she joined us," Bailey commented.

"What do you think of our newest human forms of life?" I asked.

"You mean Max, Snowball, and her brother, Sam?"

"Yes, that is exactly what I mean."

"I think it's rather cool to see them all as people."

"I do too, and I hope they like it, and I hope they can stay that way for as long as they wish. And what about this little item you have in your lap?"

"You mean Tabby?" she asked.

I said, "Yes. That kitten of yours sure surprised me today."

"They won't be able to do that when we go home though. Correct?"

"I really don't know, but it would sure be great if they could," I said.

"Yes, it would be fantastic," she said.

"I know we can do things over there we do here, like speaking to each other mentally. I know my grandmother can heal as I saw her treat my mother. She does other things she calls magic, and then she would tell me that's all it is, but it can't be. I have a feeling some of what all of us can do here, we will be able to do at home, but I just don't know the limitations of it all," I replied.

Bailey declared, "I know my parents are the same way, and Steve was saying that at one time, his father could move things without using his hands. So, maybe other things work the same way. Could you imagine Max going to school?"

"No, I sure can't, but if he could, I am sure we would see some very interesting events taking place."

Both of us laughed at that one.

"What if Sam and Snowball came over and went to school? I bet kids would really love the way she looks, but what about her name? I mean she would have to come up with a new one if she was in school." I voiced.

"That would be like Ziggy and Agatha going to school. Agatha could get away with her name and, I guess, Ziggy to some degree," she said.

"One thing we have found is Vanessa, and her sisters have animals that change along with ours. We have even seen some kinds of birds do that," I said.

90

"I sure hope all animals in this land can't change and turn into something like elephants and sit on us," Bailey said.

"Bailey, you're trying to be cute. I never wish to see something like an elephant sitting on you."

"Marty, if all other animals can change, we could be in for some big trouble over here."

"For some reason, I don't think a lot of animals over here can really change, at least not like our pets do when we need them. I have been thinking about George and April, the girls and their pets, and how they can communicate and their pets can change. Most others over here can't do that, so why is it they can?" I asked.

"Well, we know Jack can speak mentally and a few others can, along with Sky and Jasmin, but I think you're correct. We have seen things that are already ugly and just have a way of hiding it. Of course, I know there are going to be some that can't hide it. I mean, we have not seen any other birds turn into humans or things like that."

As we traveled along for a few hours, what we saw was mostly forest and a few animals, streams, and, once in a great while, a person in the distance. We were on more of a dirt road now than just a path like we had traveled the days before. I was finding it a lot more comfortable on this trip than that last one.

"This is a very quiet place, isn't it?" I asked Bailey.

She said, "It is, and I think I would love to lean against you and take a nap. Do you mind?"

"Of course, I don't mind," I replied.

She said, "I don't want you getting upset with me snuggling up to you in front of that new hot chick."

"Stop that. You know what hot chick I like."

"I do?" she asked.

"Sure. It's Ziggy," I replied.

"Oh, Marty, you are pathetic." And she poked me in the ribs and snuggled up close.

"You know better than anyone else who is important to me. You and Ziggy rate the highest always."

91

"I hope I never must compete with Ziggy," she said.

"Bailey, you will never have to do that. Ziggy is always my sidekick, best friend, and protector. You, on the other hand, are my sidekick, best friend, and the one I love."

"Hold on just a moment. What did you just say?"

"What do you mean?"

"You just said I'm the one you love."

I pulled back a bit and looked at her, and she was looking right at me, as she always does when she knows what I am thinking. Of course, this time, I let it slip. Yes, I know she understood what came out of my mouth, and I asked, "You're telling me I said I love you?"

"Yes, you did, and I heard you."

"Bailey, that must be some mistake. I'm almost positive I could not have said that."

A little voice in my head said to me, *Yup, I heard you say that.*

I looked down at Ziggy, who looked like she was sleeping in my lap, and spoke out, saying, "Quiet, Ziggy."

"What's that? Did Ziggy tell you she heard you say that to me?"

"Ziggy's asleep. Bailey, how could she even know what I said?"

Suddenly, Bailey went silent, and I knew she was communicating with Ziggy. She said, "Marty, she heard you say it."

"So maybe I said it, but it was just a slip of the tongue or something like that."

"You know, Marty, I love you too."

"Bailey, I already know that, just like you know I love you, but why make it all mushy and stuff?"

"Mushy and stuff?" she asked.

"Well, you know what I mean. The two of us saying the words of love. Then comes the kissing and holding hands, dating and romance. Next, we would be engaged and married. After that, I would be watching you gaining weight, having difficult time fixing dinners, taking baths, and even walking because of the fact that you would be carrying a baby. Of course, one baby would not be enough, so we would have to have half a dozen kids, and then we would have no more adventures at all."

"Marty, are you about done?"

"Yes, I am."

"Good. So let's just forget you told me you love me, even though you didn't say you loved me a lot or just a little, and we can just go on as we have for the past years. You and I both know what kinds of feelings we have for each other, and we always want to be close."

"I have tried to tell you several times and hoped you could see a future with us in it. You know I've never been good with words when it comes to you and me. But I have always felt you are the most special woman in my life."

"Marty, I know. I feel the same way about you."

"That I am the most special woman in your life?"

"No, you know what I mean."

"Of course, I do, and I know I had never had to say those words to you before today as you always knew, just like I have always known."

"Did you say you wanted to snuggle?"

"I did."

"Are you sure you won't get upset about that in front of that hot beautiful-looking chick?"

"I don't know. She might get upset and want to whip up on you," I said.

We both laughed, and I snuggled up to her and held her tight.

CHAPTER 15

A Good Place for the Night

After both of us had fallen asleep, the travels continued until it was almost dark. Then Tasha, Jack, and Datilina started looking for a suitable place to camp for the night. They found an area with an old abandoned building on it, and they pulled up near it.

Datilina said, "Let me have a look before we get everyone ready to unload." Then she climbed down and walked over to the building. She walked all around it, entered it, walked through it, and then came back out and said, "So far, it seems safe."

Jack turned around and said, "Hey, Burdock, looks like we have a place for the night here."

Burdock opened his eyes and shook his head and asked, "Did I hear you correctly about a place for the night?"

"Yes, we have found a place that looks good so far."

Burdock asked me, "Did you hear what Jack told me?"

I said, "Yes, I just did. So I guess we must offload everyone. I am sure some are ready for a break anyway. Do we need the ramp anymore?"

Everyone changed to people and just jumped down.

"Well, I guess not," I said.

Tasha and Jack climbed down, and Jack said, "Let me give you a hand with the horses and wagon."

Both waited until everyone was out of the back, then guided the horses and wagon to what looked like an excellent place to set the wagon for people to sleep in.

Tasha said, "This should work for the wagon if we unhook it here, and it looks like that is an old horse paddock."

"I agree," said Jack.

They left the wagon in a good location and walked the team of horses to the shelter area.

Datilina walked over with feed sacks and water for them, and Sophia then asked, "Who do I help with dinner?"

I commented, "That would be Vanessa."

Sophia turned and saw Vanessa and asked, "Can I help with dinner?"

"Sure, you can. I will never pass up help with dinner," she said as she laughed.

Bailey and I walked around the area and were checking it out with Ziggy and Tabby at our side. As the four of us walked, we discussed a few different things. We noticed the others were wandering around and checking out the old buildings and laughing it up. Tabby and Ziggy were both speaking of today's events. They were discussing the feelings of being human, while Bailey and I deliberated something different.

"What if we get down there and we can't help them?" I queried.

"Marty, if there is a way to help them, I know we will make it happen."

"I sure hope so," I responded.

"So did you feel embarrassed about saying what you felt earlier today?"

"Bailey, I have wanted to tell you for a long time and just never knew how to."

"You did a pretty good job of it today."

"Well, thank you. Okay, now back to what is needed now."

"What's that, Marty?" she probed.

"I think we need to make sure everyone finds a place to bed down for the night while we still have daylight. And we need to make sure Vanessa and Sophia have help with fixing dinner."

She looked at me, gave me a shove, then asked, "You did that on purpose, didn't you?"

"What's that, Bailey?" I asked.

"You changed the subject, and you know it," she said.

"Me?" I asked.

"Yes, you, as we were talking about our feelings."

"Oh, I'm sorry. I thought we had finished discussing that," I replied.

"Oh, forget it. I should know better than to discuss love with you."

I turned my head and looked at her, and she had this ticked-off look on her face and was shaking her head, and I said, "Bailey, I'm sorry."

As we walked back to the group, I noticed that Sophia and Vanessa were teamed up with Krystle and Heather and fixing dinner. Burdock and Jack, with some of the others, had already found places for sleeping bags.

Bailey said, "Looks like everyone was ahead of us."

"I guess we have mind readers in our group."

Dinner was being set up in a space that looked like it had been an outdoor picnic area. Logs were spread out in different directions to sit on. What seemed like a few split logs had been placed so the flat side of the wood was facing up. There were two good-sized trees that had been split in half, giving us a table space of about ten feet by four feet in size.

Steve was walking toward us with a plate in his hand. It looked like he could not shovel food into his mouth fast enough. Suddenly, he jumped, dropped his plate, hopped up on a log, started looking all around, and yelled, "Snake!"

We looked around, and we did not find it, but it was Ziggy who had walked over, picked it up, and headed for the trees, leaving it there. As she came back, she commented, "Steve, it was a little one."

"Well, it was big to me. I bet this was a nice place at one time, and I bet they didn't have a lot of snakes," he imparted.

I spoke out and said, "I think I would have to agree with your comment about this being a nice area. Someone really took their time to create it, even the location we are sitting in. But as far as snakes go, I would bet they have always had them."

"Have you seen the inside of the old house?" Steve inquired.

"No, I haven't. What about you?"

Steve said, "I walked in and looked around, and I found it to be roomy and nice. I mean, it has some cobwebs here and there with lots of dust. It looks like animals have been camping out in there as well, but it looks like the place could be fixed up."

As I was thinking, my mouth opened, and I uttered, "I wonder who owns it as it might make a good place for some of the people, we rescued to live in. It seems to have a good amount of land with it as well. That is, if this fenced area is the property. One thing is for sure. I think they would really find this a great place. I guess we would need to ask around and see who owns it. Of course, they may not wish to sell it. If they do, we would have to come up with the script or whatever they call money here."

"They call it scriptable, Marty, and soon you will remember that," Bailey commented.

"Well, my fine-looking word wizard, you keep me up to date on names and things because I am not sure I will have them all down pat."

"I know the feeling," she said.

"Word wizard?" Steve asked.

"Well, this is the one who has always used words that seldom get used today. If she can keep me up to date with all the new words and meanings over here, she will be a word wizard for all of us."

"Well, I will do my best, but it's not easy for me to remember them all, just for you two," she said.

Steve asked Bailey, "Have you talked with your mother and father lately?"

She replied, "No. Is there something going on we should know about?"

"Not that I am aware of as I was just wondering if you had contacted them."

"Maybe we can do that after dinner and find out how things are going and speak to April as well," I expressed.

"Good idea as we need to make sure everyone is safe," Bailey affirmed.

Soon, plates were being distributed with food on them along with knives, forks, and spoons. Sophia handed plates to Ziggy, Bailey, Tabby and me, and we said thank you. Following her was Krystle with cups and Heather behind her with a jug of water that had the flavor of orange juice. So, thank you was heard a few times.

"Do you have any idea how long it will take to travel to your area, Tasha?"

"I only know we spent a good couple of weeks traveling up here. But first off, we did not have any idea what it was like up in this area. We got lost. Then we lost our horses and had to leave the wagon."

Burdock spoke up and said, "I think at the rate we are moving, we may be there within the week."

As I was sitting there, I sent a mental note to April. *This is Marty.*

Hello, Marty. How is it going on your end?

Well, we have been making good time. How are things going with all of you?

Going well, and I do enjoy talking with Meesha. She is a wonderful person. George thinks we should be home soon as we have traveled without problems and are making great time. Meesha gives George a break now and again, and that way, he can rest. How are our girls, Marty?

Always great and safe.

Thank you.

You're welcome. I am wondering if there is any way to contact Mike and Marilyn to see how things are going there.

I will have to send a crow when I get home because she can't communicate as we do.

That would be good. Please let me know if there are problems.

I will, and all of you stay safe.

I will talk to you later, I replied. Next, I mentally communicated with Mom and said, *How are things, on the farm?*

She came back with *Things seem to be going well. We have been taking care of horses and chickens, goats and pigs, and doing some house cleaning here and there. So how have you been doing?*

Good, Mom. George, April, and Meesha should be back there within a day or two, it seems.

That will be wonderful as it will be nice to see them again.

Well, I am going to get some sleep. We still have a few more days of travel to go.

Be safe, son, and tell the others hello.

You do the same, Mom, and let Gram know I am okay. Bye for now.

"Bailey, are we sleeping in the wagon?" I asked.

"Yes, I already put out our sleeping bags and packs up toward the front by all the equipment and trade goods."

Ziggy are you eating? I mentally asked.

Yes, I am. The food is great.

Good, just checking to make sure you're okay.

I'm fine as I am standing near you, as always.

I turned, and there she was.

"Okay, everyone, if you have found a place to sleep, I suggest we help clean dishes and put things away and get ready to bed down. We should have a person keeping watch. I can take the first shift or second, whichever works for the other person or persons."

Steve spoke up, saying, "I can take a watch if you want to get some sleep."

"I have been sleeping, so maybe Ziggy and I can take the first watch and wake you and Max later."

"Okay with me, buddy," he responded.

So, everyone got things picked up and cleaned up and then settled in for the night.

I said, "Bailey, I will be taking the first watch, so I will try not to wake you when I get ready to get some sleep."

"Don't worry. I will be fine. But you will probably have to climb over the side of the wagon to slide in next to me as I did put our bags up in the front."

CHAPTER 16

Night Watch

Everyone seemed to be finding locations to sleep. Finally, it was totally silent. Ziggy and I sat near the fire and kept it burning. Every now and again, we would get up and walk around and listen for noises. I didn't feel anything out of place.

Ziggy inquired, "What do you think we will be facing in that Denarian zone?"

"I have no idea, but if it's invisible, that may be a real challenge for all of us."

Ziggy was saying, "Too bad we don't know what everyone has for powers. Then we could pick and choose what will work in different situations. I know Vanessa and her sisters have powers, but we have not seen them yet. I am not sure they even know what they are. I do know one thing—that anyone with powers is gaining strength from you and that their powers are increasing as we go along."

"You mean all those traveling with us are gaining strength and power from me?"

"Yes. I have gained strength and agility as I travel with you, so I know for a fact the others are gaining more power in whatever it is they control."

"That is interesting," I responded.

"Well, think of Max and all the things he can do. He says your mind is the only limitation of all you can be," she said.

"He was right about how you three could grow in height, that's for sure. I am totally amazed at some of the people and animals he can change to."

"Marty, look at all the others. Sam and Snowball probably never thought of being people in all the time they have been alive, but now they have been just that. We don't have a clue as to some of the power that is in that wagon, not a clue."

"You, my little wonder warrior, if you keep getting stronger, that is one thing that will really astound me."

"Marty, it's also been working with you when it comes to gaining knowledge, strength, and power. You have become more powerful just in the past week or two. I can feel all your strength as I am the one person—well, besides Bailey and Steve—who can tell what is happening to you."

"Well, just keep me clued in so I won't be messing up."

"I will, and if not me, it will be Bailey, and if not her, it will surely be Steve."

Soon, it was about two in the morning, so I poked Steve. Then he and Max got up. I asked Ziggy to become a pup and set her in the wagon. Then I climbed up and slid in next to Bailey and fell asleep.

As dawn was lifting its head over the horizon, people started to stir and climb down for a morning ritual. Vanessa and Sophia were out of the wagon and unloading things for breakfast. Steve had kept the fire burning the rest of the night, so there was a flame to cook by. I was so comfortable next to Bailey and Ziggy. I felt like a warm and lucky guy between a beautiful woman and my pup.

Bailey rolled over and was soon facing me. Then she suddenly pulled back and said, "Sorry, Marty. I have morning breath," and she kissed me on the cheek and got up.

Soon, Ziggy and I got up and followed her lead to get out of the wagon. Most of us were out of the wagon and enjoying the smells of meat and eggs.

Vanessa said, "Good morning, all."

Sophia said, "I see some are still asleep, but the smell of food will wake them up."

Eventually, everyone was enjoying a good breakfast as mouths were being filled. Of course, there were orange drinks to top it all off. Since everyone was now in the form of people, it became easy for everyone to locate the food they enjoyed eating.

"Ziggy, how is everything with you and the others?"

"Everything has been perfect," she replied.

"I see you decided to wear something different today, and you know, it looks good on you."

She was wearing a skirt and a blouse. One of the girls had combed out her hair and made it look better than that rough-and-tumble hairstyle she had as a warrior. She still had her boots on, but hey, the skirt made her look great.

"So how does that feel to you?" I asked.

"I like it, Marty, as it's not tight fitting like the warrior armor, and I feel more relaxed."

"That's good. I am pleased to see you dressed like this as you look excellent."

"Thank you, Marty."

After everyone ate, with plates cleaned, stacked, and back in the wagon, a few were just standing around, talking. Some took time to do a few things like wrapping up bedrolls and puffing up the straw.

I noticed Sophia walking toward a few trees that had been blown down or simply just gotten old and fallen over. *Do old trees really do that? I mean, just get old and fall over?* I watched her as she was picking up branches, and I walked over to see what she was doing and asked her, "Are you planning on collecting some of those for campfires in case we run out of trees?"

"No, I wasn't, but that might be a good idea. I am looking for branches I can make arrows out of as I have a feeling, I will need a good number of them."

"Well, tell me what you're looking for. Maybe I can help you find some."

"They must be straight, to begin with. We should look and see if we can find dead wood as that is the best to work with. It can be shaped and, by using a knife, can be whittled and cut to length. I try to cut my arrows to the length of half of the size of my bow, as that will give me good draw and release."

"Well, it sounds like you have done this before."

"I have many times. Sometimes I just wet them down and then use heat to make sure they are straight. Then I trim out a small notch on one end where the bowstring will fit, and on the other end, I must create a sharp point or make an arrowhead that will work. It's often easier to just whittle a point as that will do the damage. But whatever it hits, I can pull it out without being hung up. So, if I can find material to make arrowheads with, I will make a few."

I asked, "Can't you buy ready-made arrowheads over here?"

"I could, but most of the time, you find them in the larger cities, not in little towns like ours. How are you doing?" she asked as she picked up a few more branches.

"I have about a dozen here that I think might work, but then you are the expert, so what do you think?"

"You did very well, and I found about the same, so now I have a few arrows to make. I can do that when we camp or take breaks along the way."

I asked, "How about teaching Heather and Krystle or some of the others how to do that as well? That way, if we need more arrows, people can help make them."

"That would be a great idea if they don't mind doing that."

"Well, I have this old saying—which, of course, is not that old— that if you don't ask, you don't get an answer."

"Very true. I will ask them in that case and see what they say."

"I think you will get all the help you need."

"I hope so. That would really be great to have a good stock of arrows."

"Let's get back with the others and get this show on the road," I said.

"I am with you."

As we walked back to the wagon, I noticed Bailey giving me the evil eye. Well, it was not a real evil eye as it was just a look, and she said to me mentally, *I may have to find a sharp knife.*

I mentally replied *No worries, and you know that. We were looking for dead wood on those trees so she could make arrows.*

She replied, *I know, but I also like giving you a bad time. I think it keeps me in your mind.*

As I walked up to Bailey, she asked me, "I see Ziggy has a new look. What do you think of it?"

I said, "I think she looks great in that manner. Don't you?"

"It's a good look for her," Bailey answered.

When we reached the wagon, we put our branches in a pile. Then I asked Heather and Krystle, "Would you care to help Sophia make some arrows?"

Heather said, "I would love to."

Krystle commented, "Maybe she can teach us how to shoot a bow sometime as well."

"That might be something good for you to learn," I commented.

Sophia turned to Krystle and said, "I would love to teach you how to shoot."

Everyone seemed to be settled down. Food and utensils were put away.

It seemed everyone got a good night's sleep, and I asked Jack, "Did you sleep well?"

He responded with, "Like a rock."

"How about the rest of you?"

I got many kinds of answers, but they all came back with the same fact that they had all slept well.

Jack commented, "I was sleeping having a great dream, of which I cannot remember now when all of a sudden the smell of food passed by my nose."

Burdock added, "I was sleeping very sound myself and at first I thought I was in the kitchen at home, but then I opened my eyes and noticed I was late for breakfast."

CHAPTER 17

Waking to a New Day

Everyone was picking things up, while Steve and Tasha rounded up the horses and hitched up the wagon. Soon, everyone was ready to climb on board.

I turned and noticed Ziggy had changed back to her warrior garb. I asked, "Why'd you change?"

Her reply was "You know when you sit down with a skirt that short, people can see all of what's under it."

I just laughed and said, "I guess you have a point, and that is true. There is a place and reason for everything, and a skirt is good in many places but not so much here as we travel in a wagon."

People were loading up again to travel. Then Jack said, "I think I will ride in the back for a bit."

Burdock spoke up, saying, "I will ride up front."

Sophia asked, "May I ride up front with Tasha and Burdock?"

Bailey said, "Of course, you can if you want. Just make sure you have a blanket under your butt for padding."

"Good idea," she said.

I asked Jack, "How many miles do you think we are making a day?"

"We have constantly been traveling. I would guess at least twenty-five to thirty miles a day, if not more. I mean, it's been very smooth going so far, don't you think?" he asked.

"I think so, and I was guessing about the same kind of distance as I know it's slow going in a wagon, but it just seems we are making good time with better roads here."

Jack asked, "Care to give an old man a lift?"

I picked him up and raised him high enough that he could just step forward and get in the wagon.

He commented, "Young man, you are getting stronger day by day."

"I guess I am because I never felt this kind of strength at home."

Vanessa asked, "Can I get a lift as well?"

I said, "Anytime," and I picked her up and set her in the back. "Okay, anyone else?"

Next, there was the sound of voices, with Heather, Krystle, Bailey, Datilina, Ziggy, and Agatha all lined up. It was as if they were getting ready for a carnival ride.

When I got to Bailey, she handed me Tabby and asked, "Hey, big boy, will you give me a lift and then hand her to me?"

I laughed and said, "I can do that, my lady." I saw Steve look at me, and I said, "I suppose you want a lift too."

"Sure. Why not?" he replied.

I got what I felt was all of our group in the back of the wagon and then looked around to make sure we had everyone. Agatha was like Ziggy, the warrior, and Max was a kid still. I looked at Tabby, and she was the little girl again. Snowball and Sam were both the brother and sister we had seen earlier.

I asked, "Is there anything else we are forgetting?"

Everyone looked around, and I got answers like "I don't think so," "We have everything, I believe," and "The only thing left is for all to sit down."

So I climbed over some of the others and found my position between Bailey and Ziggy, with one snuggled up on one side and one on the other. "Okay, everyone, let's get this show on the road," I said.

Tasha spoke up, saying, "I like that one almost as well as 'Let's rock and roll.'"

The next few days of travel were lots of bumps and bruises and lots of fluffing up the straw. We viewed mountains, rivers, and lakes and went from forests to wastelands with real sand dunes. We stopped each night, making camp, and, of course, had a good breakfast. On about the fifth day, all of us took a lunch break near a small lake. All of the team wanted to stretch and look around, so everyone headed in different directions.

Bailey asked, "How are you holding up?"

"I'm doing well. How about you?" I asked.

"I am good. However, I sure wish we had put two more bales of straw in this wagon."

"I know. I have been thinking the same thing."

Ziggy walked up and said, "It won't be much longer because if we are traveling, as you say, twenty-five to thirty miles a day, we may have already covered about a hundred-plus-miles. If I am correct, that means we have less than fifty more miles to go."

"Well, that could very well be true as it does seem like we are covering a great distance, that's for sure."

Everyone grabbed a bite to eat and watched as Steve and Vanessa were walking over by the pond. They were talking and, every now and again, holding hands.

I said to Bailey, "Seems like he really cares for her."

"I think he does," she said.

As we were watching, we saw Vanessa lean over to pick some flowers near the pond, and suddenly, Bailey said, "Oh no, this is where Steve goes swimming."

"What are you talking about?" I asked.

As we were watching the two of them at the edge of the lake, Bailey said, "Just watch."

Vanessa was walking and picking flowers. She was close to the edge and started to fall forward. Suddenly, Steve grabbed her and pulled her back, but as he did, he continued to go forward into the pond. Suddenly, there was a huge splash. We all looked at Steve as he started to walk out of the lake, looking like a swamp rat. Then he stopped.

Max had been standing near them, and Steve asked, "How come you didn't stop me from falling into this pond?"

Max articulated, "I wasn't close enough."

I asked Bailey, "How come you didn't warn him?"

She replied, "Because of the following events."

Vanessa declared, "Let me get you some dry clothes and a towel."

Steve cried, "Would you please add a bar of soap to that since I am already in here? I may as well take a bath."

Soon, all of us were in the pond at different times, washing not only ourselves but also what we had been wearing. Then it was a process of drying off and changing into clean clothes. After getting something to eat and taking a bath, all of us seemed to be in better spirits.

Everyone gathered up the clothes they had washed out as they took a bath and then hung them over the side of the wagon to dry.

Tasha asked, "Are we ready to wrap this up so we can get on the road again?"

Steve spoke up and said, "I am ready if all of you are." Soon, all of us were climbing in the back and on our way with what looked like a moving clothes rack.

"Steve, I don't think I have ever seen you go swimming with all your clothes on before," I said.

"Well, I guess it was a good thing since I started something great."

"What was that?"

He said, "Marty, smell the air. Smell the air."

Everyone laughed as we all recognized all of us needed a good bath. It was a pleasant smell for a change as most of us were starting to carry a stomach-turning odor with us.

Everyone looked clean and seemed to be in better spirits. As we traveled down the road, people were removing and replacing clothes hanging over the side of the wagon so they could all dry. Then it was a process of folding them and putting them in packs or the basket.

"You saw that before it happened, didn't you?" I asked Bailey.

"Yes, I viewed that about two months ago. I had to laugh as I saw it at that time, and it's still funny today," she replied.

"It was rather funny to see. I'm sure pleased Steve is okay," I said.

She replied, "I knew he would be. I saw all of us at different times in the lake. I also noticed the clothes on the sides of the wagon. So, if I had stopped him, we probably would not have all taken a bath."

For the distance we have been traveling, everyone seems to be doing well. I would have expected arguments and some yelling, but all of us feel we have a mission to complete. I sent a mental thought to April and asked, *did you stop at the Bogart's farm and find out what happened to them?*

We did. Come to find out Jeff and his wife, Susan, had plans on going berry picking that morning. They told us they took off headed east, and a few hours later, their son, Adam, showed up. Adam told them he wanted to go with them and help. So, when he found them gone, he just started to follow the wagon tracks. Adam told them he did not realize how far they had gone until he got there. He was not worried about locking up as he thought they were just over the next rise in a small valley.

So, everything is all right then? I asked.

Yes, and we all had a great time together. They had the chance to meet Meesha, Sky, and Jasmin. You should have seen the love being shared while we were there.

Sounds like you have had a good time, and I am pleased your friends are well, I replied.

I think Jeff is going to make a carving of the dragons. He said if he does, it won't be huge, but it will be good-sized. Your mothers want to join all of you, and I guess your fathers are planning on visiting soon as well.

I sure hope so as there is much here to learn and see, I said.

From all I hear, you kids are seeing and doing more than I could ever imagine, she commented.

I hope our fathers will be able to see Jasmin and Sky when they come over.

I am sure they will still be here as your fathers will be over here in the next day or two, she said.

Well, please keep us in the loop. For now, I must go, I commented.

CHAPTER 18

The Region of the Denarians

Tasha said, "I recognize that ridge up ahead of us. It's not too far from our town."

Burdock said, "Yes, we are close now."

Steve said, "That's good. I think I'm finding riding in wagons in the wild, wild West is not my forte."

Datilina asked Steve, "What's a forte?"

"Oh, it's just a way of saying it's not my cup of tea," he replied.

"So, I gather tea is something you don't like, and forte is the same?" she asked.

"Close enough as it just means it's not what I enjoy the most," he replied.

Bailey asked, "Where is the problem that you have been talking about, Burdock?"

Burdock came back with "It's in different areas in the western region. We just don't know what it is that is creating all the problems. Maybe someone has come up with more answers since we've been gone."

As we traveled along, we were lucky to have a stream that had been running alongside us for several days. I think it was the one that fed the pond that Steve went swimming in, that same pond all of us bathed in. It had made some of our stops along the way better as we could refresh ourselves.

Over the past few days, all of us had a chance to get to know each other better. We have been learning about some of the ways Denarians live and found out about some of the things they enjoyed eating, most of which is similar to the food the three of us were used to, but some of those things came with different names.

We had started out early this morning, and now it was getting close to noon. Some of the team were talking about getting a bite to eat soon.

Tasha said, "We need to cross that bridge up ahead. Then about four miles past that, we will have a location to pull up in a nice area to take a break."

The bridge was nicely arched across the stream, with huge posts on each corner. Both sides had huge stones standing upright about five feet high. I was surprised to see it was made of rock rather than wood. All the pieces fit like they were wood.

I asked Burdock, "Do Denarians work a lot with stone?"

"Often they do as a lot of them work in mines and are used to rock slabs and cutting them. This bridge has been here since my dad was a kid, and I think it will be here for a long time to come."

"That is amazing, the way they placed all the rock slabs, so they don't need any support other than being fitted together."

As we rode across it, I kept wondering if it indeed would hold our wagon and all of us, but it did not move as we crossed it.

After a few miles, we heard the water crashing into something. As we turned a bend, we viewed this beautiful waterfall and a tree that was gigantic and growing across it. The tree was so large, people had created a path on it so they could cross to the other side of the waterfall. There was even a railing alongside that path, and all of it spanned across the entire waterfall.

We could see only what was coming over the fall from where we sat. I was kind of wondering where all that water came from as it seemed like a large amount of it was splashing into the huge pond below. It fed the stream we had been riding close to for many days.

Tasha asked, "Is this good for a break?"

Sophia said, "This is an awesome place."

Vanessa spoke out and commented, "This is totally fantastic."

Bailey remarked, "This is simply beautiful."

Vanessa and Steve were both looking at the great tree with the walkway on it. Steve asked, "What is on the other side of that waterfall?"

Burdock said, "That is about the quickest way to reach the town on the other side. The road we were on would eventually get you there, but would take another hour or two. Crossing over the falls is a shortcut."

As Bailey was asking about the size of the town, Datilina told her, "It's about the same size as Molumphy."

All the pets picked human forms and then jumped down from the wagon. All of us walked over to the edge of the pond. It was so clear, and it reminded me of the well back in Molumphy, as you could see the smallest pebbles on the bottom.

Burdock said, "Ever since I was a kid, I have seen people pitch tempts in here and make wishes."

Steve asked, "Tempts? Is that money or coins?"

"It's what we end up with in exchange after we make a purchase when using scriptable. You know, what you get back in metal pieces." As he spoke, he pulled a coin out of his pocket and said, "See?" Then he walked to the edge and tossed it into the pond, closed his eyes, and was silent for a moment.

All of us watched as the coin floated to the bottom, landing on what looked like several others.

"This must be a popular spot," I said.

Vanessa asked, "Okay, Burdock, what did you wish for?" and as she said that, a few of the others spoke out and said, "Yes, tell us what it was you wished for."

He replied, "I can't do that. If I do, my wish won't come true."

I said, "He is probably correct as that is why you make a wish. It's something only you know about, and hopefully the wish will come true."

Tasha spoke out, saying, "Kids all come up here before the last days of school and make a wish that they will pass to the next grade.

114

Also, people who shop in Ledkin save their change, and as they return, they drop a few tempts in here and wish for better days."

Sophia said, "Hey, you all, let's eat," and as we turned around, she had everything set up on the back of the wagon where she had cleared a large area for the food. Everyone got in line and dished out their grub and found a place to sit and eat.

I asked Ziggy what she thought of that waterfall. She replied, "I think that it's beautiful."

"We have sure seen some pretty sights over here," I said.

Burdock said, "If all of you wish to walk over to that town, you may wish to save some room for more food."

Bailey asked, "Do they have places to buy fresh fruits and vegetables?"

"Yes, they do," he responded.

CHAPTER 19

Walking the Path of the Tree

Bailey was standing next to me and said, "I think this is probably the best of all we have seen. I love that tree. I mean, how often do you see any tree that huge with a path on it?"

"I must agree with you. I mean, with or without a path, how often have we ever seen a tree that size before?

She replied. "Never before."

I said, "Bailey, I am pleased you are at my side as we view it, of course, along with our protectors." As I talked, both Bailey and I looked at Ziggy and Tabby, a little warrior and a little girl.

Steve walked up and asked, "So there is a town on the other side of that waterfall? Do we have time to walk across and check it out?"

"I am not sure, but it would be nice to see that waterfall from on top of that path."

"Burdock, how much weight will that tree hold?" I inquired.

"Why do you ask, Marty?"

"I was just wondering how far to that town, and will that tree hold all of us if we walked across it?"

"That tree has been here forever, and people come out and prune it and take care of it, so it will always be strong and ready for people to use."

"Well, how far is the town from here?"

"If you walk across the bridge, as we call it, you will find the town on the other side. It's only about double the distance of what that tree is in length."

"Great. Do we have time to check it out?"

"Sure. If you want, after we are done eating, we can go over there. Maybe someone will have news of what has been happening as well."

Everyone finished eating, then I asked, "Who wants to walk over to that town?"

It seemed everyone was ready to go but Tasha, and she said, "I will stay and make sure the wagon remains here."

"Do you think someone would steal it?"

"There are some Denarians who like to take things that are just sitting around, and I know we are very close to a village that I don't trust."

Datilina volunteered. "I will remain with her as we already know the town."

"Okay, so the rest of you are with me?" I asked.

All the animals, being in human form, were ready to make the trip on the path across the tree. We started our little trek, and we found it stretched farther than it looked. We finally got to the center, which was the highest point in the arch, and we all stopped.

Heather exclaimed, "Look at how fantastic and beautiful that is!"

Krystle revealed, "We don't have that at home."

All of us looked at the sight beneath us. We were finding it to be almost hypnotic as we viewed it. We just stood there and watched as the water cascaded over the ledges below. The water and those ledges were creating a real thing of total beauty as it entered the pond.

Bailey said, "Steve, whatever you do, don't fall in now, please."

Ziggy commented, "I won't jump in there to save him."

Steve stepped back, away from the rail, looking at Bailey and then Ziggy, saying, "Bailey, not this time. And, Ziggy, thanks a lot."

Jack shouted, "Well, let's get on to the town and see if there is any news of what has been going on!"

I articulated, "Good idea. Let's get moving."

Everyone turned from the view, and we followed Burdock the rest of the way over the tree and toward the town.

As we finally finished our hike across the tree, we could see the town. It was terrific as it was all built in and around huge trees, like the one we just walked across. There were shops and vendors in the streets with people showing what they had to sell. I mentally said to Bailey, *This looks pretty cool.*

Yes, it does, she replied.

Chapter 20

Entering Ledkin

The entire town was surrounded by huge trees, showing me that the tree we walked across was not the largest of all those around. I was looking at a village of houses and shops that were created with exceptional stonework. Along the streets were carts with vegetables and fruits of different kinds of which I had never seen. I could not believe all the colors and shapes of some of the things that were there.

Burdock ran up to one cart and yelled, "Dohadie!" and tossed his arms around one of the street vendors, and they hugged. He yelled at me and said, "Marty, come! Come and meet my brother."

I had been watching Vanessa and Steve walking down the street. I turned to Burdock, then walked over to him and his brother, and he started to introduce me.

His brother raised his hands as if to deflect something, and Burdock said, "It's okay, brother. It's okay. This is the prophecy of old come to life."

He looked around his hands as if peeking to see if it was safe and then slowly lowered his hands and just stared at me.

"My brother has never felt the kind of power you put forth. Most of the time, if we feel any kind of power, we know we must be ready to defend ourselves. He was doing only what we have always been ready to do. That is to prepare to shield ourselves and get ready to run or fight."

I walked closer to his brother and said, "Dohadie, I am your friend as I am your brother's. We are here to help you and your lands."

As I walked toward him, he stepped back and said, "Brother, what is this you bring to us?"

Burdock looked at me and said, "I don't think he is ready to accept you yet as he can feel all your strength, as all the rest of us do, so he still worries."

"It's okay. You spend time with your brother. When he is ready to get to know me, maybe we can shake hands as friends. I still don't feel like I have a lot of power that all of you tell me about, but I guess it must be true from all the reactions I have been getting."

Jack walked up and joined us.

I said, "Introduce your brother to Jack. Then maybe that will ease his mind." I turned around and noticed the girls looking at veggies and walked up to them, asking, "Bailey, how are you doing?"

"I am doing great. Sophia was just telling me about some of these vegetables. It sounds like we are in for a treat."

I said, "Well, that's good. So where is your daughter?"

"My daughter?" she questioned.

"Yes, the little one whom you call Tabitha."

"Oh, she is over there with Ziggy and Agatha. They're watching them make bowls out of clay and straw."

"Well, maybe I'll walk over and check it out."

Bailey said, "I will be there in a few minutes. I'm going to find out more about these veggies."

"Ziggy, are you learning how to create bowls?"

"Yes. This is interesting," she replied

Heather and Krystle joined us. They were followed by Sam and Snowball.

Krystle said, "I have seen this done with only clay but never with straw added. This is different and looks so cool."

Tabby finally spoke and said, "I would like to try that."

There were about seven men and women, all working together to produce beautiful bowls and pots, excellent examples of fine art.

One lady said, "Come here, little one, and I will show you how it's done."

As Steve walked up with Vanessa, the three of us stepped closer to the area where they were working on the pottery. Suddenly, I got feelings of fear, along with some very strange looks, and all of them got up and moved back.

The woman who was going to show Tabby how to make the bowl looked at me and said, "We feel your power, sir, and that is something that makes us think you are a danger. You must step away from us or all the people here will leave."

"I am not here to harm anyone. I am here to help all of you and save your lands." As I said that, I stepped back. Then I yelled at Burdock. "Hey, Burdock! I think you might wish to come over here and speak with these folks as well."

He yelled back, "I will be right there!"

I turned to Steve, saying, "I think you and I need to step away from here. So come with me."

As we stepped back, he asked, "What the heck is going on?"

I said, "They feel our strength and force."

He said, "I think they feel you."

"You have power as well, so it's not just me."

Bailey walked up and asked, "What's going on with you two?"

"Well, it's not just us two. It's us three. Evidently, my powers are growing, and that must be happening with both of you as well."

Bailey said, "I know a lot of people can feel your power."

I returned, "When we first got here, some of the people could feel our powers. But now it seems just about anyone we walk near feels us. Burdock told me, 'Most people who can feel the kind of power we have will go on the defensive and get ready to fight or run.'"

Steve remarked, "Well, let's have Burdock speak to the town and let them know why we are here, and we will just find a good place to wander."

I mentally asked, *Ziggy, why don't you and Agatha join us? But ask Krystle, Heather, Sam, and Snowball to stay with Tabby as she learns how to make that bowl.*

Ziggy said, *I'm right behind you but will send the others that message.*

I looked over my shoulder, and there she was.

Steve said, "You two need to see something Vanessa and I just saw."

"What's that, Steve?"

"Come with me, because to tell you about it would be unbelievable."

We walked what could have been about a city block. Then suddenly, we viewed the greatest-sized tree I had ever seen in my entire life. We were surrounded by trees—and most of them more significant in comparison to the ones I had ever seen before, but this one was the tree of all trees. This one was the great-granddaddy of them all.

Steve asked, "Do you see what I mean?"

I replied, "I do now."

Ziggy said, "I have never seen anything like that. What are all those things all around it?"

Bailey said, "Those look like little houses with walkways. It looks like they are all around the tree."

Vanessa said, "This would take a long time just to walk around."

As I was standing there, trying to compare it to something, the closest thing I could think of was a stadium at one of the schools in Walla Walla. The circumference of the tree was almost the size of a football field. It was huge.

It had a large entrance going up to the tree. Then it had walkways all the way around it and up through all the branches. About every fifty to seventy-five feet was what looked like a small house. Each house was built on the outside of the tree and was not cut into the tree to avoid damaging it. It seemed like the lumber must have come from old branches and other trees to make all the homes and the walkways.

Think of a stairway that winds up the inside of a tall cylindrical lighthouse. Now think of those stairs and walkways on the outside and around this tree. If you can envision that and place little houses along the way to the top, you would have in your mind what this tree full of dwellings looks like.

Snowball and Sam came running up with the others, and Tabby was holding a brand-new bowl. She said, "Marty, look, look at this. See what I made."

"Tabby, that's awesome. So I guess we now know who an artist is in our group."

Everyone checked out the bowl while it was passed around so all of us could see it. As all those who just came running up started looking at us, they soon noticed what we had been viewing. Suddenly, all eyes were looking up at that tree. You could just see a few mouths drop open, with eyes going wide.

Burdock walked up with Jack and said, "We have a town to meet."

Jack spoke up, saying, "I have never seen anything like this. Burdock, are those all houses all the way up that tree?"

"Yes, and if you look at some of the other trees, you will see more."

I turned to him and asked, "You have talked to the people in the town?"

Burdock said, "Yes, we spoke to them, and I feel they understand now."

"Well, let's do it," I said.

As we walked back down the street, I noticed people were not backing up or running away. They were gathering in great numbers as we approached them. However, all of them were keeping their distance. They were chanting something, but I was not sure what it was. I mean, it could have been a death march or something like that because I had never heard the words being used.

Jack walked over and stood next to Burdock's brother. They were talking, so I got the feeling it was not the words to a death march. Jack and Dohadie seemed to be coming closer to the crowd, but Dohadie was still keeping his distance. I stopped and allowed all those behind me to catch up. We stood there, and the town seemed to grow around us. So many of the people from the township wanted to know more about who we really were.

They were all speaking to each other, asking questions. As we grew closer to them, many of them stepped back. We knew all of them wanted to hear the answers from us because of the questions they were asking. Every one of them wanted to see if we were really the beings from another world who came to help save their lands.

There was the sound of a voice. Then some of the people started parting to clear a path for us to walk through. It was Dohadie who had spoken, but he was still keeping his distance and being careful about getting near me.

He walked up slowly and put his hand out and then said, "I am proud to know the healer of our world."

He was still very cautious about taking my hand. I could still feel the fear inside of him, but he was making a strong effort to reach out to me. As I shook his hand, his entire body seemed to shudder. He started to speak, but the words seemed to stop in his throat.

After his body stopped shaking and he had gained his composure, it was then that I suddenly heard him say, "Dear lords, you are one very powerful kid. Please come with me."

All of us followed him to a small inn. When I say small, I do mean small. As we walked in, my five-foot eight-inch height was almost hitting the ceiling. So the beams must have been just about six feet. We were all invited to have a seat and enjoy some refreshments.

As we sat there, many of the people from town came up, saying, "Thank you, and glad you're here," things like that, but most of the people kept their space while others seemed to want to get close to the power we had. Other people were still outside. I felt awkward about not meeting them and asking them about what has been happening. I stood up, hitting my head on one of the beams, and everyone got a laugh out of that, but I suddenly had a pain in my head. I lowered my head and shook it until I felt like I had a clear head again. From that time on, I made sure I was paying attention to where the ceiling was.

I said, "I wish to thank everyone here for your hospitality, but we need to speak with all the people, including those outside."

As I said that, everyone rose and followed me out the door. When we entered the street, we noticed more people had arrived. We listened to the conversations among everyone, which covered things like "Who are they?" "Where are they from?" "How can they help us?" and "They are kids." As I walked out with Steve, Bailey, our pets, and friends, everyone started to take steps back away from us.

"Burdock, we need information, so please ask all of them to quiet down. Please reassure them we are not here to harm them in any way."

As things quieted down, I looked around and noticed several rugged-looking guys who, to me, could take on any problems and handle them without our help.

I said, "Jack, why don't you speak to them? Introduce yourself and all the rest of us and ask them if they know of anything that is happening to their lands so we can find out more information while we are here."

He said, "These people have all come to see you. They want to hear from you."

As I stepped forward and started speaking, the silence was amazing.

"We have come as a team to help your region and all your people. We are here to stop whatever it is that's destroying your lands and lives. Do any of you know anything about what is causing the problems?"

One of the women stepped forward slowly, then said, "I saw several bugs with wings all over the land as they destroyed everything in front of them. Our family packed what we could and traveled over here. We are all hoping we never see anything like that again."

Bailey said, "That sounds like locusts, don't you think, Marty?"

"It sounds like it."

"Is this the only thing all of you have seen so far that is destroying your lands?" Bailey asked.

One man said, "I have seen firestorms that have been destroying farms and homes."

Steve asked, "How far away are these things happening?"

The one woman who spoke of bugs with wings said, "Our home is about seven to eight days west of here, close to the old town of the giants."

One man said, "We have a home that is close to that same area. We watched flames destroying everything."

"Do any of you know anything more about these two things that are happening?" I asked.

Some of the people talked about others passing through and leaving the area. Some said a few of the people are staying in the towns of Etheral.

"Towns of Etheral?" I asked.

One man spoke up, saying, "Yes, we have the three town areas. Old Etheral, Lower Etheral, and Upper Etheral."

"I see. Well, I guess we will see them sometime soon," I said as I looked at Burdock.

He looked at me and nodded, saying, "Yes, we have family there."

Steve asked, "How close have you been to those bugs or those firestorms?"

The one woman who spoke out about the bugs with wings said, "I saw them from a great distance, but it looked like a huge person was walking inside all of them."

Bailey asked, "What about the firestorm?"

"I could not tell a lot about it as I was a far distance from it, but what she said about someone walking in the flying bugs is like what I think I saw in the firestorm."

"Are you both saying something or someone big was walking in both events?"

"Yes, that is what I saw," both declared.

"Jack, could there be a wizard creating these events?" I asked.

"Anything is possible, Marty. Over the years, many wise ones have lost their way when it comes to protecting the land and people."

Dohadie voiced his thoughts about what was going to happen by saying, "I, for one, want to be with you when we end this destruction. I will travel with my brother, Burdock, and all those who support the three of you. That is, if you will have me."

"You are more than welcome to join us, but we will need more wagons and supplies if we gather more people," I stated.

All of us walked around, learning more about those in the village.

Dohadie said, "I will load up my cart and take it out to the main road back to where you have your wagon by the big tree."

"How long will that take you?" I asked.

He answered, "It will take about an hour or so as it is a long way around, but I should be there by the time all of you return."

"May we join you, sir?" came the voices of a few men and a couple of women.

I asked, "Can any of you cook?"

We heard a lot of "Yes, I can," "When do we start?" and "I will bring my wagon and pots and pans."

Sophia asked, "Is there a metalsmith in the village?"

Two men stepped up. One of them said, "If you mean blacksmiths, I be one, and my name is Magnum."

The man standing next to him said, "I be his brother and the other blacksmith, and my name is Staggerbush."

Staggerbush looked like a gentle giant with huge arms. He had a bald head with a mustache, and I could feel he was a caring person. He had a scarf around his neck and was wearing bib overalls.

As I looked at Magnum, I was thinking, *He does not look like a gentle-giant kind of guy.* He had long white hair and a white beard, straps around his lower arms and big muscles, and bib overalls and was holding a substantial two-headed hammer. It reminded me of Ziggy's Thor hammer. But everything I was feeling from him told me he was the kind of person who would give his right arm to help or save others.

Sophie asked, "Can you make special arrows or maybe just the arrowheads if I give you the details?"

Staggerbush said, "Well, I have never made metal arrows, but I guess we could find some lightweight metals that will work. As for arrowheads, we have made some before for warriors."

"Will you need our services on your path to save our lands?" Magnum asked.

"We can't pay wages as we don't have what you call script," I commented.

Steve, standing next to me, leaned my way, tipped his head, cleared his throat, and muttered from the side of his mouth, "Scriptable."

I turned my head, looked at him, leaned in his direction, and spoke to him, saying, "Well, Steve, I was close."

Bailey asked, "Can you make swords and axes for those who need them?"

"We make the finest swords in the land. Plus, our axes are the strongest metals and longest-lasting, sharpest blades you can find."

"We can prepare our wagons and join you within a day or two if you will allow us to help."

"If you can join us, that will be fine. If you can create the arrows Sophia needs, that will be great. We may need good metalsmiths for other reasons along the way."

"Burdock, what is the next town we will be in? Is that the town that you want to stay in for a few days?"

"It's my hometown, and it's called Etheral. I would like to spend a few days with my wife and friends. I know that Tasha and Datilina will want to have time for friends as well. I am sure they are both wondering if we are planning on returning from this town visit, so maybe we should get a move on."

"You are correct as I am sure they are ready to return home as soon as possible," Jack commented.

Dohadie asked, "Is Datilina with you?"

Bailey replied, "She is. She and Tasha are back by the waterfall."

We noticed Dohadie got a bit excited. I could feel he just became a bubbling kettle of happiness. He turned to me and said, "I am going to get my farm cart right now, and I will see all of you near that waterfall."

People came up to us with huge bags of vegetables and home-cooked food. As I smelled the bread, I was reminded of just how much I have missed April's homemade bread. Everyone had a bag of food to take back to the other side.

As we all took the bags, Dohadie pulled his wagon out onto the street, ready to travel around and join us. He yelled out, "Just put all those in the back! Then I will bring them with me."

"Thank you, brother," Burdock said. "We will see you on the other side of the waterfall."

Everyone placed their bags of food in the back of his wagon. Suddenly, Dohadie whipped the reins, and he was headed down the road. As he was leaving, he was doing it at a pretty fast clip. I could feel his excitement of seeing Datilina again.

Suddenly, a woman came forward out of the crowd. I recognized her as the one woman who stayed near the pottery station, while all the rest of the people ran off. She was the one who told Tabby she would teach her how to make a bowl. This was the lady who told me my powers scared all the rest. I watched her as she walked toward me. In her hands, she held a beautifully finished bowl. It had the most beautiful blues blended with the white of the clouds, and the colors of the sun to accent them.

She stood in front of me, then said, "This is a bowl worthy of a great leader. It is the finest I have ever made, and I wish to give it to you. However, I dare not get closer as I can feel you from here."

"I understand what it is you feel. All of us realize it's not something you are used to. We have been told that anyone who touches us feels better and has ailments healed."

She continued to walk up to me. The closer she got, the slower she walked, but finally, she reached out with the bowl in both her hands.

I reached out and accepted the bowl, saying, "Thank you from the bottom of my heart." I held the bowl in one hand and reached out to her, wrapping my other arm around her, and said, "Thank you so very much."

As I wrapped my arm around her, she started to shake, and I could suddenly feel her grab me in a moment of fear, but it quickly changed to happiness.

"Your power is so magnificent, I think you just removed the pain in my legs and hands I have had for years. As far as I am concerned, you will always be welcome in our town."

I looked at her, nodded, smiled, turned to the others, and said, "Okay, it's time to go."

While she was walking away, she was telling everyone around her how I had healed her. Soon, many of the other people from the town wanted to be healed as well.

Jack started walking toward the bridge, with all the rest of us following. As we walked, people came up to all of us, wanting to be touched and healed. When they did, we could visibly see them shake, and we could feel the fear they had at that moment, but it soon turned to joy. Soon, we were all hiking across the bridge and back to our wagon.

Tasha said, "You took so long, we thought you got lost, or maybe Steve fell in that waterfall, and all of you jumped in to save him."

"Well, we should get loaded up again and get ready to go," Datilina said.

Burdock said, "We will, but we have one more wagon joining us shortly because my brother should be here soon."

Datilina asked, "Dohadie is coming?"

"Yes, he was in the village selling his wares and asked if he could join us. I had a feeling you would want to wait for him."

"Of course. You know I want to wait for him."

Burdock walked over to Steve, Bailey, and me and uttered. "They kind of have a thing."

Tasha walked over to us and said, "Well, she has been quiet all this time, and now I bet we won't be able to shut her up."

We all laughed, and some of us walked back over to the water and sat down. As we waited, it didn't seem like a long time as all of us talked about the food and those tree houses. I was talking to Bailey and Tabby about her new bowl.

Bailey asked me, "Have you ever seen a bowl like that before?"

I replied, "Never, and it's beautiful."

Tabby said, "The one the woman gave to you is very special. I noticed it sitting on a high shelf near her home, and I could tell she was very proud of it."

"I think you're correct, little one, as it is an exceptional bowl and one I will treasure always."

I felt something coming and realized it must be Burdock's brother, Dohadie. For a good amount of time, we enjoyed the beauty and sounds of the water as it fell from above. As we continued to wait, all of us turned as we heard a lot of noise. About that time, a wagon came around the bend to join us—and then another and another. We also noticed people were walking across that tree over the falls.

As the first wagon pulled up, Datilina ran up to the wagon, then she started jumping up and down like a bouncing ball until Dohadie stopped and climbed off the wagon. It was if they both looked like one, and I said, "I guess they really did miss each other."

Tasha said, "She really loves him, and I know he loves her."

Jack spoke out and was saying, "Okay, I guess we have a few wagons and a lot of people going our way. So, let's see if we can load everyone into all the wagons that just showed up and move out."

Steve and Vanessa climbed up front with Tasha. Datilina and Burdock climbed up in the seat by Dohadie in his wagon. Soon, we had a full load of people in our caravan. The two wagons behind Dohadie were quickly filled with people as well. When we got everyone loaded, we were ready to move out.

Heather was talking with Snowball, Krystle, and Sam. Agatha, Ziggy, and Sophia were all talking about having special weapons made. Sophia was speaking about how the metalsmiths mentioned they could create metal arrows. I noticed Max and Jack were talking about what the villagers had spoken about when it came to the firestorm and the flying bugs.

As we were getting ready to move again, everyone found a suitable place to kick back and relax. I walked around to the back of the wagon and located Bailey, Tabby, and Ziggy. Then I climbed up and joined them. As Sophia, the twins, Sam, and Snowball talked about those arrows, Agatha plopped down by Jack.

Steve looked back at me and mentally asked, *Do we have everyone?*

I nodded, and he turned to Tasha and said, "It must be time to rock and roll."

CHAPTER 21

Just Around the Bend

"Hey, Jack, do you feel anything out of line here?"

"Marty, what do you mean?"

"I feel like we are not alone."

He laughed at me and said, "Of course, we're not alone. Look at all the people with us."

As we both laughed, I explained, "I feel more than this group. I am getting the impressions of deception and hate."

As we traveled for about another hour, I kept feeling as if there were other people nearby, more than just the people we had with us. I asked Bailey and Ziggy, "Do you feel anything out of the norm?"

Both of them replied, "No," but Ziggy changed back to a puppy, and soon all the others changed as well. I guess if we get a feeling, it's better to be prepared before things happen.

We came around a curve that had cliffs on both sides of the road and huge trees, that looked like they were wrapped in branches. The branches coiled around the trees but not close to them, as if there was breathing room between them and the tree itself. Those branches rose from the bottom all the way to the top.

Tasha abruptly pulled to a stop. All the wagons stopped, and I jumped out of the back, stepped up next to where she was sitting, looked up at her, and asked, "What's the problem?"

She didn't say a word, but she raised her arm and pointed straight ahead. Then she spoke, saying, "Remember, I told you there is a group of people around here that I don't trust."

By this time, a few others had joined me. Some distance ahead of us, we noticed a large group of people standing along the side of the road. These were the extra people I had been feeling for some time, many with crossbows and other weapons pointed at us and ready to be used. There were small people and people of regular height, some black, white, yellow, and tan, with one person alone standing in the center of our path. Bailey, Steve, and our pets were all climbing down from the wagon. Our pets turned into human form to jump down until their feet hit the ground and then suddenly turned back into paws.

I said, "I will check this out." I walked toward the one in the center of the road and asked, "Is there something we can do for you?"

The one person standing in the center of the road said, "We just want anything you have of value. Then you can travel on."

I said, "We don't have anything of value, so I suggest you move out of our way."

"Kid, you need to get back with your mommy and daddy. We will take what we want. Then all of you can pass on down the road."

As he started walking in my direction, I noticed he was looking past me. So I turned around to see what he was looking at. I noticed all our pets spreading out and turning into people, one at a time. All of them were armed.

I looked back at him and asked, "Do we have your attention?"

All those behind me walked up and stood next to me.

I heard him say, "I don't know what kind of cartful act you're part of, but I told you, we want your valuables, and then you can move on."

"A cartful act?" I asked.

Tasha rose out of the seat to stand and then yelled at me, "He thinks this is all magic tricks from a big show with animals and a big tent!"

"Oh, you mean a circus," I said. I turned to him, saying, "So, you think this is a circus act? This is no circus act, and I am telling you only one more time. Clear the road."

"What do you mean, 'circus'?" he asked.

"Where we come from, it's called a circus, with trained animals and clowns."

"What are clowns?" he asked.

"I guess here it's what you call a cartful act, but where we are from, it's called a circus."

"We don't care about your circus or anything else. We want your goods," he said.

"I guess you have not been paying attention to what I have been saying."

As I spoke those words, I heard a bowstring snap and turned to see an arrow headed straight for me. Instantly, my sword was in my hand and ready to take it out of the air, but before it came near me, it was hit with another arrow and shattered and dropped to the ground. I bent over and picked up the remains of one shaft and the arrow that destroyed it. As I did, I heard a person yelling about being shot. I looked over to see a man with a bow bleeding and holding his wrist. I turned around, looked at everyone, and then noticed Sophia standing on the seat of our wagon with her bow in her hand.

"Thank you," I said.

"You're welcome," she replied.

"So, was that two shots in no time flat?" I asked.

"Yes, I am afraid I was a bit slow."

I said, "I think you were fast enough to take that arrow out of the air."

"Well, it seems that sword you're holding showed up just as fast as my arrow," she said.

"It does that when I am in danger."

I looked at all the rest of the team and then turned around to face the guy who was still standing in the road ahead of us. I said to him, "You really should move." I walked up toward the person in front of me. As I did, I stopped and turned to his group, saying, "This is no circus act. If you are a believer in the centuries-old prophecy, you will know who we are. We are here to help people protect the lands and give others better lives."

I raised my hand, which held out a glowing, beautiful sword with movements of the gods on the sides of the blade. The colors flashing blue, yellow, green, and red were as bright as the sunlight. As the feelings of anger and hate subsided, that sword vanished into thin air.

After making sure no one else wanted to take a shot, I walked closer to the leader, who was still standing in the middle of the road. He felt my power and started moving back. All at once, I lifted him off the ground, then I continued to walk toward him. I thought about waving my hand back and forth a few times now that I had him in the air to give him the ride of his life, but I could tell he was concerned at this very moment about not dying. I wanted him to feel the power and strength that scared the hell out of other people.

As he was floating in midair right next to me, I spoke to him and the rest of his group, saying, "This must end and end now. If I ever find any of you stealing or harming others, you will answer to my friends or me."

I could feel everything from those in that group as I moved their leader to the side of the road. I set him down and continued walking away. Their feelings were now filled with wondering and questions, but now they seemed to understand they needed to change how they lived.

I yelled back at Tasha, "Let's rock and roll!"

She started moving the wagon forward with everyone alongside and behind keeping pace.

Some of those still standing alongside the road were asking all those walking behind us and riding in wagons, "Who are these people?" Answers came back in a variety of ways. "Have you ever heard of the prophecy?" "Have you heard how three teenagers with pets would enter our world to make it better?" "You could not feel the power and strength?" "Did you not see those pets change to people with weapons?"

Someone said, "The prophecy of centuries past is finally here."

Another person spoke out, saying, "The heart of that prophecy is with all of us now. You have had the chance to see some of what they can do. You can now tell all your friends. It's time for a change."

I was walking in front of the wagon with Bailey and Steve, while our pets were walking in front of us. It was like we were all just taking a walk in the woods, each of them in the form of people.

I looked at Bailey and said, "I feel all those who tried to stop us have just changed and are now having feelings of caring and helping, even the one I picked up and set on the side of the road."

Bailey asked, "How did you do that?"

"I am not sure. You know, I just felt I could do it, and I made it happen."

Some of the people who had been in the group that wanted to stop us earlier were now walking with us.

The one I had set on the side of the road was now telling all the others, "I could tell he was more than a trickster once I felt his powers. Once I felt his power and strength, I was afraid I was going to die."

Chapter 22

Etheral Dead Ahead

Soon, all of us allowed our wagon to move past us so we could climb on board. Sitting in the back with Bailey on one side and Ziggy on the other, I felt warm and safe with them. I viewed Steve and Vanessa speaking together and felt the two of them were becoming special to each other.

Bailey asked, "Did Burdock tell you anything about his hometown?"

"Not much. He did say it was forest and mountains and such. However, I think we are about to find out more very soon."

"Marty, you know Jack and Max are still speaking about those firestorms and bugs that the people back there talked about. It would be nice to know what both of them think," Bailey said.

Ziggy asked, "Are they like those little grasshoppers we had in your yard before we left?"

I replied, "Well, if they are locusts, they are much bigger from what I was reading at school, and they devour everything in their path. I thought maybe that is what has happened over here, but when that woman said someone large was walking with them, that makes it a whole new ball game."

"Yes, and that one guy spoke of what looked like someone walking in that firestorm, saying it was a big person," Bailey said.

"Well, I guess we have a lot of research to do to put an end to either one."

Max asked, "Tasha, how much farther?"

Her reply was "We will be in the outer parts of our town in about an hour. It will be nice to be home for a while."

Jack said, "You know before the Denarians took over this part of the lands, giants used to roam through here. They used to have homes and farms here as well."

"Could there still be giants around these parts?" Bailey asked.

"I have not heard of any around these parts as they mostly live in areas around the mountains a great distance from here. It's where the dragons and all us wise ones live," Jack replied.

"Well, we need to look at all ideas, then get a closer look, if we can, at what we are going to be dealing with. That's one thing for sure."

Steve broke away from Vanessa for a few moments and asked Jack, "You said giants traveled around here. So they lived here. Is that correct?"

"Yes. This region is where all the giants lived. They lived in all these lands from here to the far western high lands and mountains. They took mates and tried to live in peace. It was seldom you would find giants causing trouble or creating problems."

"So, none live around here now?" Steve asked.

"I think if any of them lived around here, we would know all about it since the Denarians can feel that power from them, as they do with all of you and Marty."

Suddenly, Tasha said, "Home sweet home. Welcome to Etheral."

We all rose out of the wagon enough to see what was up ahead, and Heather said, "I don't see anything yet."

Krystle said, "Maybe it's hidden."

Heather commented, "It's hidden well."

Max said, "I need one of those invisibility spells."

Tasha laughed then replied, "It's just around the next bend. I am so used to seeing this area. I guess I know just how close we are."

As we turned the bend, there was indeed a town but not a city as I expected as what we saw reminded me of a ghost town. The road we were on was just a dirt path as it had been since we crossed that last bridge back by that huge tree. I guess I keep expecting to see a paved road sooner or later.

As we entered this town, there were rocks with lots of brush on both sides, with huge trees like the ones we have seen for many miles. We could see in the distance a massive mountain, but here, it seemed like a town that had really seen its better days. We passed an old house built of stone with a roof that seemed to be lots of lumber and shingles made of wood.

Just as we were about to cross a bridge, someone came out and waved.

Tasha yelled, "Hey, Babble! We are home."

As we crossed that bridge, I noticed it was like the last one we crossed made of stone. All of us looked down into the stream and viewed water so clear it reminded me of the water we have seen so often lately that almost seemed to be pure. On the right side of the road, we found what must have been a horse barn as it looked like an old corral and shelter fenced in. Sitting along the side were a couple of old wagons, and I noticed a few horses in the corral area.

On the other side of the street was what looked like an old bar or an eatery. Behind that was another old barn with livestock in the pasture. The next old barn we passed appeared to have seen better days as the roof was missing lots of its wooden shingles and the slats they were attached to.

We were passing many old buildings, so I asked Tasha, "What is this? Is this Etheral?"

"This is the original townsite of Etheral, which has been here since who knows when. Some people I know still live here. They take the chance of being attacked by wild animals, beasts, and things like that."

Bailey asked, "This is where your town started out then?"

"Yes. When people first came here. However, you will be amazed at seeing the next towns."

"So there are three towns by the same name?" I asked.

"They are all Etheral, but this part is the oldest," she replied.

We passed a few older buildings in the old townsite. One of them had been constructed out of rock slabs with half of it destroyed, leaving visibility to the rooms inside. Of course, there was not a lot to see on some of the structures. I am sure the weather along with animals have taken care of what was once there.

The grounds around us were full of greenery with lots of trees. Some of those trees had a funny look to them. Branches were twisted and gnarly looking. Some stretched out so far, you would think they should have busted off and landed on the ground. It reminded me of some of those adventure movies where you could see all kinds of weird trees with a forest behind it, but you would never know for sure what was there. As I viewed some of the areas, it made me think of that guy called Indy and his adventures for all the lost cities and searches for artifacts.

Then it dawned on me. I have seen trees with branches sticking out like these back home in Walla Walla. *Yes, in Pioneer Park.* Of course, the park did not look as overgrown and destroyed as this place. I always loved that park as they always seemed to have bands or events there, with many people enjoying the day.

Looking further down the road, we could see what looked like a mountain among pillars of rock. I mean, those pillars looked like enormous icicles sitting upside down, with the points way up in the sky. There were stones that climbed hundreds of feet in the air on each side of the city. Huge pillars along the cliffs were all over the landscape, many on the outsides of the walls for the town. In the center at the base was this big mass of buildings and homes and that wall around all of it.

I guess the most impressive part of what I was looking at was the same thing many of the others were staring at and discussing. I could hear all of them making comments about it. I looked around the wagon, seeing all the others gazing at three waterfalls. The one in the center was an enormous waterfall cascading down the face of those cliffs. It was as if it was flowing inside of a substantially transparent pipe because it was not splashing all over the place like the ones on the outside walls of the town. The waterfall flowed down into what looked like a pond, then poured out to another large basin below. All this was what we could see from the location we were at as we rode to the entrance in front of us.

We could see what looked like a road that zigzagged back and forth from the bottom of the lower town all the way to the top of that mountain. It went back and forth about four times, and it was funny how that waterfall flowed behind that road in many places.

"Is that Etheral?" Steve asked.

"That be her," Tasha said.

As we approached the area of this town, I noticed the path was winding around different objects and a castle that looked like it had been in a war and was destroyed in many places. There were huge walls with stairs and windows, but most of the walls were no longer complete. It seemed to have a lot of open spaces and an enormous amount of overgrowth around it, in it, and even over it. Everyone was staring at what looked to be the ruins of what might have been a beautiful structure at one time.

Steve said, "I would love to explore that."

"So would I," Bailey said.

Of course, everyone else agreed.

Tasha said, "That is some of what is left from when the giants lived here so very long ago."

It looked like the road we were on would worm around past it. The next thing we viewed directly in front of us was an arched gateway.

I asked Bailey, "What is it with these towns and large arched gates and tall walls?"

"I think there are things here we should find out more about," she said.

Ziggy said. "You know, they have them for a very special reason."

"What reason?" I asked her.

"You're asking the wrong person, Marty. You need to ask Tasha or Burdock."

CHAPTER 23

Entering the Gates of Etheral

As we arrived at the gates, I could see patrols walking along the tops of the walls. The walls stretched for close to a mile. That entire wall must have been at least twenty feet tall. It extended from the cliffs on one side of the town where those massive columns were pressed up against the mountain to the other side of the city where more of those pillars were located.

Everything that surrounded the city, the walls, the cliffs, and the pillars were almost vertical with a height that would make it impossible for a person to negotiate. The entire front of the entrance came out from the cliff face about as far as the wall stretched across the front. Soon, we were passing under one more entry arch. Of course, my mind kept yelling at me, *Find out why they need these things!*

As we entered, what we saw was amazing. Tasha pulled the wagon over, turned, looked at all of us, and said, "You saw the old Etheral, and this part is what we call Lower Etheral." As we traveled further into town, Tasha explained, "You will see what is called the steps to Upper Etheral, which is that road that we will be climbing to reach the top of the mountain. That waterfall in the center behind the lower town flows out from the top of the mountain and creates that waterfall you all saw where the tree bridges it."

Sophia asked, "How many people live here?"

"There are thousands," Tasha said.

Soon, we were moving again and looking all around. We passed small farms and homes along the way and noticed that water that ran from the top of the mountain. It was flowing right past us, and now we understood what created that waterfall we viewed earlier. The last waterfall was really something to see, but what we were viewing currently was a more magnificent sight to enjoy as the cliffs were so tall, you could hardly make out the people on the top who looked like they were scrutinizing us.

Everyone in the wagon was now staring at the waterfall behind the lower city of Etheral as it was beautiful. Two other waterfalls fell over the sides of the mountain just on the outside of the walls of the town. They created an impressive sight as they splashed into man-made ponds of different sizes all the way to the bottom.

Dohadie pulled his wagon up next to ours and asked, "Have you ever seen anything so beautiful in your life?"

I said, "I must admit, that is it, right there."

The waterfalls looked like they were being poured out from under large archways. As the water flowed down from the center waterfall, it seemed to stop at various levels. It disappeared as it ran under what looked like a roadway. It moved to one side, then spewed out and flowed to the next lower level, and vanished again. Suddenly, it was coming out in another location near the road below. It did this all the way to the bottom. It must have stopped and changed its flow about four times. The water would crash into a pond, then the next until it reached the base.

Burdock said, "Marty, I knew you would like our homeland."

Bailey asked, "Why do you have such high walls and guards around your town?"

"You have not yet had the chance to see some of the creatures of destruction in our lands that take more than an army sometimes to kill."

Steve asked, "So you're saying there are huge monsters down here?"

Tasha declared, "Well, we have a number of things in our world that are dangerous and can destroy people."

I said, "And here I thought all you had was something invisible destroying your lands. You never told us about monsters that take an army to destroy."

All of us laughed.

Burdock said, "Well, what's one more monster?"

Bailey said, "Some of our powers should take care of just about anything we face."

Jack spoke up and said, "I feel there is nothing in our lands you cannot protect the people from as it has been told you are the protectors and healers of our world."

Steve tossed back, "We will protect the people and lands if we don't get killed."

As he said that, the actions of dying started with coughing, choking, and more coughing. Then he started laughing, and the rest of us joined him.

Tasha moved our wagon forward, then Dohadie pulled back behind us again. We were continuing to ride along the road that allowed us all to see the side of the mountain in front of us.

I stated, "One thing's for sure. You have a lot of homes on the face of those cliffs."

While we viewed all of that front section, we could see hundreds of homes that had been carved out of the face of the mountain. It was as if they figured out where they would build a dwelling and created walks they could use to reach each one. They cut the face of the cliffs, so there were walks in front of every one of those home locations, then carved out the homes. The walks looked like they must have been about five feet wide, and there were about four levels of homes on the face of that cliff area. The builders created elaborate railings on each of those walkways so no one would fall to their death.

"How did they create all those homes and walks up there like that?" I asked Tasha.

"They created the first level by cutting out a large path. As men and women created the path over the first level, all debris had to be removed. The crews of people then started on the next level, doing the same things. They continued to cross the face of the mountain, locating places for good-sized homes."

Bailey asked, "So all those homes are tunnels in the mountain?"

"To start with, I guess you might look at them as tunnels, but they are just like regular houses, much like what you saw at Mike and Marilyn's. They created tunnels. Then they carved out rooms, like bedrooms, living rooms, and things like that."

"How do they cook in those?" Steve asked.

"Each kitchen in each home is located next to the front wall. They have all been built to allow all smoke and fumes to vent out in individual tubes," she said.

"So what do they do about toilets?' Ziggy asked.

"Well, each of those homes has a form of plumbing that acts like a regular toilet with water and can be flushed. All the waste from those enter a system that runs out to a special plant that separates, filters, and purifies it, then the water is recirculated."

Max asked, "It does not stink?"

"No, when the water leaves the purification process, it's as clear and clean as the water you have seen in those streams."

"So, how do they see inside of their homes at night if they need to get up?" Bailey asked.

"Long ago, people found they could set up a jar, and bugs would collect in them, so they developed a lantern using the night bugs that would give off light."

"What happens when the bugs die?" I asked.

"They have a long life. They do not die for a long time. In each home, people set up a place for them to live that looks like small forests. They leave the lantern in the mornings to return to their own forest home. Then when darkness comes, they bring the light back. If a person does not want the light, they have a shield they raise to block it, but the light is still a glimmer in case someone gets up."

I said, "Now that would sure be an energy saver."

Jack questioned, "So with one level finished, they create another level and do the same thing?"

"Yes, and with each level, they cut back into the mountain so the waterfall would always be behind the walks, roads and travel around the homes. The water cascades behind the roads. Then it's funneled into a large pond. As the pond fills, all the water leaves that location, and about thirty feet away, it pours over another ledge. The water then fills a new pond, then the next one, continuing to flow to the pond at the bottom. At every location where the water leaves the ponds, there is a water wheel that creates a system for all the homes on each level to give them fresh air. They can clear out any stale or strong odors."

"Wow! You actually created fresh air for all those homes on the cliff area?" I asked.

"Yes. It was one of the things travelers found in the larger cities. After viewing those ideas, our elders had workers drill and create the same plans. I guess there are still a few problems with a few of the homes, but they have been working on it."

"That is amazing!" I exclaimed.

Vanessa spoke up and said, "It is too bad you did not have that when they built those homes on the cliff face because I am sure fresh air would have really been needed."

"Yes, indeed. It would have been nice," she replied.

"This is totally amazing," Steve said.

"Steve, you should remember most Denarians are good at working in mines and have experience with tunneling into the sides of mountains. You will also find they are superb craftsmen as well. All of us will see some fascinating work on the way to the top of that mountain as we will be traveling on the roadway that was cut out of that rock."

Vanessa asked, "Can we get out and walk around for a bit?"

"Tasha, are you in a big rush, or can we all get out and look around?" I asked.

"Be my guest," she replied. Then she pulled the wagon over to the side of the road, and the other wagons behind us did the same thing.

Everyone was in human form. All of us stepped down from the wagon and started discussing the town and the people. As we walked around, many of those who had been following wandered up to see what was going on.

We walked past a few farm areas that were probably an acre or so in size, but they did something different. They had built levels over portions of the ground locations that had crops. They did not do that to all of the land they had since they only did it to specific sections. It reminded me of some of those new parking garages back home.

As we were walking past a few homes, we had the chance to meet a few of the people, and I stood back some ways, along with Steve and Bailey, so as not to scare them, but it didn't seem to work.

Suddenly, three or four men ran back into their homes and came back out with crossbows and demanded, "Who are you?" "What are you?" and "Where are you from?"

Dohadie walked up and spoke to them. Then everyone seemed to take a deep breath as I knew I sure did. Soon, we had people all around us again. However, they did keep their distance.

Jack asked, "Do any of you know what has been happening to the lands and homes in this region?"

One person said, "I did not see what caused it, but I heard where there were once trees and bushes, now there is only dirt and branches and leafless trees."

Bailey said, "The more I hear that kind of story, the more I think it must be locusts, and I am not sure how to really get rid of those."

"We need to contact our parents and ask them if they have any ideas on how to destroy locusts."

"I will reach out to Mom," Bailey said.

"Steve, you may wish to do the same thing as our parents may have ideas on how to destroy them, and I will contact my parents as well," I commented.

"Got it, buddy. I will contact Mom and have her ask Dad."

I mentally thought while the others were doing the same thing, *Mom, I need some information. I hope you or Dad can help us.*

What is it, son? she asked.

Do you have any ideas on how to destroy locusts? I asked.

Locusts? she queried.

Yes, it seems something or someone is creating them to destroy the Denarians lands. I mean, that is what we are hearing, but I am not sure that is the case. But if it is, we need answers before we face them.

Let me ask your father. I will also ask George and the others and see what we can come up with.

Thank you, Mom. It sounds like April and George have arrived. I hope they had a safe trip.

Yes, they are here. Plus, they brought with them a young lady and two beautiful dragons.

I hope there is a way that they can find someone to watch the farm so all of you can come over here. I also hope our fathers have the chance to see those dragons.

We are trying to work on that now, she replied.

Mom, that would be great.

Tell everyone I said hello, and I hope all of you can join us soon.

People were starting to congregate, and I asked, "When did these problems start happening around your lands?"

A woman who was about the same height as Ziggy walked up and said, "This started about a year ago. Since that time, we keep hearing about more things happening."

"So what happened a year ago?"

"We just heard from people in the far lands that their farms and property were being destroyed by different stories."

"What do you mean different stories?" Bailey asked.

"Some say fire. Some say bugs with wings. Some say winds and heavy rains."

"But all this started about a year ago?"

"Yes, that is when we first heard of it here."

"So, these are the only things that have been happening in your lands as far as you know during this last year?"

Another person spoke up, and this time, it was a man with a large set of arms who looked like a bodybuilder. As I looked at him, I thought he looked like a short version of a bulldozer on two legs. At least, that's what this guy looked like to me. His beard was black as coal, and his hair was cut well, and his nose was just peeking out from behind that beard. He looked like a very gentle person as I viewed his face, but I got the feeling whoever crossed him would wish they had stayed home that day.

He said, "We have several excavations going on all over the outlands because of historic cities and dwellings of the giants that lived all over these lands almost a thousand years ago. We heard the very first place that was attacked was near our furthest excavation area. We have yet to hear from the people who were on that dig."

"Did they just start excavating that area?" I asked.

"They had been working some ruins there for a number of years, but one of the men who came back for supplies a little over a year ago said they found the Hector Pie."

"What is the Hector Pie?" Ziggy asked.

"It's the great winning or the ultimate prize," he said.

Steve said, "That sounds like what we call the mother lode."

"Well, after he left with the supplies, no one has returned for more."

Steve asked, "This happened about a year ago. Then the first of those events started to take place?"

"As far as I can tell, it was about the same time that everything started to happen."

"We need to find out more about that. What is your name?" I asked.

"I am known as Nomi, Nomi Tinder, sir."

"Please, Nomi, just call me Marty."

"Well, our crew will be heading out that direction again in the next couple of days to a week if you wish to join us," he commented.

"So you will be here for a few days to a week, but we don't know what we need to do around here for the people. I understand we are supposed to meet the elders."

"Yes, I understand that will be one thing you will need to do. We will be here making sure we have things ready to go. We have friends and family here, so just let us know when you are ready. A few of us have been getting ready to travel, but I have a feeling another week won't hurt."

"Okay, I will be looking for you when we get our timeline established. So please keep an eye open for us when we come back. We will join you to find out more about what is going on," I remarked.

"I will do that, sir—I mean, Marty."

"Thank you, Nomi."

Jack asked, "And you, young lady, what is your name?"

"I am Manna Day."

"Manna, who told you about the things you heard?" Jack inquired.

"I learned it from a few who live in the faraway lands when they came through here to find a safe home."

"Are they still around these parts?"

"I think they are in the old town area. I have seen them a few times over the past three weeks, off and on, shopping here."

"Okay, please do me a favor and, if you see them, tell them we need to speak with them so we can learn more. Would you do that for me?"

"I will help any way I can. I see you have a good-sized group, and if you need a good cook or laundry person, I am at your service."

"Manna, we may very well need your services."

"Thank you, and if I find them, I will tell them you will be around for the next few days. Is that correct?"

"Yes, my friends and I will be looking for answers to this problem."

All the people around us talked about feelings and power regarding Steve, Bailey, and me. One of them said, "I was scared at first, that's for sure. I ran in and got my crossbow and was ready to shoot them. Especially that guy called Marty because it's almost like he can knock you over with the power he exerts."

Others were saying, "They look so normal, yet they say they are here from another world. So how do they travel between planets?"

"I was wondering that myself," another person said.

Many of them walked up to us like a person would with anyone else. However, we watched as their stride changed to a slow crawl.

150

All of us took the time to allow people to walk up to us and shake our hands. Of course, as we did, the reaction was always the same. I guess you could say they shook, rattled, rocked and rolled. Finally, everyone was speaking about how they had just been cured of some kind of ailment or ache or pain. It was nice to know we could help them in that manner.

We spent time speaking to a number of those who had gathered, and they kept saying, "If you need anything—a good meal, laundry, a good bath—you just let us know." I don't think I've ever felt the kind of welcome we have found over here. If we were travelers from another planet and landed on Earth, would they treat us the same way? I'm not sure they would. It seems lately so many people back home worry about only themselves, and they don't take the time to care about others.

Steve spoke up and said, "Hey, a good bath would always be a welcome idea."

"I agree. Let's gather the others, get some clean clothes, and find that bath," Bailey verbalized.

Everyone wanted to get cleaned up and get into fresh clothes, so we took advantage of the offer. Many who lived here just headed home to do the same thing, saying, "See you in the morning."

After a good bath and returning to the wagon, I noticed it was sitting in the street and was wondering if we could find a better place for the night. I asked Tasha, "Is there a good place to put the wagon so we can camp for the night? I am getting tired, and I am sure many of the others are as well."

"Sure. Let me move it to a field," she said.

CHAPTER 24

Sleeping in Lower Etheral

Some of the people wandered off to different parts of the town to visit relatives. Others followed us as we found a large field where we could feed, water, and brush down the horses. We placed them in a small corral next to the wagons, then set about fluffing up the straw to sleep on.

Tasha and Burdock soon said, "We will see you in the morning as we have a family to visit. We want to tell them all about you three and what we have been doing."

By this time, we must have had about four wagons with us. Many people who had remained looked like they were searching for places to get some shut-eye. Some were trying to figure out how to fit in those other wagons or under them for the night. All of us and our pets found a spot for a campfire because we knew where we would be sleeping. It would be the same place we have spent nights for several days. We sat around chatting about many different things.

Bailey finally spoke up and said, "Marty, we must find a way to conceal our powers."

Steve said, "It would be a good idea since it seems every time we get close to anyone, they step back and run for a weapon."

"Well, I have to agree. We need to be able to hide our powers as not everyone needs to know who we are," I said.

Bailey said, "Mom was saying we need to do that, but she did not say how. Maybe I need to reach out to her and see if she can tell me how to achieve that."

I commented, "I think all three of us need to contact our parents and ask since they have done a good job of hiding what they have."

We were all sitting around, almost in a trance, when the one person who stood in the road to stop us earlier walked up. As he looked at all of us, with Ziggy and Agatha in their Amazon warrior looks, Ziggy said, "They are mentally speaking with people in another world."

"You're kidding, right?" he asked.

"No, I'm not kidding. They are trying to find out information about different things that have been involving the people of this world and what has been destroying the lands. They are not sure that's what's really happening, but they want to be prepared."

Soon, all of us came back to the here and now. As I did, I looked around and noticed I had someone who was sitting close by and staring at me. I asked, "You're the one I removed from the roadway, aren't you?"

"Yes, that is me, and I am pleased you didn't slam me into a tree," he answered.

"We are here to help people, not kill them. You seem to have different feelings now than you had on the road. I can tell the difference."

"We used to spend most of our lives removing things from others. After meeting you, feeling the powers, and understanding the age-old prophecy has finally come true, that has changed. We discussed all that happened, and to be honest with you, I am not sure what it is that has come over us."

"Well, I feel you have changed, and I hope all those who were with you feel the same way," I said.

"It's not just me. All of us will soon be returning to our village to tell everyone else about meeting the three of you and your pets. We will be letting all the people we speak to know what all of you can do. I want to say I thank you."

"Thank you for what?"

"For arriving in our world to help others. There is something about all of you that gave us the feeling we can be useful as well. We have been discussing how we can help the old town of Etheral. Instead of just taking from others, we are going to bring our entire village over here to build walls or structures that will protect the people, something they can be safe in or behind during attacks. Who knows? Maybe we can rebuild the entire old town itself," he said.

"What do you mean?" Bailey asked.

"People just outside of the walls face creatures, or they run for the gates to get inside. Often, they don't have time to run and even get near the gates. Over the years, we have seen many of those people, some of them friends, who have been killed."

Steve said, "What they need are bunkers to hide in."

"Bunkers?" he asked.

Bailey spoke up and stated, "In our world, people years ago dug out places and used concrete, rock, or blocks to build a small building underground. If things happened that could be dangerous, they would run to it, open the door, get inside, close the door, and be safe."

"You called them bunkers?" he inquired.

"Yes. If you need ideas, maybe we can help," I said.

"That would be great as I am sure with your help, we can create something to protect all the people on the outside of the wall," he answered.

"Well, I am not sure how long we will be in Upper Etheral, but we should be back here in a day or two. We can give you some ideas and maybe some help when we return," I spoke.

"We are all leaving now and will return hopefully tomorrow or the next day," he replied.

"We should still be here," Steve declared. As he turned to walk away, Steve asked me, "Do you think we will have time to help them build a few bunkers out there to help save those people's lives?"

Bailey said, "I would think that if we can help in any way, that is something we should consider doing. What do you believe, Marty?"

"I suspect we must help all the people we can," I replied.

"I remember some of the ideas people had at home for fallout shelters. I guess something like that could work."

"Did either of you get a response on how to hide our powers?" I asked.

"I didn't get anything solid as of yet," Steve replied.

Bailey said, "My mom knows how to do it, but it's rather complicated. She said she will figure out how to make it simple and get back with me."

"Well, that is a step in the right direction. What about you, Marty? What did your parents have to say?" Steve asked.

"Mom was telling me, 'Your mothers will be joining her soon, and when they reach us, they will help us with that.'"

"Well, I hope they have a way to fly here and catch up soon," Steve said.

As he made that comment, all our pets and Bailey looked at him. I noticed that as I was viewing all of them. I found that to be somewhat different, and their feelings seemed to be hidden, but I just passed it off as a simple reaction to a statement.

Some of the people started speaking louder. Suddenly, there was a crowd gathering around, but they were leaving an opening as if to allow someone to walk up. However, it was not someone walking up to us as it was a person on a horse who was in a uniform. As he approached, he slowed, and finally stopped and dismounted.

One of the people standing near said, "I will hold your horse, sir."

"Thank you," he replied.

It looked like a soldier, and he was stepping lively until he came in a range of my powers. Then he abruptly stopped. He looked around at Bailey, Steve, and me and said, "The king heard rumors of the prophecy of old becoming reality, so he spoke to the elders, who in turn asked me to come down here and find out if it is true."

Some of those around us spoke out and said, "They are the prophecy of centuries past," "These are the three with their pets that can change," and "They are the three."

I put my hand out in friendship, but I could tell he was very skeptical about shaking hands. I said, "I understand how you are feeling at this time as I have seen it so often lately. But believe me, I am not here to harm you."

It took all he had to approach me. Then he slowly reached out to take my hand. As he did, I could see him shudder at the feeling that was running through him.

Then it was as if his entire body rippled and he said, "I have never been near or ever felt such power before in my life from any being." He stepped back and looked at all of us in total amazement, saying, "You are for real."

"We are here to help protect, save, and stop all harm to all people and animals. We are here to help protect your Mother Earth. As we travel and do all we can for this world, there will be times we must go back to our own world, but we will always return to do what is needed here," Bailey replied.

"I never believed that old prophecy from the past, but I sure do now. The elders have asked me to make sure you travel to Upper Etheral tomorrow as they wish to greet you, feed you, and honor you. I am part of the guards who protect the elders in our kingdom. They told me if you are real to remain with you and travel up the hill when you are ready. So, I guess I am an escort for you and your friends when the time is right."

"Well, allow me to introduce myself and those on our team. I am Marty."

"I am Phillip, Philip Danassia, and my friends call me Phil," he replied.

After introducing him to everyone who was on the team and giving him the chance to see one or two of our pets change, we sat and talked for a bit. Many of the people who were still around us could not believe how fast some of our pets could change.

Then Bailey said, "It's getting late, and I don't want to sleep until noon tomorrow, so how about everyone find a place to sleep?"

All the surrounding townspeople wandered off as they must have figured out where they would be sleeping.

I said, "Hey, Jack, how about you introduce Phil to the elite sleeping quarters up in front of our wagon in the seat and floorboards?"

"I will do that, Marty. Phil seems you and I get the luxury quarters. However, I am sure you will wish to remove some of your uniform. That way, you might keep it looking nice and neat."

"Well, lead the way, my friend. It's interesting, finding a wise one and those three in the same place."

"Oh, you have seen nothing yet as we also have two dragons that will be around as well."

"Real dragons?" he asked with total excitement.

"Yes, two of them, and they came to help protect this team."

"Well, that will be something to see. I have forever heard stories of dragons, and in my mind, they have always been magical. To see one even in the distance would be wonderful. Are they nearby now?" he asked.

"Not at this time as they are escorting a few of our friends to another location but will be joining us soon."

"Oh, I do hope I have the chance to see them," he said.

Jack imparted, "Well, follow me so I can show you where we will be getting some sleep."

They walked to the front of the wagon. Then Jack showed him how they used the blankets and straw for sleeping and said, "You have your choice: the seat or the floor."

Soon, most in the camp were sleeping as the fire in the fire pit crackled, with one or two of the townspeople still sitting around it. They were talking about what it would be like to rebuild the old town site of Etheral.

All of us managed to find soft locations to get some sleep. As I viewed Steve and Vanessa, it seemed to me my friend had finally found a real girlfriend. Bailey was already situated with Tabby. Ziggy and I moved in next to them. Soon, everyone was cutting logs and sound asleep. No. No one had a chainsaw or a hand saw. That is merely a way of saying everyone was going to sleep. So, no one was cutting logs of any real kind.

CHAPTER 25

The Road to Upper Etheral

Bailey and I walked around our camp, and we could smell the coffee and breakfast being cooked. It was just a beautiful morning, with feelings of happiness and love all around us. We had returned to our wagon after speaking to a few people who wanted to join us as they wished to help.

Soon, Burdock walked over and tapped me on the shoulder. He asked, "Phil seems to think we should move out. Are we ready to go up the hill to meet the elders?"

"I guess if that is what we must do, we need to get it done," I said.

Burdock exclaimed, "Okay! All of our team needs to get loaded up. We will be back down here soon, I would think."

It was not long before we had a few wagons following Phil, taking a few different streets through town. All of us were on our knees, looking over the side rails of the wagon so we would not miss a thing. We were headed to the cliffs that the upper town of Etheral was established on. Looking at a road that seemed to weave back and forth all the way to the top, all of us were amazed at how that one waterfall flowed down the hill. It ran behind all the roads at various places and came out as a good-sized flow, feeding that stream we were used to seeing. It was not long before we were at the base of the road we would be traveling on, which would take us hundreds of feet to the top.

Tasha had only one person sitting up front this time, and that was Sophia. Maybe it was because of where we were taking this wagon.

I asked Sophia, "How are you doing up there?"

"I am doing fine, Marty. I think that soon the view will be incredible, and I am so happy to be with all of you."

"If you're happy, then I'm happy."

Then I just kind of looked up at the cliffs and thought, *That's a long way up there.* It seemed strange to be on a road finally as we were now traveling up to the top of the cliffs, not just a worn-out path or a well-traveled dirt road. It must have been about twelve feet wide and was created by cutting away the cliff areas just to make the drive.

There was a wall on the outer edge about three feet tall. I thought, *That must be a small bumper in case a wagon got out of control. But I'm not sure how much it would stop anything from going over.* I noticed it was grooved with a crisscrossed design. *I guess in case of snowfall or something like that. The surface was not smooth, that's for sure.* It looked like they had blasted the sides of the mountain away to get an excellent pathway to ride on.

I asked Jack, "Have you ever seen anything like this before?"

"No, I have not seen this kind of combination of road and waterfalls before. I do understand they are great craftsmen, but I did not realize how great."

"I find it interesting, the way they feed those walks off the roadways out to those homes on the side of the cliffs," I said.

"There was a lot of thought that went into the design of this entire area," Steve said.

As we kept riding along, we found the road was not steep, but it did have an incline to it. Suddenly, we came to a bend that would take us back over and above where we had just been riding, and there was a vast building stationed near the curve.

Tasha was talking to all of us over her shoulder, telling us all about the road, and said, "This was built during the construction to house those who were building this road."

"So they created a place for everyone to live in as they built this?" I asked.

She replied, "Yes. It was designed to be a huge living area, but they simply cut around where it would be and came back later and carved out the insides. Once that was finished, they started the next section of the road. Today these serve as guard locations that are designed to stop anything that might endanger our people. You see, if our town is attacked below, we can get everyone up to the top of the cliffs and keep them safe, or that is the way it is supposed to work."

Jack said, "So everyone can find safety at the top of the cliffs if need be."

"That is correct."

I was looking at the building, which was two stories and had a walk around three sides. It seemed like the entire building was virtually part of the mountain at one time. I was trying to picture in my mind how they chiseled around what would be the building and then created it. The structure sat on what was not removed below it. Guards were only needed on three sides.

We turned the corner to rise further up the side of the cliffs. Then Bailey looked over the edge and said, "They must have taken years to do this."

Ziggy looked over and said, "Well, I sure would not want to fall from here."

Steve said, "You know, this is really a feat of construction if you think about it. I mean, they built this road, created homes on the side of the cliffs and huge buildings on every turn for the workers to live in. Someone had to be a great engineer to set this up."

Jack said, "I find that Denarians are very hard workers and they simply know how to create things out of just about anything, but even I am surprised at this creation."

It took some time to travel on the road as it stretched across the face of the mountain. So, as all of us viewed the waterfall coming down the hill, we had a better vision of how it vanished between the side of the cliff area and the road.

"Amazing," Jack said.

Of course, all of us had our own spoken versions of that word, *amazing*—"Beautiful," "Wonderful," "Fabulous," and "Unbelievable."

The next curve swept back over the road we were just traveling on. On that curve was another house with the same design and planted on the side of the mountain the same way as the last one. I got a better look as we turned the corner, and it looked to me as if they had cut down the side of the mountain to a point they knew would be the roof, leaving a large flat area that would be the top of the building and, of course, not removing any of the mountain under that.

I asked no one in particular, "Do you think there is more to those buildings than what we see?"

Heather asked, "What do you mean, Marty?"

"Denarians are miners, aren't they?"

"From all I have heard, I believe many of them are," Jack commented.

"So, I wonder if there are tunnels all over this mountain area."

Tasha said, "One more turn around after this one, and we will be heading to the top. And to answer your question, Marty, yes, there are tunnels throughout this entire mountain for the people to use as a refuge if needed."

As I looked over the edge, I had this sudden urge to toss everything I had eaten today over the side. Well, I had that urge, but I managed to keep it in. I have never enjoyed heights, and this view gave me a feeling of lightheadedness. It seemed all my blood just washed away. I remember flying with Max to help Anubis, and I felt safe, but this was scary.

Ziggy asked, "Are you okay?"

"I will be when we get to the top of this mountain. How is everyone else doing?" I asked.

I was surprised to hear some of the replies. Even the pets in their human forms were saying, "I am not sure how I like this because we are a long way from the bottom," "I will sure be glad to see my feet on solid ground again," "I can't even look anymore," and "I bet landing on all four paws would still not save us," but then I heard Max say, "Looks like the view I see when I fly."

Steve commented, "Max, it's a good thing you don't mind heights."

"I think you can handle it, Max, as it's part of your being," I verbalized.

"Oh, so now you are a philosopher?" Bailey asked.

"Bailey, you know better, I would think."

Ziggy spoke up and said, "I think Bailey is correct as you did sound like someone with great knowledge and well-being."

"Wow! I think this Mother Earth education is working on all of us by the sounds of it, Ziggy."

"Not sure about that. I'm your cute, wonderful, loving protector."

"You're too much, Ziggy. So, tell me, are you really an animal, or are you a god posing as an animal?" I asked.

"Why would you ever ask that? You know where you found me."

"Yes, I do." I looked back behind us, noticing Burdock, Datilina, and Dohadie were just talking away, not even paying attention to the road. I said, "I sure hope those horses know where they are going."

Jack said, "I am sure they do, Marty, as I get the impression Dohadie has been all over these towns."

Suddenly, we turned a bend, but it did not sweep back over as we had been doing the last three times. Now we were heading toward what looked like another tall wall and—guess what? Yes, another arched entrance. Tall walls, a huge entrance gate, and what looked like large crossbows off to the sides. Now I mean those crossbows were extremely large as they would have to hand crank the bowstrings back, then place a vast shaft in the guide of the crossbow itself. They were in various places near the walls where a target could be shot if it was coming up the hill. They seemed to be movable in all directions. We also viewed what looked like catapults.

Steve said, "I guess they are serious about protection here."

"It seems so from what I can see. I sure hope those crossbows are not for shooting down dragons," I replied.

Bailey asked, "I hope you're correct about that. Do they really need that much protection around here, or is this all new because of the impending threat?"

Tasha said, "Some of those were not here when we left, so I guess it's because of what is coming. We have never seen dragons here, so

I think those are for the creatures that look like huge birds but have wings, like the tanners you find in caves."

"What are tanners?" Steve asked.

"They are the creatures that live in caves and hang from the ceilings with their wings wrapped around them as they sleep," she said.

Bailey said, "That sounds like what we call bats. They are small and scary. I have heard they carry diseases and such, but I would not think anyone would use a huge crossbow that size to take them down."

I asked, "Don't mean to interrupt you two, but can we stop the wagons for a few minutes now that we are on the top?"

Tasha said, "I guess we can do that as I am sure some of you have never been on a road like that before and this high up."

As we stopped, our escort stopped and rode back to see if there was a problem.

Tasha said, "No problem. They just want to see the view."

We all got out and walked back to the road and looked over the edge. There was fencing all along the side of the cliffs to help protect the stupid who had to be on the very edge. Yes, you may have guessed it. I was not one of the stupid. I was looking out and over the side of the cliff, but I was standing about thirty feet back away from that edge and the fence. What we could see was a view of the entire landscape and it was dramatic. There were forests with gnarly-looking trees and rocks that seem to just grow out of the ground.

The entire valley we had passed through was beautiful from up here. The waterfall was off to our side, away from the road. We could see where the water ran, and as it neared the edge, there was fencing that reached back a good hundred yards. I am sure it was there to prevent anyone from going over. I could sure hear the water as it rushed in a spectacular flow over the side, and standing there, I could see it.

I stood there and just pictured what it would be like to be a person going over the edge, down, down, down, and I could not see the bottom, but I could sure imagine what it would be like. I suddenly said aloud, "*Thump, thump, thump—kerplop!*" and as I said that, my head was lowering as if I was watching the entire event.

Steve, standing next to me, turned his head and looked at me with an unusual expression as if I had just opened my mouth and a rock had fallen out. "What was that all about?" he asked.

"I just thought if a person went over this cliff and hit the roads and continued to the bottom what it would be like. You know, you hit one road, the next, and the next—then *kerplop.*"

"*Kerplop*? Is that the best you could come up with? I mean, you could not come up with a splat, crunch, or just plain dead?" Steve asked.

We both laughed, and Bailey walked up and asked, "What are you two laughing at?"

Ziggy said, "They are discussing the results of a person falling off this cliff and hitting every road all the way to the bottom."

Bailey said, "I can just about imagine what they had to say."

I said to Steve, Ziggy, and Bailey, "Looking at that old townsite makes me feel we are viewing a board game with all kinds of small pieces."

We all stood and looked out across the land as Bailey asked, "Is that the other waterfall by the tree, way over there?"

"I'm not sure, but it does look like that tree that is bent over that waterfall," I said.

Bailey bent over and whispered into Tabitha's ear as she was standing next to her at the time. Of course, with her small height, she could not see all we could see.

She walked over to me, tugged on my sleeve, and asked, "Hey, Uncle Marty, would you give me a lift so I can see what you see?"

I looked down at this little girl standing next to me with a sweet innocent look on her face, looking up at me, and asked, "Who put you up to that?"

She turned, looked at Bailey, and then turned back to me with a big smile. Of course, Bailey just smiled as well.

I lifted her up and asked, "Okay, little one. Now, is that better?"

She said, "Oh yes, this is awesome. But can you step back a couple of feet away from that cliff, please?"

As I had started to reply to her question, I was taking a few steps back. I said, "Well, I am pleased you think it's awesome because you won't see this back home. And yes, I can step back away from the edge a bit more."

Next, it was Ziggy who walked up and asked, "Hey, Dad, how about a lift?"

So, she turned into her cute little puppy self. Then I picked her up and let her see more of the landscape. I twisted around to place Ziggy on the ground, and as I did, I viewed Agatha, Sam, and Snowball, who were all in line, right behind me. They had all returned to the small animals they initially were.

I asked, "Okay, so who is next?"

As each of them viewed the sight before them, they asked about specific locations we had traveled past. Sam asked, "How old do you think that castle is?"

I replied, "I am not sure, Sam. I have never even seen a castle before in my life. I have seen photos of them but never one up close. They said it was left from when the giants lived here, so that would have to have been hundreds—if not thousands—of years ago."

I was listening to all the comments from the others as Jack, Heather, Krystle, and Vanessa all spoke of the distance we had traveled and were saying, "It sure does not look that far, does it?" Everyone seemed to be totally impressed with the view. We each had our comments about the landscape and thoughts of how far we have traveled.

However, our thoughts and feelings about this view were interrupted like a bubble being burst as Tasha shouted, "We should get going!"

All of us piled back into the wagons and followed Phil.

CHAPTER 26

Upper Etheral

As we entered through the main gates of the town, it was larger than it looked. Streets were going in every direction, with what looked like hotels or motels and beautiful houses all over the landscape. I noticed that the entire city was spread out over the hillside and flatlands. It reminded me of the difference in what I had seen the last couple of times my parents and I drove over to the Tri-Cities. As I looked at Kennewick, the first time I had the chance to see, there were no homes on all the hills behind the town.

This now gave me a view like I had seen in Kennewick the last time we were there, about a month ago. Houses were being built all over the Horse Heaven hillside. This area has had many years of growth, and we could see homes well off in the distance and all around us, but in the center was what looked like a castle.

I imparted, "This place is huge."

Heather said, "Not only that. It's wonderful."

Everyone agreed with that.

Krystle and Vanessa were busy talking about the castle. The rest of us were involved in a conversation about the guards, crossbows, and catapults.

Jack was saying, "It seems they have a city that has grown greatly behind its walls. If there are attacked by something, I am not sure what would protect those distant homes and businesses."

Steve spoke up and said, "I bet they never expected the city to grow so much and spread out so far."

"It seems they planned everything else, so I think they probably planned for that as well," I said.

Bailey had a gazing expression on her face, saying, "I think if you look in the distance, you will see towers in various locations."

"I am sure they have protection from other directions," Jack said.

As we passed homes and shops, many people came out and looked and stepped back away just as fast, but this time we figured we knew why.

"Someone is going to have to travel ahead of us and warn people not to be afraid," Steve said.

"I think I must agree with you," Bailey said.

"I should think that might be a good idea. I am not sure how well anyone here can heal us if we have crossbow arrows sticking out of our chests," I said.

"Good point," Steve said.

Bailey asked, "Was that a pun?"

As we rode through the streets toward what looked like the castle, I kept wondering why we didn't see more soldiers or guards. I would think if the king and queen live here with lots of homes and thousands of people, we would see protection for them. I expected to see soldiers or guards here and there. Every now and again, we noticed what might have been constables or police, but they just seemed to be walking around, visiting with the people as they passed by.

Almost everything we saw was created from stone or lumber. Alongside the streets, some entries reminded me of what I had seen in movies of subway entrances. As we passed people, they stepped back but then started to follow us in large numbers.

Krystle said, "Marty, I sure hope those people like you three because some of them still have spears, swords, bows, and such."

"Oh, I see. It's just the three of us who will get whacked as you look on. Thank you, Krystle."

"What do you mean, 'whacked'? Is that like killed or hit or something like that?"

"Right, something like that," I said.

Ziggy said, "I think they are just following because they sense we are not harmful or a threat to them but want to know all about us and what's going on."

Agatha said, "I get that kind of feeling myself."

I imparted, "I don't feel any hostility from any of them myself, but I do feel fear when they come near us."

Vanessa asked Bailey and Steve a question, and then she asked all of us that same question, looking for answers from everyone in the wagon. "Do all of you who have skills and powers feel you are growing in strength being around Marty?"

Bailey said, "I've always felt stronger around him. I know he generates energy and strength, which, I think, enhances all of us."

Steve said, "I must agree as I never used to think I had any kinds of powers. But lately, I have had feelings I have never had before." As he looked at Vanessa, he said, "Well, of course, I have exceptional feelings for certain people. I have noticed, however, that I feel stronger, and ever since we grew in height, I keep getting this tingling feeling like I'm growing—and not just in size."

Vanessa said, "I think we are all experiencing that, Steve. My sisters and I know we are gaining strengths we never had before."

Max spoke up and said, "I think all of us have been gaining more strength and power since we have entered this world. I know that being around Marty has been helping a lot, but could it be Mother Earth?"

"Well, I am not sure, Max, as I have always been in this world and have not started feeling this way until I met him and all of you," Vanessa replied.

Steve said, "Whatever it is, I, for one, like the idea of having more power with some of the things we have run into so far. I wish I knew what my powers were."

Jack said, "I know I have been gaining more strength as well since I have had the chance to meet all of you."

"I know for a fact I have been finding I have more powers than I ever could have imagined before I came over here," I said.

Bailey said, "Well, we have all seen you do some very amazing things lately."

CHAPTER 27

Meeting the Elders

Tasha said, "Well, I think this is where we should be as Phil is stopping."

As we pulled up to an entrance, Burdock, his brother, and Datilina pulled up alongside us. Many of the pets had been changing into human form since we left that view of the valley so they could look over the edge of the wagon and see all the buildings and the castle coming up.

Tabitha was standing and looking up at the walls of the castle we were about to enter and turned to me and said, "Uncle Marty, this is a very big house."

"Yes, it is, little one," I said.

As I looked at her, she stood about a foot shorter than Agatha and Ziggy. I kept wondering, *what kinds of things can she really do?* I have been getting this feeling from her that she has a few great powers, but I can't figure out what any of them are. Of course, I can't figure out what everyone else has for capabilities, either.

My mind returned to what was happening as Phil said, "With this crowd of people behind us, I am sure the elders know we are here. So, let's present ourselves to the guards and go meet them."

As we approached the guards, they raised their weapons. Many on the wall seemed to be ready with their arrows.

I said, "Maybe you should warn them, Phil."

"Okay, all of you, wait here. I will return in just a moment."

As he spoke to the guards, they all waved the others off, letting them know it was safe. But as we entered, Phil walked ahead of us, warning anyone else who may find the powers behind him a threat to step back. The guards allowed only those in our group to pass. The rest of the people had to wait outside, but they all stayed because they still wanted to see what was going on and about to happen.

Two men and a woman were standing in a courtyard as if they were waiting for us. Phil spoke to them, walked back to us, and asked Bailey, Steve, and me to step forward.

As we did, he said to the elders, "This is why members of our region were sent north."

As the elders looked at us, the woman said, "You are so young, but everyone around you can feel just how powerful and strong you are. It is said you also have pets. Am I correct?"

"Yes, ma'am, we do." So, I turned to Ziggy, Max, and Tabby, asking them to join us. As they came to stand next to us, I asked them, "Will you take your regular form, please?"

As they returned to the small animals they originally were, we heard, "Oh my lords," "That is truly unbelievable," "How can that be?" and "This is so amazing."

"So, the prophecy is real. After so many centuries of stories and tales, we have the fortune of experiencing it firsthand. Your group—including Denarians, of course—have been the stories children have heard about for centuries. They are the stories all of us grew up with. Never in my entire life, until a year ago, did I think all of us would be standing in this courtyard together, seeing those old stories become reality today."

Bailey revealed, "We are not sure what your prophecy has said all these years, but we are here to do whatever we can to help you if you need it."

"I would like to introduce all the members of our team who have joined us as we have entered your world because it is all of us working together who create better things," I said. "Those of us from Earth are Bailey, Steve, and our little friends Ziggy, Max, and Tabitha, and I am Marty."

"We are the elders of Etheral. My name is Averell. This is Mincer and Tangent."

"All the rest of you, please join us," I said. As the remaining members of our team walked up, I introduced them. I said, "Many who travel with us have special powers, and some of them can change as well. This is Agatha, Sam, and Snowball, who can also turn into animals. Here are Vanessa, Krystle, and Heather. This is our wise one, Jack, and this is Sophia, who has joined us lately. I am sure you already know Tasha, Datilina, Burdock, and his brother, Dohadie."

Tangent spoke up finally and asked, "We sent more north. What has happened to all of them?"

"They have stayed to help people we saved. One of them, Meesha, is traveling with two friends to protect them as they travel north, but she will be returning soon. Oscar and Ruther are helping create a new base camp for all those who are now starting new lives and wish to join us. Magic is doing a fine job of helping cook for all those who are already there, and Winterish is there with her bear, protecting that camp."

"Well, it sounds like you have all been busy since you entered our world," Mincer said.

"We have, and we have more to do."

Datilina spoke up and said, "Yes, they have been busy saving people, and on top of that, we have two dragons who are part of this group."

Averell and the other two looked at Datilina as if she had spoken out of turn, and Tangent spoke first, asking, "What did you just say?"

"Did I speak out of turn?" she asked.

"Oh no, child. You said something about two dragons," Averell said.

"I said we have been busy and we have two dragons who are part of this team as they came to protect the three and their pets."

Averell, Mincer, and Tangent, all three, looked at me as if they did not believe that was true. I looked back at them and nodded, and as I did, so did all those with us who had already seen them.

172

"Oh, dear lords," said Averell, "it's true."

To understand this better, you must keep in mind it was just like home, where many different religions believe that one unique being or creator is what they call on for guidance. Of course, all of them have different names and faces and are different colors. However, that is what they believe in, and all love to call him or her a god.

Here, they have the same thing. Many people have beliefs and enjoy raising families with the feelings they have. They understand completely that all people have the right to believe as they wish without trying to influence others. Everyone believes in a god or, in many cases, do not believe in any god, but those who do are worshipping the same entity but by different names and faces.

Averell walked toward me, and as she did, her hand was reaching out for mine, but I could tell she was feeling my power already. She slowed as she approached me and suddenly had to stop.

She looked at me and said, "The feelings I get from you are unbelievably strong."

I held out my hand and said, "We have heard that often since we entered your world."

She took another step forward, and I said, "Do not be afraid."

She took my hand, and I could feel fear building up inside of her. She seemed to go rigid and shake a bit. I was watching the guards as she did.

Phil walked over to them and said, "She is going to be fine."

After he did that, I got the feeling they were more relaxed, but before he talked with them, I got the feeling I would soon look like a pincushion with a lot of liquid pouring out of my body. I looked back at Averell, and she looked like she had just awakened from sleep and rotated her head from side to side as if to loosen up her neck.

Then she spoke to me and said, "I have never felt so free and full of life as I do right now. You have a gift and power that is totally superb."

Mincer and Tangent walked up very slowly. I had the feeling these guys were not as daring as the woman I had just touched. As they came closer, they moved very slowly, doing the same things as Averell did.

Both went rigid and were shaking as guards started to rush in, but Averell said, "Stop. There is no reason for any of us to be alarmed."

Mincer said, "I don't know what it is about you, son, but all those aches and pains I had, are now gone. Thank you."

"You are welcome, sir."

Tangent said, "You just made me feel like I am ten years younger. Thank you."

"You also are welcome." I looked over at the guards, and I asked them, "Would all of you care to find out about our powers?"

Some of them were nodding and others shaking their heads, but I walked up toward them and held out my hand.

Averell spoke up and said, "You will not be harmed, but you will feel cured of your ills."

Suddenly, I was being touched by very cautious guards and watching the surprised looks on their faces.

Phil walked up and said, "I am pleased you offered to share that with my fellow soldiers."

"If any of us can make others feel better or help them create better lives, we will do what we can," Bailey said.

"Well, you have traveled a long way, and it is now time for you to enjoy our hospitality. We will make sure you have a healthy meal, along with a good night's sleep. All of you, please come with us," Tangent said.

The dinner was excellent. I don't think any of us have sat at a table with so much food on it before in our lives. Everyone seemed to be enjoying every mouthful. The discussions covered just about everything we have experienced so far. Soon, all of us had our fill. The table now cleared off, everyone wandered around the grounds, just enjoying all the beauty of the city.

Tasha walked up and said, "You did what you said you would do."

I asked her, "What was that?"

She said, "You told me I would see the high city again, and we did that, but you forgot to mention eating with the elders and enjoying an evening on their palace grounds."

"Well, it seems no matter where we go, we are offered more hospitality than we count on," I said.

Steve and Vanessa were wandering around, holding hands, and talking about the differences between each of their own homes and here.

Steve said, "I could have never imagined that before we came over here, all of us would be in a huge city high up on a mountain, walking around a palace."

"Well, to be honest with you, Steve, I feel the same way and could never even picture in my mind all this," Vanessa said.

Ziggy asked Agatha, "Does all this seem real to you?"

"Not to me, but you must keep in mind my only knowledge of things like this has been brought about because of all of you. I never even knew of things like this before we traveled here."

"I am the same way," Ziggy said.

Jack and Burdock sat on a bench and were talking about how amazing everything was. Jack was saying, "You have lived here all your life and known about all this, and all of us have now had the opportunity to view and enjoy its beauty."

"Yes, I have lived here all my life. I have even helped create some of what you see, but that is what all of us do. We all work together to create a better way for everyone around us."

Dohadie and Datilina were standing next to a large fountain. He was telling her, "I have missed you greatly, and to be honest, I was concerned that you might not return."

"Oh, don't be silly, big guy. You know nothing would stop me from getting back here to be with you."

Everyone else was standing around, chatting with Sophia. Bailey and I leaned against a wall and spoke of how much we have accomplished so far.

"Marty. I did not see all of what has happened and all this. I did see glimpses of Steve going swimming and us picking up Sophia. I even saw a quick view of you and me standing here as we are now."

"One thing's for sure, Bailey. With you at my side, I feel complete knowing our small protectors are safe. I don't think I could ask for more. I know Steve must feel the same way now with Vanessa at his side."

"He sure does seem to care about her, as I have not seen him try to hit on Sophia once."

We both had to laugh at that comment.

The sky was getting dark, and the night was setting in, and most of us were ready to get some sleep. The feel of a real bed was something I have been dreaming of but now find it's exactly what I needed. All of us were shown to our rooms. Ziggy and I went one direction, while the others all went another.

I said to Bailey and Steve before they walked away, "I am really looking forward to a good night's sleep and a real bed."

Bailey said, "I hope they have good ones, but you know, anything beats the heck out of that wagon and straw."

Steve said, "Well, Max and I are going to just crash. So, see you all in the morning."

All of us were given rooms with baths and even new clothes as they took the old, saying they would be cleaned. I never imagined I would be with friends in a strange new world, being treated like royalty, but right now, it is as if we are just that. It was like someone just gave me knock-out drops because I was out like a light. No, no one gave us any drugs. We were just so tired, we placed our heads on our pillows and fell asleep.

CHAPTER 28

Meeting the King and Queen

There was a knock on the door, and I said, "Yes?"

The door opened, and a young woman entered and said, "Your breakfast will be ready when you are, sir."

"Thank you very much."

"You are very welcome, sir."

I got out of bed. Then Ziggy, who had been sleeping at the foot of the bed, woke, shook, and jumped down to the floor.

The young lady who just woke us said, "My, what a beautiful animal," and, as she petted her, said, "I will make sure you have something special this morning." She turned and walked away.

Ziggy mentally asked, *Did you hear that? She said I am beautiful, and she must like me because she is getting me something special.*

I heard that, so don't rub it in. You already know I love you any way you are.

I know, she said.

As I got dressed and ready, we walked out of the room, looked down the hall, and noticed doors opening and others walking out into the hallway.

Bailey said, "I slept so well last night, I could not believe it."

Steve said, "So did I."

Burdock walked up and said, "I never could imagine I would be sleeping in one of the elders' palace rooms in my entire life. But, Marty, you made it happen."

Datilina, Dohadie, Tasha, then Sophia walked up to join us, and all spoke of a good night's sleep. Soon, we saw Vanessa with her sisters, along with their pets.

Jack walked around the corner and asked, "What is this? A convention? I have been waiting for all of you to wake up for hours."

All of us looked at him, and then we all just laughed when the young woman who woke us walked up next to him and said, "Don't let him give you that. I had a tough time getting him to leave that bed, and he was the last of you to rise."

Jack just looked at her, turned red, gave her a big smile, then said, "Well, it's been a long time since I have slept in such a fine bed."

"Okay, let's all go to breakfast," I said.

Conversations were lively as we ate, talking about where we came from and what it is we like about this land. We heard about the construction of this empire, all the lives lost in the creation of it, and the achievements that have been made. We spoke of what might be in store for all of us as we traveled further west. Of course, no one had a real answer to what we might have to face.

Breakfast being over, all of us gathered to walk outside. As we thanked our hosts, they said, "We have a surprise for all of you." So we walked out with them and entered the same courtyard we walked into yesterday. However, this time, we were greeted by different kinds of guards and more than we saw before.

These guards were dressed in brightly colored clothes and had sashes across their chests over breastplates of armor. They wore armor on much of their bodies. Each had a helmet that reminded me of the head of a creature but only the skull with the eye sockets, a place for the nose, and huge sharp teeth.

As we walked out, the guards all stood between two people and us. I looked around to see if we were about to be surprised in a manner we would not like. As I did, I felt hopefulness and wishful thoughts. I felt happiness and friendship.

Averell, Mincer, Tangent, and Phil all walked out ahead of us. The guards stepped back and created a walk for all of us to approach the king and queen of this region.

"Please come forward," the queen said.

We all looked at one another, and Bailey nodded. So did Steve. I turned and started walking forward. As I did, the first guard I walked toward pulled his sword.

Within a split second, I was suddenly holding a beautiful glowing sword in my hand. The colors shimmered as the designs on the side that looked like gods were moving in motion to the feelings running through my body.

The other guards at once pulled their swords and gathered in front of the king and queen.

All of them had swords of the most wicked-looking kind of design. The blades looked like they had the design of a demon on each side. The steel seemed to flow like a large wave off the ocean. Then it reduced in size to where the last part of the blade took on the shape of a diamond and extended out to a point.

On top of the blade was what looked like many small waves from the ocean, as if they were rising up and forward to sharp points. They reminded me of one of my mom's new serrated bread knives. To me, they looked quite deadly. The protection over the hands almost looked like a claw of some kind.

I spoke out, saying, "I am finding things in this world are different for sure, but I know what you feel is my strength and my power. We have had people tell us this since we entered your world. We are not here to harm anyone. We are here to help protect your Mother Earth and all the people on her. I am sorry my sword came to my hand so quickly as it is a defense for me against any dangers." As I said that, I raised my hand above my head with my sword, and the sword vanished as quickly as it had arrived.

The elders said, "These people are not here to harm anyone. Please put your swords away and meet them. Feel the power they have and know they are here to work with us, not against us."

All the guards slowly put their swords away as if they were still not convinced and did not trust us.

The king said, "Remove that guard."

I said, "Your Majesty, it's not his fault. It's what all of you feel as the three of us walk toward you. Allow him to join our team as we may need a good soldier or two who know how to react and quickly."

He looked over at the guard and then back to me. "Let it be so," the king said.

I looked at the guard who, by now, had lowered his sword with his hand on top, with the point placed on the ground, and was kneeling next to me. Then I said, "If you wish to join and help us, please rise and walk with me."

He looked at his king, who nodded, and he stood then looked at me.

I reached out to shake hands. "On my world, when people meet and wish to know each other, we shake hands."

It did take some doing for him to gather the strength that was needed to step forward. As he did, I could see he felt my power with the look in his eyes and the expression on his face. He took a deep breath and slowly raised his hand to meet mine.

As we shook hands, he said, "I could feel your power before, but now that I have touched you, I feel you just gave me the strength I have never had. I am not sure what it is I can do to help you and your friends, but I will be at your side, helping in any manner that is needed. I must say, I am pleased to meet you."

I said, "The three of us scare the heck out of most people we meet over here, so we try to keep our distance."

All of us walked closer to the king and queen. The guards around us were visibly showing the effects of our power and strength. All our pets were in animal form, walking with us at his time. As we stood in front of the king and queen, I turned to all those with me, turned again, and kneeled in front of them. Everyone behind me did the same, including the animals, who had merely lowered their heads.

"We have heard that you are the prophecy of centuries old. It seems you have magic or powers no others have. So, is this true?"

"I am afraid I have no idea of what your foretelling really says. However, just about everyone we meet tells us we are the prophecy."

"I see you have pets as well, but the prophecy says they can change. Can these animals change?" the queen asked.

Turning around, I asked, "Will all of you please show Her Majesty what you look like as people?"

It was amazing how each of them changed one at a time, one after the other. As I was viewing all our pets change, I felt the king and queen suddenly giving off a feeling of shock. I turned to see them both looking at all our little peaceful, cute animals as they transformed with looks of disbelief on their faces. Even the guards were giving off feelings of amazement, and I was sure they were standing there with open mouths and looks of skepticism behind those helmets.

"Praise the lords," the queen said.

"Yes," said the king, and as he stepped forward, he hesitated. Then he said, "Whatever you need, all you must do is ask."

"Thank you, Your Majesty," I replied.

He walked up, and the closer he got, the more he seemed to slow down, and he said, "Now I understand why this guard feared for our safety."

I reached out to shake his hand. Hesitantly, he reached out and slowly touched my hand. As my power surged through him, he gripped my hand firmly and started to shake. Once he felt the power and recovered from shaking, he pulled me close, then embraced me, and the queen stepped forward. Very slowly but she also reached out her hand.

Both the king and queen looked at each other and then at me as the queen commented, "I have never felt such power before. It seems you just gave me a renewed life."

The king commented, "Son, I have no idea what you just did, but right now I feel less pain and fewer aches than I have for years. Thank you."

The elders, king, and queen all talked with all the rest of the team and gave them all big hugs. I walked around and spoke to all the guards. It took some time before they would shake hands, but soon, they overcame the fear that had built up inside of them. One by one, we shook hands. Then they all seemed to have gained something special.

I spoke to Jack and asked him, "Please find out what items we may need to travel with the group that is going to those excavations. Please make arrangements for all of us to join them."

He spoke up and said, "I will make that happen, Marty."

"Thank you, Jack," I replied.

I noticed the king and the guard speaking, so I walked over and stood as they talked. I could hear the king as he said, "I am proud of you, young man, and I should not have doubted your feelings."

He replied, "Your Majesty, I may have overreacted."

I spoke up and said, "No, you didn't. No matter where we travel, people who are not used to us have reactions like your own. As we entered your town down below, people came out, then ran back, grabbing crossbows and other weapons because they could feel us and the powers we have. I could feel the fear they held inside of them and knew they were all ready to use those weapons on us. We now have figured out that we need to send a person ahead of us to inform others we are not a danger to them."

"Marty, please allow this young man to be your personal envoy so he can reach out ahead of you and let people know you are coming."

The young soldier excused himself, then walked away as the king and I continued to speak.

"I do appreciate that, sir."

"I am also going to be sending eleven more of my guards along with you for protection. That young man who just left us will oversee them. They will, however, all answer to you."

"I hope, sir, you will allow Phil, who is the captain of the elders' guards, to join us as well.

"We will make that happen," he replied.

"Thank you. He has been with us since we camped down below," I said.

"I am also sure you will need supplies, so I am going to make sure my guards take one wagon for a few extra horses. There will also be plenty of room on that wagon for food and water for all of you and your animals."

"That will be wonderful, Your Majesty," I replied.

The young guard walked back over and said, "Please excuse me, Your Majesty." Then he and the king walked a short distance away. When they returned, the young soldier walked off again. Then the king came to speak with me.

I said, "Your Majesty, we have a few things we are going to need, and I do hope you have a person who can help our wise one plan for those."

"I will make sure you get what you need. In fact, that young man, Philip Danassia, you have chosen will carry with him a note from me. It will allow others to know you are representing the crown. He will also have one larger wagon for all the men to sleep in because I don't want my men to have to just sleep on the ground. It was just brought to my attention you do not have a covered wagon. You may need one where you will soon be traveling. So, I just authorized a wagon from our group of wagons for you to use and have."

"That is very considerate, Your Majesty. Thank you."

I looked around and found Steve and Bailey and sent them a mental thought. *Please join me and bring your pets.* I sent a thought to Ziggy. *I think it's time we get ready to leave.*

The king and queen were both surprised to see both Steve, Bailey, and our pets all walk up to me at the same time. They both looked at me and those walking up, then they looked at each other.

I said, "I spoke to all of them and asked them to join me so we could say our goodbyes. We have a lot to do before we leave as it seems we have a long way to travel yet."

"We did not hear you speak to them."

"It's just a mental thought thing, Your Majesty."

"Well, you must not be in a big rush to leave. We are going to have a good lunch and then a dinner in your honor this evening. All of you can leave in the morning after you have a good night's sleep," the king said.

"Well, I guess I can't argue with a king," I said.

All of us walked around the courtyard, looking at everything. As we looked out from the courtyard, we could see for many miles in most directions, so I asked, "I see you have very high walls with sentries on them. Why is that?"

"When those of our past came to this part of the region, they found a few beasts that attacked the people and destroyed anything they created. Soon our past generations started building walls. The one down below was the first. Many of the groups decided to create this area up here. They started with narrow paths that became roads and enhanced them as years went by. It has been a lot of work and lost lives that created all we have today."

"One other question I have is 'Those large crossbows are used for what?'"

"We have some huge birds with long heads and wings that look like a tanner from the caves, and they attack us often lately. We are not sure where they have come from, but it seems much of what is happening now started about a year ago. Why do you ask?"

"Well, two more members of our team have not joined us yet but will be with us soon. We were concerned you might wish to use those crossbows on them."

"Why on all we stand for would I do that?" he asked.

"Because the prophecy is well known throughout your lands, and many people, animals, and other life forms have become our friends. We have two who have joined us as they were sent to travel with us and protect us. Today we are protected by all dragons and those two other friends are dragons."

I thought he was going to get sick as he lost all color in his face as I said that. His face gave me a look that lacked expression, but then turned into the look of excitement.

Suddenly, he said, "Praise the lords you are the prophecy as it says you will have wise ones, Denarians, archers, pets that change, giants, and dragons at your side. It is said that as you travel, you leave behind people in all areas who will help build and protect all."

Soon, all of us entered the palace where everyone got the grand tour.

Dohadie walked up to me and said, "Marty, you have made my brother a very proud man. From now on, I am not sure I will ever be able to be around him for any great length of time as he will never shut up."

We both laughed. Jack joined us. Then we all talked about the fact that the palace was not elaborate.

I said, "Back home, I have seen photos of palaces that were filled with fine furniture and wall hangings. Most of them have gold everywhere and servants all over the place. However, I don't see a lot of fancy items or furnishings here."

As we talked about it, a young lady who was passing by must have heard our conversation and said, "The king and queen are more like the people. I think if they could, they would live in a regular home just like anyone else, but they are royalty. Many times, they will have meals fixed and invite all the working people to join them."

"I got the feeling they were very calm and understanding, and the only time I felt they were afraid or were having problems was when I walked up to them."

Jack spoke up and said, "Most people you walk up to start having problems and want to run or grab a weapon, Marty."

"I know most of them come out with crossbows," I said.

CHAPTER 29

Viewing Our New Ride

Phil came over, saying, "Marty, first off, thank you for requesting my company as you travel."

"You're very welcome, and it will be good to have you riding along with us."

"I would like you and your team to join me for a few minutes as the king and queen have asked me to show you your new coach," he said.

"A coach, you say?" I commented as I laughed.

"What's so funny?" he asked.

"I guess I have not heard of any old wagon called a coach before," I said.

"It's just what we call these, and I am sure you will see why. If all of you will follow me," Phil said.

I looked around to make sure everyone was with us and sent a mental note to Bailey, asking, *Are you with us?*

I am right beside you and Ziggy, she replied.

I turned, and she was about five feet away and staring at me with a great big beautiful smile. I said, "I guess you are."

All of us walked out to an area that seemed to be a large barn or garage full of different carriages and wagons. I noticed one was being set up for horses, so we walked over and looked inside, and it had stalls for about four horses, two horse stalls on each side. We also noticed lots of storage compartments in the front and rear and on top.

Then we walked to the next wagon, which I gathered must have been for the guards to use for sleeping, and I said, "Wow! Now that is fancy."

As I viewed it, I noticed how tall it looked. Even Steve noticed it and commented, "Look at the height of that wagon."

All of us looked at it. Then Bailey said, "That is a weird design." It had windows and what looked like a cab of a truck—without the front-engine compartment, of course. It was wide and longer than the wagon George had created that we have been traveling in since we left his place. There were compartments on both sides between the wheels for storage. There also seemed to be more storage area on top of the cab.

All of us looked it over. Bailey opened the back door and stepped up inside. After seeing her disappear for a minute, we all heard, "Hey, this even has a bathroom."

Phil poked his head inside of the wagon and said, "Well, I guess you will like your new wagon."

She asked, "Is this ours?"

"No, this one is for all of us guards, but come with me. I will show you yours."

All of us walked to the next section of the garage. Sitting there and being fitted out with supplies was what looked like a new wagon. It was very much the same as the one we just viewed. So, everyone walked around it and looked under it and noticed the springs for a better ride. Some took turns climbing inside and checking it out. Two people were loading up barrels of water on both sides just behind the wheels. They were not big round barrels like I have seen in wineries back home. They were about two feet around, and they stood about four feet tall.

I noticed the windows and asked Steve, "Do you see what look like shutters next to the windows?"

"I do. I noticed a person can slide those into place if needed. I imagine if people are sleeping during the day, you could close them to keep it dark," he replied.

Ziggy came over and asked, "Did you notice that front section is fancier than your father's truck?"

"I have not seen it yet," I said.

As I spoke those words, all of us walked to the front of the wagon. It had two doors, one on each side with windows. The window in the front had two parts where the lower section could be tipped up so the driver could control the horses and still have protection from the weather. If the weather got too bad, you could lower that window and run the reins through slots and still have control of the horses. Of course, with no one around, you would have both windows in place and have full protection from the elements. I guess that way, you would not have any upholstery damage.

The entire roof was not part of the back section since they were separate but all enclosed. We each had to take turns climbing up and sitting in a cushioned seat.

Tabby walked over and said, "Uncle Marty, can you help me up so I can find out what it's like?

I turned, looked down at her, and just shook my head. I then picked her up and set her in the seat. After all of us found out how elaborate our new wagon was, we all walked back to the main room where the king, queen, and elders were all chatting away.

As we walked in, the queen walked over and asked us, "Well, what do you think of your new coach?"

Bailey spoke up and said, "It even has a bathroom."

We all broke out laughing.

Steve said, "That is awesome."

Everyone around us agreed.

I said, "I am not sure we can take that wagon."

All those around me looked at me with squinty eyes, opened mouths, and what-are-you talking-about faces.

Then Bailey asked the question "What are you talking about?"

"I am really starting to enjoy the ride in our old wagon, I would miss all the bouncing and bruises just to ride in all that comfort. You know a soft ride, and as you said, it has a bathroom. Not sure I will be able to handle sleeping on a bed and having running water."

Steve and Jack started laughing. Then everyone else joined in.

Then I said, "That is one of the finest-looking wagons I have ever seen, and I know everyone else here looks forward to riding and sleeping in it. Thank you very much."

The king and elders all walked over, and we all discussed that new wagon and all its comforts.

CHAPTER 30

Lunch with New Friends

Soon, a well-dressed lady walked out and rang a small bell and said, "Lunch is ready whenever you are."

All of us followed all the royalty in and then found seats. This time, all our pets were people and would enjoy the food as they should. We were all offered diverse types of sandwiches and soups, along with salads and extra trays of veggies. They poured out glasses of water and offered us a special drink they produced in the city below.

I asked, "What is it?"

"It's a blend of berries and herbs. Try it and let me know what you think," Averell commented.

As I gave it a try, I found it tasted familiar and said, "This, tastes like grape juice we have at home."

Suddenly, everyone else was grabbing their glass and holding it as one of the people came around and filled them. Many of the expressions were a nod or a nod and smile. I was getting the feeling from everyone of excitement and happiness. Everyone was speaking about the palace and the town. They discussed the beautiful wagons and craftsmanship that went into making them.

Steve asked, "All the work on those wagons was done by your people?"

"Yes, every part of the workings on those wagons was created by skilled labor. They are rewarded for what they do," Mincer replied.

"So, do they have like an apprenticeship for people wanting to learn those trades?" I asked.

"A what?" Tangent asked.

Steve spoke up and said, "That is where the younger generation can learn about a special trade, and it's called an apprenticeship."

I said, "Yes, it's as if you are a carpenter and have someone working with you, learning about how you do your job."

"What is a carpter?" the king asked.

"I was speaking to Ruther about that just before we headed down here. I explained to him that a carpenter is a person who creates with wood. They are most often a master cabinet maker or wood craftsman as they build homes and all the wooden structures inside of them," I said.

"Oh, Ruther is one of the creators of the wagon you will be receiving from us. He is very skilled at his work and has built many items for us out of wood," the queen said.

"He is helping build our new base camp, about a five day ride to the north. Oscar is drawing up the plans for new homes and buildings, and Ruther is teaching others how to create them," I said.

"Oscar designed our carriages and wagons and is very knowledgeable when it comes to putting on paper how to place things and what they should look like. I think that without the two of them, our wagons would still have the look of an ordinary old wagon that most others use to transport goods and supplies."

"Well, I have given Oscar the title of engineer and Ruther the title of carpenter. They both seem to love the fact they will be building a new community," I said.

The king said, "It would be nice to see your location after it is built."

"You will always be welcome. Of course, you will have to understand we don't have the elegance and fancy places to sleep and eat in like you have here," I said.

The queen spoke up and said, "Marty, one thing's for sure. The two of us don't need all the fancy trimmings and elegant ways. We would enjoy just having the chance to visit and enjoy your company and those around you."

Everyone finished eating and rose from the table, then offered to help clean things up.

Those who waited on us said, "No, you just relax and enjoy."

CHAPTER 31

Walking in Upper Etheral

All of us walked outside.

Phil asked, "How would you like to walk around the town and see what's here?"

Of course, I said, "I would love to as long as no one pulls out a weapon and shoots us."

Steve said, "That would be cool."

I replied, "What's cool? Us getting shot?"

He started laughing as he shook his head and finally said, "No, not that. Walking through town would be cool."

Phil stated, "Our royalty suggested we get you some new clothes."

Bailey, Vanessa, and all the rest of the girls all said, "Let's go shopping."

Jack shook his head and looked over at Steve and said, "You know, I almost had a feeling someone would say that."

All of us hopped in a wagon. Then we rode into the shopping area of town. After stopping, we climbed down, and this time, we were not alone. Some of the guards escorted us so no one would use us as a target. We still scared the bejeebies out of a lot of people as we approached them, but at least with the backup team, we had no one running for a weapon.

The guys went one way, then the girls went the other, as half the guards were with each group. As we looked at different clothes, I found a few stores didn't have my size. I was thinking back to when Dad ordered something online that was made in China. He thought it would fit him according to the size chart, but when he got it, he found he was too big for it. Well, now I understood what that was like.

We walked into one more shop after our guard entered and spoke to them, and we found this was one store that had our sizes. Phil had told our guard that if we wanted something, we were to let him know, and he would take care of it. Soon, all of us came out with a few bags of different items.

I looked over at Burdock and asked, "How do you feel?"

He looked at me and said, "I think I will soon feel like a new person with a new goal in life."

Jack walked out and stood next to me with a big smile.

I asked him, "What did you get?"

"I got some of the finest material I have ever seen or found to make a new robe out of, along with new pants, shirt, underwear, socks, and new footwear."

"Steve, what about you?"

"Hey, buddy, look at this." Suddenly, he opened one of his bags a bit and pulled out a hat, not just a ball cap or something like that, but one that reminded me of that Indy guy with a whip.

I said, "That is awesome, and it looks good on you."

"I also got new pants, shirt, underwear, and boots," he said.

Everyone had bags in their hands with new shirts, pants, underwear, and socks.

Dohadie asked me, "What did you get?"

I opened my bag and pulled out a new pair of boots. "I got these new boots, along with a new shirt, underwear, socks, and pants."

All of us guys, including Max and Sam, pulled out the boots and had to put them on. Soon, all of us seemed to be walking taller.

I looked over at Burdock as he looked back at me, and I tipped my head to the side and said, "Maybe all of us need a haircut and a trim."

Burdock tipped his head at an angle, gave me a sly grin, then asked me as he stroked his beard, "Was that directed at me?"

I looked at the other guys. Dohadie, who was cleanly shaven, said, "Brother, I really think as they do. It's time."

Soon, all of us were getting our hair washed, then getting haircuts. Burdock got his hair and beard shampooed and soon had a new haircut, along with a trimmed beard. We all walked out and stood outside of the shop and looked at each other.

Burdock spoke up and said, "I must admit, now I feel much better."

"Hey, there are the girls," Max said.

As we all reunited, all of us spoke of what we obtained. The girls had several items they had purchased. It seemed all of them must have hit a leather factory as they came out with big bags filled with all kinds of new clothes, leather tops and skirts, with boots and huge smiles on all their faces. Of course, they bought pants and underwear, socks, and jackets as well.

All of us guys walked up to them as they opened the bags to show us all the leather, I said, "You girls are just trying to work on our imagination."

Vanessa said, "No, we are just working on who we are."

Steve looked at Vanessa and said, "Well, working on who you are is always impressing me."

I looked over at Vanessa, her sisters, Ziggy and Agatha, who also had bags, and asked, "You didn't just purchase warrior items, did you?"

Agatha spoke first and said, "No. We got pants, blouses, socks, underwear, boots, and a few other things for comfort."

Vanessa and the girls all stood there with big smiles, and Heather said, "We got some things that make us look like we should if we visit the king and queen."

Ziggy commented, "All of us took advantage of getting clothes we really like."

"I am pleased, ladies," I replied.

All the girls walked over to Burdock and were checking out his trimmed beard and haircut. As they surrounded him, he started to back up.

Vanessa said, "Burdock, this is a very nice change."

The other girls all had comments as well, —"Very nice," "Is that really you?" and "It's nice to finally see you, Burdock."

He looked over at us, and we were all smiling and nodding. Soon, all of us were loading our bags in the wagon and traveled to another section of town because I had asked Phil to show us the less fortunate side of the city.

He told me, "Most of the people are taken care of, even if they are poor, as just about every person contributes in some manner to the creation of better lives here. You see, in our cities, all people help everyone else."

We pulled up to a street that looked like it had older homes or, in some cases, shacks. I asked Phil to pull over so we could meet some of the people. As we climbed down, some of the guards walked ahead of us and warned people about the feelings of power and explained who we were.

We walked up to people in the street, having the chance to meet them. Often they still had a great fear of us, but after we touched them, all that changed. Some told us they had not been working, and we sat with them on the steps of what looked like a town courthouse and discussed what they did for a living. Soon, more people were joining us. It was as if we must have had all the people from this part of the town around us.

Steve, Bailey, and I touched everyone we could as it seemed to heal or help them in some way. It was not just the three of us anymore, as we found out. Even Vanessa and her sisters had the power to help others.

People lined up to be touched, and I stood on the steps and said, "Tomorrow I hope to meet with others who want to rebuild the old town of Etheral. If you wish to help, you should all think about joining us down in Lower Etheral."

"Many of us don't have a horse or wagon to ride up and down the hill," a man said.

Phil spoke up and said, "If you wish to travel down the hill and help rebuild the old city, I will see if we can make sure you have wagons to ride back and forth in."

It seemed that was about all it took to get half of the people here who were not working willing to help others. He continued to say, "I am sure our king and queen will do what they can to help all of you in any way."

One of the women walked up to him and said, "I'm sure most here would love to help, sir. We don't need a lot as most of us are pleased we are treated well. I, for one, will be in one of those wagons because they will need cooks and helpers."

Soon, many other voices were heard yelling, "I am with you!" "Count me in!" and "Let us know when to meet the wagons!"

As all of us walked through the crowds, one woman who had not been touched came toward me. She suddenly stopped and backed up but still wanted to speak to me.

She said, "Please help me."

I said to her, "I know you can feel my powers and strength but reach out your hand and touch mine."

She walked slowly to me, and as she did, she took a huge breath. Her body shook all over before even touching me. Then she started to fall. I rushed over and caught her. I stood her up and was looking at her.

All she could say was "Praise the lords you have come."

I asked, "Are you okay?"

She said, "I have never been better in my entire life thanks to what you have done for me, but can you visit my daughter as she has been ill and no one can understand why?"

"Where do you live? I asked.

"Over there," and she pointed to a home about two houses away.

So, all of us walked over to her house. As she opened the gate, I noticed a girl about the size of Tabby sitting on the porch.

The woman with us walked up and said, "Honey, this man is not from around here, and he may feel very strange to you, but please don't be scared. I want you to reach out and touch him."

The little girl seemed to struggle to get up. Her mother helped her, and I reached out my hand as they both walked to me. I could see the girl shake, and her expression changed, and I could feel she was afraid for her life, but she put her hand in mine. Suddenly, she stood up, turned and looked at her mother for a long time, and took deep breaths. Then she turned back to me and looked up. I viewed her beautiful eyes. Then she wrapped her arms around me, giving me a big hug. It was just like getting a big hug from Tabby.

I looked at her and asked, "How do you feel?

She hugged me more and said, "I am well. Yes, I am well."

Then her mother knelt next to her, looked up at me, and said, "I praise the lords because you have come and saved the most important part of my life. Thank you."

People out in the streets were telling others what just happened, and all of them started cheering and clapping their hands. Many in the back were still learning about all that had taken place, but as soon as they understood, they joined in with the cheering.

The guards with us all looked totally amazed. Phil was standing there, and as I looked back at him, it almost appeared as if he had tears in his eyes.

We spent a good amount of time talking to the woman and learning more about her and what had happened to her daughter.

She was saying, "One day she came home and found it difficult to even walk. In the mornings, she could not even get out of bed."

The girls were all talking to the little girl. Suddenly, they all broke out laughing.

Steve said, "Well, it sounds like things are better now."

"I agree, Steve," I said.

Soon, all of us started to walk back to the wagon, with a few hundred people opening a path for us. Many of them who had not been touched struggled to step up and contact one of us. The expressions were fantastic, but the feelings I was getting were amazing.

As we climbed on board the wagon, I stood up in the back and said, "I speak for not only myself but every member on our team with me when I say we have been very fortunate to meet all of you today. I do hope some of you will join us in the lower city as we meet with others who wish to rebuild the old townsite."

Soon, all of us were heading back to the palace with many happy feelings and faces. People waved as we left.

Phil said, "I have seen you do amazing things, but to heal that young child was an incident of real beauty."

I asked him, "Did I see you start to get a bit misty at one point?"

"Misty?" he asked.

"Yes, I could have sworn I almost observed watering eyes as I looked back at you."

"I found it to be"—and he paused a moment, then continued—"a very moving situation as that is one of my best friend's daughters."

"I am pleased we could help her," I replied.

CHAPTER 32

Dinner with Royalty

Soon, all of us were in our rooms, taking a bath, putting on all those new clean clothes we just bought, and getting ready for a dinner with a king and queen along with the elders.

The meal was something you only imagine people of wealth to place on a vast table. We had our choice of just about anything we could possibly enjoy eating. There were salads, meats, and vegetables as well as milk, water, and fruit juices—I mean milk for the first time since we have been over here, and it was cold and amazing.

Everyone was eating, talking, and I was concerned that maybe some of the pets would mess things up, not being used to sitting at a table like this. However, it was not the pets as it was me who managed to spill some of the dressing on my shirt. One of the people waiting on all of us just walked over and gave me a cloth. I rubbed it on the stain, and it was gone.

I looked down and then looked back at the person who handed me the cloth and said, "Wow, this is one thing we don't have in our world that I know of. Thank you."

She nodded and replied, "You're very welcome, sir."

We were asked questions about our powers and what kinds of things we could do, but most of us still have little or no idea about our capabilities.

Bailey said, "Most of what we use comes to us as we need it."

Dinner was fantastic, but that was not all because as soon as the dinner plates were removed, dessert was brought out on trays, and everyone had a choice of what they wanted.

I looked over and had my eye on a nice slice of chocolate cake and said, "I know I should not do this, but I do love eating my grandmother's chocolate chip cookies, and that slice of cake reminds me of those, so I bet that cake will be awesome."

The night seemed to go on for a long time as it was still light outside. So most of us walked back out around the buildings near the garage, and all of us found interesting things to look at and learn about. Phil introduced Sophia to the metalsmith for the royal family. Soon, she was showing him a design for arrowheads.

He said, "I think this would be an easy design to work with. Let me see what I can do." He then walked into a small shop, with all the girls trailing in after him to see what he was thinking about. As he pulled out some small pieces of metal, he cut and shaped a few pieces and asked, "How would these work for you?"

Sophia said, "Let me get my bow and arrows. Then we can compare them." Soon, she was back, talking, and comparing the arrowheads.

"Let me have some time so I can make a few for you and give them to you tonight or first thing in the morning," the metalsmith commented.

Sophia and the girls all walked back to the courtyard and wandered around, talking to all the others.

Heather said, "If we can get arrowheads made, that would be half of the problem of making arrows."

"Yes, it would be, and we have to keep in mind we will have two blacksmiths riding along with us as well who said they would make a few, too," Sophia commented.

Our team members were still speaking with the elders and were asking, "How did you know we would be in your world at this time?"

"It's not just us, Steve, as we have people who view all those stars and planets. It has been seen that the planets have been aligned with historical events. Many people who study events have been telling us for several years you would arrive. Most of them just did not know exactly when. All of us realized all of you were going to be entering our world within a short period. So during the past year, we spent as much time as we could trying to find out more facts on when you would arrive. When we finally felt the time was close, we set up a plan to have people meet you so they could help and protect you. We sent our team to find you, hoping everything and all the timing was correct. However, to be honest with you, it was a guessing game."

As the elders spoke to Steve and Max, I was chatting with the king. In an earlier conversation, he had told me his name was Haskin and his wife's name was Natalie.

We were talking about what the king thought might be the problem in the lands west of here, and he said, "I don't know what is going on because about a year ago, things started to change. People have run from weather, fires, bugs, and so much more, and there is no reason for any of it to be happening."

"Someone said they have a dig close to the giant's old town. Is that correct?" I asked.

"Yes, it is, and we have had people going to those digs to bring back artifacts and the remains of bodies that were never buried. But it seems some people are just going out there to steal everything of value."

"Do you know someone by the name of Nomi Tinder?"

"Oh yes, Nomi checks the digs and brings things back that some people would like to keep. How do you know him?" the king asked.

I replied, "We met in the lower city, and I told him we would like to travel with him the next time he goes out to those digs."

The king commented, "He should be a good guide as he has traveled those areas often and returned with many wagons full of items we plan to place in a specific area of remembrance."

"What kinds of things are they finding?" I asked.

Haskin replied, "They are searching out the old townsites and building sites of the empire of the giants. They are finding old skeletons of families and groups of people who died for no reason anyone can think of. We have people trying to figure out what happened to them. Nomi has brought back may things like furniture and tableware, items with jewels and precious stones. We want to set up a building in recognition of their lives."

I said, "That would be a wonderful idea."

"Some people have traveled out to that area and created paintings and drawings of different places to hang in the halls of that building."

As we talked I looked around at all of our team and thought of how lucky we were to have each other.

CHAPTER 33

What About Tabby?

Tabby was over near the flowers, and all I could think of was the time I noticed her in the flower garden at Bailey's, chewing away on the plants, but this time, she was a little girl and seemed to just be enjoying the beauty of the flowers.

Some of the guards were around Sophia, looking at her bow. I think she was enjoying all the attention she was getting from the guards, who would soon be traveling with us. All of them seemed to be heavy in conversation about weapons.

The metalsmith returned with a few arrowheads and told her, "If you need more, just let me know, and I will make them for you."

"Well, I am not sure how I will get them because it seems we leave tomorrow for the western parts of your region."

"I will see if I can create more before you leave," he said.

I was noticing a new feeling as it seemed to be coming from a distance and not one I had before. In a way, it reminded me of a dove I once healed as it felt like a bird that was flying.

Many of us were discussing what it would be like to ride in luxury, and Ziggy asked, "Well, who gets to ride in the old wagon?"

Jack, Tasha, and Burdock all said at the same time, "I can."

As they talked about the difference between the old and the new, everyone was really impressed with the new one, but they also knew how dependable the old one George had created has been.

Jack said, "I guess we will have to get up early and make sure both wagons are ready to go. Tasha, maybe you and I, along with Burdock and Steve, can get together first thing and check things out."

Suddenly, there was what sounded like someone pounding on one of those enormous church bells about five times some distance away from us.

I thought, *What the hell is that?*

Then Steve said the same thing I had been thinking aloud. "What the hell is that?"

The elders split up. Then some headed our way, and the one left with Steve said, "All of you must get inside to be safe."

Everyone looked around as all the guards ran to separate locations near a few huge crossbows, and the king and queen were escorted inside.

The elders came over to us and said, "It looks like we will soon be under attack, so all of you must go inside now for protection."

"What do you mean, 'for protection'? We need to see what this is," I said.

All of us were looking at the sky. I still felt something, but at that moment, whatever it was just seemed to be calm, as it did not seem to present a threat. It always felt like a bird, and it seemed to be just flying. It was still a reasonable distance from us.

I asked, "Where is this attack happening?"

"Our outer towers have rung the alarm bells, so now everyone in our city and around it must get inside."

"So you're telling me it's not near us now, correct?"

"Yes, that is correct."

"I feel something, but it's a huge bird. I don't feel anger, hate, or hostility, but it is coming our way," I told the elder.

"That is probably what will attack us," he said.

As it got closer, I told everyone to get ready in case we must protect the people. Most of the team were in different areas. Sophia pulled out five arrows and stuck them in the ground near her.

We waited while the king and queen were inside looking out, and I noticed many of those who waited on us standing next to them.

205

Some of the elders were brave enough to stay just outside of the building but close enough to get inside if need be. The guards were set up by the huge crossbows, ready for whatever it could be that would attack us.

I was looking around to see where everyone was, and out of the side of my eye, suddenly, I noticed something huge. Then that feeling I had of a calm flying big bird turned into thoughts and feelings of food, along with hunger. As I turned, I was viewing what looked like a prehistoric bird.

I yelled at everyone, "Get ready!"

Suddenly, Bailey yelled, "Tabby!"

All of us looked around to see our little kitten, who was now a little girl, being picked up and hauled off in the claws of a huge bird.

I turned to Sophia and yelled, "Shoot it!"

"What about Tabby?" she yelled back.

I yelled again, "Just shoot it, and I will take care of Tabby!"

Suddenly, two arrows took flight and the bird was hit. As the arrows penetrated that bird, it released Tabby. Now she was falling about fifty feet to the ground. I could feel her as I already had reached her, I had gathered up the fear of losing one of our own. Everyone was screaming and yelling. Tabby suddenly stopped falling as I slowly brought her back to the courtyard and set her down.

She ran up to me, wrapped her arms around me, and gave me a big hug. Then she said, "I could feel you holding me all that time."

"Are you okay?"

"I think so," she said.

Everyone looked to the skies to see if there were more.

Steve said, "I think I see one more."

I told Tabby, "Get over by Bailey and stay there."

Abruptly, one more looked as if it was diving for all of us. I guess it felt a meal was close at hand. As it did, I raised my hands and let some of my anger and fear of losing one of our team go. Suddenly, a flame and a blast of wind encased that bird, and it fell to the grounds below the cliff.

I wanted to run over and look over the cliff and see both those creatures as I knew I had seen them before in books or movies. I bent over and braced myself by placing my hands on my knees while trying to gain back all I had just pushed into the air.

Steve ran up and put his arm on my shoulder, knelt next to me, and asked, "Hey, buddy, are you okay?"

"I believe I am, but I was so afraid of losing Tabby, I must have lost it."

"Well, you and Sophia took care of that first one and saved Tabby. But whatever it was you did to that second bird captivated everyone as you blew the hell out of it, that's for sure."

"You know, I value life of any kind and really hate the thought of destroying anything. I tried to use only a part of my power and anger," I said.

Steve replied, "I understand that, Marty, but something as dangerous as that creature left you little or no choice. If you and Sophia had not done what needed to be done, those guards would have let those crossbows take care of them and could have probably killed Tabby."

"I guess so, but that does not make me feel any better about being an instrument of death," I said.

"Marty, you saved Tabby," he said.

Bailey walked up to me and said, "Thank you for saving Tabby."

I heard voices and had the feeling many were behind me, so I turned to find everyone standing there, looking at me. Some of them were crying. Others were yelling with joyful voices. All I felt now was warmth and love.

I looked at Bailey and said aloud, "I will always do my very best to protect all the people around me," and I said to her mentally, *I will not allow something to happen to anyone on this team.*

I looked over at Sophia and said, "Thank you," as I bowed my head and turned to find a good bench to sit on. I was still trying to recover from what had just happened because it seemed I pulled a considerable amount of my power and forced it to the surface as I discharged it.

We all heard the bell one more time, so everyone was back on full alert and ready to do whatever they could. All of us stood and looked at the sky. We all looked around to see if more of those creatures were coming, but the only things coming our way were all the guards, the elders, the king and queen, and everyone else who worked in the palace.

All of them grouped around us as the king walked up, grabbed me by my shoulders, pulled me close, gave me a huge hug, and said, "By the lords, we have indeed been honored this evening by all of you."

"I will want to see what that was in the morning when we go down there, so I hope it will still be in one piece. I am sure the residents will want to get their share of whatever that was," I said.

Steve spoke out and said, "We have come to a strange world, Marty, because that was a dinosaur. I saw those before as they all flew out of their cage in that dinosaur park movie."

"That is what they looked like to me," Bailey said.

"I got that same impression myself," I replied.

Ziggy spoke up and said, "Please tell me we don't have any of those back home."

"We don't," I replied.

"Thank goodness," she responded.

"Well, I have had enough excitement tonight. Do you think that is all of them, or will there be more?" I asked.

"Chances are that was all tonight. It seems we have seen fewer and fewer over the past few months," Averell said.

"Well, in that case, do you think there is any more of that chocolate cake left?" I asked.

The king looked at me and said, "If not, we will bake another cake for you."

CHAPTER 34

Heading to Lower Etheral

The morning seemed to arrive too soon. I heard a knock on my door.

"Yes?" I said.

The door opened, and instead of a cute young woman, a man entered and said, "When you are ready, sir, your breakfast will be as well."

"Thank you," I replied.

"And for you, little one, I am sure I can find something special for you." With that, he was out the door and gone.

Hear that? He's going to find me something special, Ziggy mentally said.

Oh yes, I heard. I'm sure they spent a lot of time gathering the bones of that bird I took out of the air last night for you to chew on, I said.

She tilted her head, then shook it saying, *No way. You're just saying that because you're jealous. He is going to give me a good treat.*

As we all gathered for breakfast, I noticed Ziggy got a good plate of scraps, and along with that, she received a bone. So I mentally said, *See? I told you they went down the hill, picked the bones off that bird, and saved you a nice one.*

As she was eating some of the scraps and listening to my message, she suddenly raised her head, shook it, coughed, and then replied to me. *I am going to take my bone with me so I can enjoy it as we travel. But he did give me a generous portion of scraps.*

I am sure the guy who gave it to you will wrap it up for you if we ask him politely, I said. I excused myself from the table and got up so I could speak to the king.

Everyone else started speaking about last night and the events that took place.

Steve was saying, "I knew he had power but never realized just how much until that second creature was upon us."

Dohadie said, "I was totally amazed at how much power he created, and one thing's for sure—any enemy or monster that will not change is in for a huge surprise."

Burdock spoke out and said, "When we were leaving the location where we met this team, many of those who traveled north stayed to build the new home base. I felt we had lost any of the real power or people who could fight. I was telling Marty, 'There goes most of our fighting force.' He turned and was looking at me. Then he said, 'Burdock, we will have more power and strength going with us than you can even imagine.'"

Vanessa commented, "I know he does not feel good about having killed that big ugly bird."

Bailey spoke up and replied, "I have known him most of my life, and for him to kill anything, it has to be in defense of those he loves, or he has no choice. I have watched him with the smallest of creatures as he studies them and places them back where he got them from. Right now, I can feel what it is he feels. Both of us can feel each other's pain, and I understand he wishes there would have been a different possibility."

As all the others were sitting at the table and talking, I spoke to the king, saying, "It must be about time for all of us to travel down to the lower town. We must meet a few people who can tell us more about what has been happening in the far lands. I am not sure what we will be doing next, but I know the trip up here and back down takes a lot of time."

The king said, "Please just have the young man who is your guard tell them rooms are taken care of if you need them. Your new wagon is ready for you to take with you as well. I am sending the captain of the guards, along with all the guards you have already met, with you. They will do whatever they can to protect you if need be."

"Thank you, and I hope we see you again soon," I voiced.

The king lowered his head a bit and asked me, "Will you walk with me?"

As we walked a short distance from all the rest of the people, he turned to me, turned his head a bit, leaned toward me, and spoke. He made sure no one else was watching or could hear. I leaned toward him and heard him say, "I may be the king, but from now on, I do hope you and your team will always consider my wife and me your friends."

"Gladly, sir, and I hope we can cure the ills of your lands and help all the people," I said.

"I want you and your group to always be able to show you have my support. So I want you to take this and wear it at all times. It is my crest, and people in this land know it well."

It was a beautiful ring, a ring like I had never seen before. It was made of gold. One side of the ring had what looked to be the king, and on the other seemed to be the queen. The entire crest itself was surrounded by what looked like silver, and inside of that was a lower area of gold. Rising off the gold was a brilliantly colored blue metal in the shape of a dragon as if to protect both the king and queen. I found it was not small, so I had to try placing it on all my fingers and finally found it fit on my thumb.

I said, "I will treasure this always, Your Majesty."

We walked back to the group, where we got a few perplexed looks, but no one dared to ask.

The king stepped back next to the queen and said, "We do hope you can stop whatever it is that is destroying our lands. We will be waiting to hear any news."

As we were standing waiting for our wagon, two large wagons appeared with the guards and Mortice riding a beautiful horse. I must admit the horse he was riding was smaller than the ones I have seen before, but I guess when you're a little person, you don't need a huge horse.

The first wagon to pull out was the horse wagon we had viewed in the garage that had two doors on each side. That carriage was an interesting design as the rear wheels were not under the wagon itself. They looked like they were following it on the very back end. Items had been stacked on top of that space as storage. All the doors could open without hitting anything, and the wheels up front were directly below where people were sitting.

Soon, the second wagon pulled out behind it. I found the view of what I would consider the cab of the wagon very cool. Even though I found that interesting, what I noticed about both carriages were four strange-looking animals in harnesses pulling them. I mean, they looked like horses but more prominent as they were beefy and tall. I thought, *Maybe a Clydesdale or something like that.* All of them were bigger than a regular horse. They almost looked like a cross between a Brahma bull and a Clydesdale, and they were all white.

That second coach was large, with one door in the rear. As I observed it, I noticed I had not paid close attention to the design when we viewed them last night. Today I saw a regular wagon bed up to the top of the sideboards. There looked like a metal band for about two feet on top of that. Then what fit over that was what looked like a roof that spread out about a foot and a half on each side. As I looked closer, I noticed it was the top part of the wagon. It was lowered over another section and fitted to the top rails of the wagon bed. I could visualize this thing now as I viewed it, as if it was a tent trailer. You know, you could get in it and push the top up, attach it, and have more room.

That one also had a cab with two riders in it. The back part was empty at this time from what we could see.

All of us were staring at those wagons, and I knew just about what all of them were thinking because I was sure I was thinking the very same thing. I thought they were amazing. We were all shaking our heads, and we took a deep breath and started looking around to see what was coming next. The next wagon was our old one, which had been created by George, with Jack and Vanessa sitting in the seat.

Suddenly, another coach pulled up on the side of the road and, as soon as our old wagon passed it, that one pulled into the line. It was our new fine-fitted coach, with two soldiers riding behind it. Dohadie's wagon trailed behind our new wagon. When all wagons were in line, they stopped. It gave everyone a chance to check them out and allow us to decide which one we wanted to ride in.

I said to Bailey, "I guess that's the wagon the king gave us."

Some of us climbed into our old wagon, me being one of them as I was not ready to be enclosed in a box going back down that winding road with a long drop. One of the guards was handling the new wagon, with Tasha next to him. A few of the others climbed in the back and were looking out the windows. Dohadie, his brother, and the love of his life were right behind all of us in his wagon.

Mortice yelled, "Okay, everyone, let us move on down the road!"

One after another, all the wagons drove out of the palace gates and through the streets of the town. We stopped at one point where two more buckboard wagons pulled up alongside us. Phil told them to pick up the people who wanted to go down the hill to help rebuild the old town site of Etheral. He gave the drivers directions as to where the people were waiting and then returned to Mortice.

Then I heard him say, "The townspeople will follow all of us down to Lower Etheral, but it will be about a half hour before that happens, so we can carry on now."

Mortice said, "Okay, I will get them moving." He rode to the front of all the wagons, and soon we were in motion again.

As we left, people must have heard all about our leaving. It was as if we were part of a festive event. There were cheers, waving, and some running up with cakes and baskets of food. One guy walked up and then stopped as if being cautious.

I looked at him, saying, "I won't harm you."

He smiled, then finally continued over to me and handed me a bottle. He said, "I could feel your power, which bothered me a bit, but this is for all of you. This is home brew you won't find any place else."

I said, "Well, I am only sixteen and not of age to drink in my world. Maybe I will save it for a special time after we take care of the problems here. Then all of us can try it."

As he was walking along the side of the wagon and we talked, he said, "That would be a good celebration drink for all."

I reached out, and we shook hands. As we did, the man swayed his head to the side and let go of my hand. I thought maybe he was not impressed and just wanted to see us leave now. But when he noticed he was being left behind, he ran back up to me and said, "Whatever you just did, I want to thank you as I have not lived many years of my life without pain, but now all that pain is gone. Thank you."

I replied, "I am pleased I could help you, sir."

"Stay safe, my friend, and come back soon," he said.

Heading back down the mountain gave me a queasy feeling because I was on the side, close to the edge, and each time I snuck a peek over the sideboards of the wagon, I got light-headed and felt weak. I really do hate heights, but the view was extraordinary since I could observe the levels below and even catch sight of that waterfall and how it traveled behind the roads, along with the side of the cliffs.

As we made the next turn to ride back across and down the face of the mountain, I was now facing the homes that had been carved out of the cliff and walks they used to get to their homes. People were standing out front, waving and cheering, and it gave me a good feeling and took away some of the fear of the height. Of course, the next curve placed my side of the wagon facing open space again.

We were lucky to see so far in the distance and enjoy all the beauty of these lands. I understood why so many people live here. They had a view as far as the eye could see. My feelings seemed to expand, and most of what I felt was love, caring, respect, and the fantastic sense of friendship throughout. I thought to myself, *Why can't all countries throughout all worlds have that kind of feeling and care I am feeling right now?*

After arriving back in the town below, our wagons pulled into a largely undeveloped area. As Steve and I walked around, I looked back to the top of the cliffs and said, "That is one trip I really don't care to make very often."

"I hear you, buddy. I didn't mind going up too much, but when we came back down, the foot brake on that wagon was really heating up from what I could tell. All I could think of was our wagon racing down that hill at a hundred miles an hour and crashing."

"I am sure pleased I was not aware of that fact and you didn't tell me as we were coming down the hill."

We both laughed, and he said, "Well, we made it safe and sound. I was really impressed with the king and queen and those elders."

"I was too," I replied.

Bailey had walked up, along with the rest of our group, and everyone agreed that meeting the king and queen was one of the greatest things they had ever experienced.

One of the guards approached us and asked, "Do you have someone to move your wagon, or shall we drive your coach over to the shops?"

"Not sure what you are asking," I said.

"Sir, we have been told to make sure all the wagons are stocked with supplies and provisions that you may need. We set up many things before we came down here, but we still need some supplies for all the wagons. So all the wagons are being moved to the shops now and will be returned in a brief time and be ready to travel."

I asked, "Will they do that for your townspeople who will travel with us as well?"

"Yes, they are doing that for all the wagons, including those traveling to the excavations. In that manner, we will have supplies for a respectable number of weeks. I believe your old wagon will end up being loaded with a few more good bales of straw and supplies, with a tarp added to it to protect everything you have in it."

"Well, if you have a driver, please have him do that as we have to find out what attacked us last night."

"I will have a driver come over and get your wagon," he said.

"Thank you," I replied.

CHAPTER 35

A View of the Past

As we all got settled in a camp area, I said, "Phil, I want to see what that bird was we took down last night."

Steve said, "So do I."

Everyone around us said the same things, and soon, we were trying to figure out what area it landed in.

Phil said, "I would think from what I saw last night it would have landed near a large area with lots of trees on the south side."

"Can we travel over there to see it?" Bailey asked.

"Sure, we can, but we will have to take the horses as the wagons are being set up with more supplies," Phil said.

"Okay, let's get the horses and saddle them up and ride," Steve said as he laughed.

All of us found the guard's horses and one empty wagon with a team of horses. The owner of the wagon said, "We can take mine if you want."

Soon, Phil, Bailey, Steve, Vanessa, and I were riding on horses. Everyone else in the team was situated in the wagon, and we were on our way. As I rode along, I felt rather huge on this horse. It reminded me of riding a Shetland pony at home when I was about twelve years of age. My legs hung almost to the ground, and I was wondering if I was harming the horse by riding on him or her, whichever the case.

I looked over at Bailey. She looked too big for the horse, and so did Steve, so I knew I looked too big.

I yelled out, "Just a minute!" and everyone stopped. I climbed down from my horse and said, "This horse needs a small body on it. I will ride in the wagon."

Soon, Steve, Vanessa, and Bailey were doing the same thing. Smaller people climbed up on the horses as all of us got in the wagon and continued on. Finally, we found the area Phil had talked about.

"I am not sure where it would have landed, but it should be around here someplace," he said as he looked up to the top of the mountain, about where we had been last night.

Everyone climbed down from the wagon, and all the pets turned into their standard forms, saying, "As animals, we should be able to smell it and locate it faster."

I said, "I'm not so sure that is true anymore because all of you have gained stronger senses and feelings. In human form, you may find it faster with the added height to locate it."

Suddenly, all of them stopped as if discussing the issue, and soon all of them were in human forms again. We all spread out over an area that must have been twenty acres and searched for a good two or three hours.

Everyone was yelling back and forth, "Have you found it yet?"

"Not yet!" someone yelled.

Ziggy yelled out, "Hey, Steve, I have a snake over here! Do you want it?"

Steve yelled back, saying, "You can have it!"

Finally, Sam yelled out, "Over here!"

All of us ran over to where it sounded like he was yelling from, and some were shouting back, "Where are you, Sam?"

"Follow my voice. Then you will find me."

Suddenly, he started singing. I was not sure what the song was, but it gave everyone direction. Soon, we were standing over the bird that had flown over us last night.

Steve said, "That is exactly what I thought it was."

Bailey and I were standing there, nodding, and I said, "It's what I was afraid it would be."

"What do you mean?" Bailey asked.

"I was afraid, like you two, that we would find a bird that flew during the same period that dinosaurs roamed our Earth. Now we have to keep in mind a different world with a different set of events."

"Oh, I think I am getting your drift," Steve said.

Phil asked, "What is drift?"

Bailey said, "What he is saying is he feels he understands what Marty is thinking about."

"What is that?" Phil asked.

Steve spoke up and said, "You tell me if I have this correct, Marty. We are dealing with two very different worlds, and one world was hit by a huge asteroid, destroying all the dinosaurs on that one planet. But maybe that never happened on this planet."

"I think you got my drift correctly," I replied.

Bailey asked Phil, "Do you have other large creatures with huge bodies around your planet?"

"We have many here. Some are used for helping move huge rocks and clearing large fields. In some parts of our world, people use them for transportation. Of course, we also have the ones that attack our towns," Phil said.

Vanessa asked, "So what is this thing?"

Steve spoke up and said. "You see, this big bird on the ground in front of us was part of a period where huge animals roamed our world about sixty-five million years ago."

"Sixty-five million years ago?" Heather asked.

I said, "Yes, it was when life forms were developing, but some say a large meteorite hit our Earth. I have heard some say more than one hit our Earth, but what most have agreed on is the fact that ash and dust was so thick that all the sunlight was blocked out for several years. Of course, Heather and Krystle know what happens when plants don't get sunlight, don't you?" As I asked them that question, I turned my head and looked at the twins.

"Of course. Without sunlight, plants cannot live," Krystle said.

Heather added, "Without sunlight, you have no warmth."

"That is true, and not only do plants die from the lack of sunlight, but also the temperatures drop to the point of freezing as well. So, all those creatures like this one died. Some say it was not just the lack of sunlight but also tidal waves and forest fires around the entire world," Bailey added.

"That must have been awful," Ziggy said.

"Well, it was because it destroyed more than 80 percent of all life on our planet at that time," Steve said.

Phil asked, "So, if our planet was like yours and never had that happen, you think we may still have huge beasts roaming our world?"

"I'm not sure, Phil. Why is it that all the cities need huge walls to protect the people?"

"There are a few beasts that are probably fifteen to twenty feet tall and stand like we do, but they have big bodies and small arms and hands and long tails."

Steve was shaking his head back and forth and then said, "Man, I was afraid you would say something like that."

I looked at him and at Bailey. Then we all looked at the thing on the ground in front of us.

I said, "Last year, we talked and wrote reports on dinosaurs, and this one was called a pterodactyl. It was not really considered a dinosaur since it was more of a flying reptile, but lived during the same period in our history. So, maybe this is a freak of nature. Maybe there are no dinosaurs around here."

"But what about the beast Phil just described?" Bailey asked.

"I have no answer for that one, but I do for this one as it's a pterodactyl," I said.

"Well, we have at least one answer," Steve said.

"Yes, but the one Phil described sounds like what they call a T-Rex," Bailey said.

I said, "Yes, I must agree with you, Bailey,"

"You both know we have already seen things in this world that just don't add up. I mean, let's face it. I never in my entire life thought

I would see dragons or run into some old worn-out-looking dog that's a god called Anubis," Steve said.

Bailey and I both agreed.

"Well, all of us need to get back and see if we can help the people who want to rebuild the old townsite of Etheral. If they have monsters here, we need to make sure those people are safe," I declared.

CHAPTER 36

Finding the Problem

All of us were either looking around to find the others or talking about how we just got a brand-new wagon that was fit for a king.

Looking at the people with many different faces I did not recognize, I said, "Let's find a few people who are going to the old town of Etheral."

Steve walked up and said, "You probably remember this guy."

I looked at him and recalled he was the person I spoke to the other night and the same person that was standing in the road as we were headed to Etheral.

I said, "Yes, I do, and I don't think we really exchanged names, but my name is Marty."

He replied, "You're correct, and my name is Anthony. I have rounded up several people from our community who will be working with us to create safe places for the people in the old townsite. I hope you and your team can help with some ideas."

Vanessa commented, "It seems we have a respectable number of people who are coming down to help."

She pointed to the road coming down the hill from Upper Etheral. All of us noticed wagons and hundreds of people as if in a parade was coming down that hill.

As all of us looked around, I said, "It looks like the entire town is coming down that hill to work with us."

Steve was standing there and suggested, "The first thing we should do is look closer at that townsite. It seems we don't have a great distance to walk to get outside of the gates. So why don't all of us go for a hike?"

"A hike?" Anthony asked.

Bailey spoke up and said, "It's like saying let's go for a walk."

"Okay. Well then, let's go for a hike," Anthony said.

Soon, it was as if we had the entire town walking with us to the old townsite, and Anthony turned around and looked behind us, then said to me, "I sure hope that beast won't attack now as I am sure most of these people will not survive."

It was Ziggy who spoke up and said, "They have more protection right now than they have ever had before."

I looked down at Tabby walking next to Bailey and me, then I asked, "Hey, little bit, what are your powers?"

"I can't tell you because that is my secret," she said.

I looked at Bailey then both of us looked down at Tabby, then started to laugh.

Steve asked Anthony, "What does this beast do when it attacks?"

"It seems to simply walk all over everything and crush anything it can, and if people are in his way, he just eats them."

"We need something he can't crush. How big is this thing?" I asked.

"I am not sure what to compare it to, but it stands about four times your height," he said.

As he made that statement, I looked at him, then looked up as if to figure out how tall this thing would be. As I looked back at Anthony, he was shaking his head as if to say, "Yes."

We had walked to the center of the old townsite, and as he gave me that answer, I said, "Okay, let's stop right here. Max, I need you to come over here with me."

"What do you need, Uncle Marty?" he said.

Steve, Bailey, and I all looked at him and just shook our heads. Then I said, "So, now I am your uncle too?"

"Of course, you are, and you're Sam and Snowball's uncle as well."

"Okay, okay, I can see I won't win this one. I need you to come with me. All the rest of you, stay right here."

As we walked, I explained to him that I needed him to imagine in his mind a beast that has a head similar to that of a dragon with no scales, just a head that size. "It has a shorter neck and a body about the same size as Jasmin but walks on two strong large legs and has short arms and small hands. Oh, and you need to have a tail about seven feet long. Do you think you can create something like that?"

"Wow, I thought you were going to ask me to do something simple. Marty, that is an ugly vision you just put in my head."

"What do you think? Can you picture something like that in your mind and create it?"

"I am not sure I can, but give me a bit of room."

I turned and walked back to what looked like the entire town of people. As I did, I started to feel fear and anger. Then I heard yelling and screaming.

Soon, Anthony said, "That's almost what it looks like."

I turned around to see Max had already changed, and he scared the bejeebies out of me. People were yelling and screaming, so I started to grow in height. As I did, people began to quiet down.

I was now about fifteen feet tall and saying, "All of you must understand we can do many things. Max has changed so we have a better idea of what that beast is that is killing people and how big it is. Do not be afraid as we try to learn more about this beast." Then I became my regular size again, turned to look at Max one more time, spun around, and said, "That is what I thought we would be dealing with, Anthony."

"How did you know?" he asked.

"Just a good guess," I said.

Everyone on our team came forward. Bailey and Steve explained what the beast was that all the people had been facing. We knew it was not an exact reproduction of a T-Rex, but it just had to be the vision of something close.

People were saying, "He looks a lot like that monster. Can you make him turn back to the boy we saw, please?"

I turned to Max and said, "Well, we found out what we needed, and now we need to build something that monster can't destroy, and you need to be a boy again."

Max said, "It was bad enough to have that vision in my head, but to try to create that thing was terrible."

"You did an excellent job. Thank you," I said.

Soon, all of us were viewing the structures that were still standing and trying to find out why those have stood all this time and all of the others had been destroyed. Many ideas came into play, and Phil walked up and said, "This is where we need Oscar and Ruther."

I said, "You may be correct."

CHAPTER 37

Creating a Solution

"Okay, we have a few ideas, but I still want to know why some of these walls are still standing when the ones next to them have collapsed," I said.

Many of the townspeople who traveled down from up above started inspecting all the walls that had been destroyed, then checked the ones still standing.

One of the men came over and said, "I am not sure as it seems to me those walls that are still standing are solid slabs of rock to begin with, but they look to be placed in the ground a good depth."

"Okay, we need to find out how deep," Anthony replied.

As we walked over to the one wall still standing, I did notice there was also a wall extending from the main wall, which gave it the shape of a T, so it would have reinforced that main wall, along with the slabs buried in the ground. As I looked around, I could see places that would be great bunkers because so many of the rock slabs were all over the place and could be used for walls and a ceiling if need be.

"Anthony, I saw what looked like subway tunnels in your city. Well, you probably don't have a clue what that is. They are tunnels with steps going down to lower levels. So why can't we do that here and have them go to bunkers where they can be protected? I feel we need to create places that have rock walls and thick rock ceilings that could withstand the weight and movement of the beast?"

"I suppose we could do that as we didn't start creating those tunnels until we were behind walls."

"Okay, let's get some people over here and find out who created those tunnels and find out if we can use some of those rock slabs for the walls."

Jack walked up and said, "Marty, this man worked on designing those tunnels inside of the town."

"Well, it seems this is one of the men we need to put to work right now designing tunnels out here."

He spoke up and said, "I suggest that whatever you build, do it near the face of the mountain or cliff. That way, we can create tunnels into it where people can be safe as the entire mountain will probably remain and not be destroyed."

"Good idea. It's your baby. So run with it," I said.

"I gather 'run with it' means to do the job?" he asked.

"Yes, and it sounds like you're the man for that job."

"Hey, Marty, we have a few more people here that worked on those tunnels and created what the designers gave them!" Steve yelled.

"Okay, Anthony, I need you to get up higher so you can yell at all those people and find all those who worked on those tunnels. Just yell it out and tell them to come up front."

Once he found a suitable location to yell from, he got the attention of many in the crowd. Soon, men and women were coming forward in large groups. Then we had to figure out where we needed to build different exit routes. Bailey was asking everyone coming forward what they had done to help make those tunnels, and she placed different people in separate groups.

Soon, we had construction workers, designers, carpenters, sheet-metal people, and even plumbers. A few in each group worked together to figure out where to start the tunnels, and soon, people were ready to excavate the areas. Others were getting ready to move slabs of stone so they could be placed in positions to make four-foot-wide tunnels that ran off to bunkers where people could be hidden and not seen or heard. Other people started clearing and cleaning up areas, placing old tree branches and brush in piles, and yet others were setting up a place to cook.

Ziggy walked up and said, "Hey, Dad, you got this."

I looked at her and said, "All of you pets are too funny."

"Yes, but you love us," she said.

Over the next few days, we worked with the people to create a safe zone for anyone outside of the gates. We watched and helped all the people building new walls and bracing them so they would not cave in as the last ones did. The process was amazing as every person seemed to have a mission to rebuild this old townsite.

I said to Mortice, "I need someone to go over and speak to Nomi about when he plans to head out to those digs."

"I will send one of the guards to find out and let them know what you're doing here to help these people."

As I was listening to some of the workers, one of them said, "We need some cardo."

I was shaking my head and trying to think about what that was as I have heard that word before. *Cardo, cardo . . .* I was thinking, and then it came to me. "Dynamite." I looked around and asked, "What do you need cardo for?"

"If we dig a huge hole in the ground about ten feet and drop a few sticks in that hole and run, we can make that ground easier to work with and remove it faster," he replied.

"I see. So, that is where the bunkers will be?" I asked.

"Yes. Anthony told us your idea was a good one. We can create solid rooms closer to the cliffs and drill to establish tunnels into the mountain. In case those rooms become unsafe zones, they will have tunnels to enter with exits someplace else."

The entire process was taking less time than I had imagined it would since people were digging, others were cutting slabs of rock, and a few had huge dug-out areas in front of the mountain that would be rooms. Some of the others were already tunneling into the side of the hill at a depth of the bottom of those rooms for more protection.

I noticed Steve, Bailey, and our pets all standing around and discussing something, but could not tell from where I was what they were talking about. When they saw me looking their way, Ziggy said something, and then all of them spread out.

Now what was that all about? I wondered.

As Steve came by with a few new workers, I asked, "Hey what were all of you discussing over there?"

"Not sure what you're talking about, buddy."

I said, "All of you were talking about something a short time ago over there, and when I noticed all of you, Ziggy said something. Then everyone of you scattered."

"Oh, that was nothing at all, just talking about the workers," he said.

"Okay," I said, but I got the feeling he was hiding something. I just brushed it off as something that did not concern me and walked over to the big hole in the ground.

As I did, one of the men yelled at me and said, "You need to get back away from that hole, son, as we are about to set off a charge in it."

So I backed up a reasonable distance and was glad I did because even where I was, I felt the explosion. Soon, a handful of people were jumping into the hole, and others were lowering large buckets in for them to fill. Within hours, they had a room-sized area to put slabs in.

I was watching the operation, and it was taking about twenty men to move a massive portion of rock, so I asked, "Can I try to help you?"

"Be our guest" was the reply from all of them.

I stood there and was not sure I could move it even a small amount, but soon, with all the men around me and some of the strength I had, we were redeploying those enormous slabs of rock.

One of the men said, "How wonderful is that?" and all the rest of the people cheered.

Soon, we had rock slabs in place for the floor, with the walls being put in place, and the roof was next. They had cut that one about two feet wider all around so the ground would be giving more support to the entire project. That way, it would not be just the walls. Men had been tunneling and finally came out in a different location just about the time we were ready to place the last rock slab. Bailey was there, along with the rest of the team, and they were watching all that we had been doing. Once the roof was in place, people went to work, drilling into all the slabs and connecting them all together.

We had not planned on spending a lot of time on this project since we looked forward to traveling west. However, we spent four long days helping with the construction. We walked back to the wagons at night and returned in the mornings. On the fourth day, all of us walked down steps to enter a tunnel that was about six feet high and around four feet wide. As we walked along, we observed a sizeable wooden section that could swing out in place with two large wooden beams next to it. Once closed, those beams would be put in place to keep things out. I was feeling very safe inside of this structure, and soon, we entered a room that had four different areas for people to be secure in.

The walls between the rooms all served as braces for the roof area along with the side walls. It was like walking into a little house made with concrete walls and dividers. In the back was another tunnel that took us into the hillside. We walked for a few minutes where we found another large room inside of the mountain itself.

As we all looked at everything and the construction, Steve said, "They sure know how to carve out a mountain and create space."

Off that large room was another tube. Anthony said, "If people need to escape, they now have two ways to enter that bunker."

I looked at Anthony and said, "All of you have done a fantastic job on this."

He replied, "You mean all of us as it was all of you who gave us ideas and the help we needed to make this happen. We now have plans on two more like this, and as you can see, we have had people working on the walls of the old buildings. Those are now reinforced and will not be easy for anything to knock down."

I asked him, "Will you be able to work in shifts to create the next bunkers and tunnels and be safe while we are gone?"

"I believe we will as we now have good crews of people for all the jobs that have to be done and we won't need the entire town out here watching. We can now work in crews and create our old Etheral one more time. If the beast returns while you're away, we will have safe places to run to."

CHAPTER 38

Locating Nomi

As all our team started to walk back through the crowd of people after four days of work, we were being touched and talked about all the way. We knew we were healing others as they contacted us, and each of us felt as though it was not something that was draining our powers, so we treated all those we could.

People were clapping and cheering, waving and yelling, "Thank the lords!" Someone else yelled, "Thank you, Mother Earth!"

By the time we returned, I expected to find an outraged Nomi and crew sitting and wondering how soon we could leave. To our surprise, we had a trail of people following us and discovered it was Nomi and some of his excavation crew. They had been helping with the design of the bunker and those tunnels.

I said, "It's Nomi Tinder, correct?"

"Yes, it is, Marty." he replied. He walked over and said, "That was pretty amazing what all of you did to help our people. I know that area will soon be a safe zone for anyone caught outside of the walls from now on."

As I turned to look at all those around me, I said, "I think we have a really great team, and you have many fantastic workers."

Bailey said, "We need to know what kinds of things we might be facing in that area we will be traveling in besides the unknown and invisible. We get the impression you have creatures and beasts here on your planet that have long since been destroyed on ours."

I said, "That is true from what we have already seen and heard. One of those beasts is what we call a T-Rex. It's what we call a dinosaur or a fossil."

"We have some extraordinary beasts, but in most cases, they keep to themselves, and it's not often anymore they travel this far," Nomi said.

"I know the wagons have been stocked, but is there anything all the people don't know that they should? I thought if we have a need for special items, Jack could make a list and hand it to the guards to fill."

Nomi stated, "I think the soldiers know more about what will be needed than we do. We always purchase what we need for a few weeks at a time. Then we add another week's worth of items in case of emergencies. From what I understand, the king has filled all our wagons this time with supplies and any items we may have a use for."

"Is he always that caring about the people?" Steve asked.

"Yes, he is. We used to have royalty that would simply look down on all the people and treat all of us as if we were slaves. People wanted change, and soon, all of us chose who would control our lives. All of us made that change. This king and queen have been our royalty for many years, and everyone loves them as they make sure all people are able to work, have a home, food, can always see a doctor, and have good lives."

"That is amazing," Bailey said.

"How soon will you be heading out?" I asked.

"Heading out?"

"Yes, how soon will it be before you head out to the excavations?"

"We can leave as soon as we all get organized," Nomi said.

"We would like to check out our wagons and make sure everything is ready. Then I guess we will be ready to move out with you," I said. As Burdock walked up from one of the shops, I asked him, "Do we have everything we need to hit the road?"

"All the wagons have been equipped with supplies they did not get up on the hill. Food, along with water, was put in place today as they figured we would leave soon. We should be ready to go, Marty." he replied.

"Steve, how are we doing?"

"Good," he replied.

Bailey said, "They made sure we have more bales of straw in the old wagon."

"Glad to hear that," I said.

"How many wagons do we have going?" Steve asked.

"We have our two, Dohadie has one, and the local townspeople who want to travel, help, and cook have theirs and then, of course, those two wagons for the soldiers. There may be one other wagon, but I am not sure. The blacksmiths arrived while we were up on the hill, and they have one. A few of the people from here are traveling along with us. I think more than anything, they just want to witness the events and actions," Burdock replied.

"Well, that's fine if those people are traveling just to see what will happen. But please be sure they have been supplied with plenty of food and water. Also, ask them if they have planned for cold or heat. Above all, if things start happening, ask them to be sure and stay back," I said.

CHAPTER 39

Checking Out the Wagons

One of the guards was walking his horse back alongside the wagons as he seemed to be checking them for any problems.

I walked up to him and said, "Your name is Mortice, correct?"

"Yes, sir," he replied.

"I understand the king considers you one of his best guards. But tell me, is that your real name?"

"Yes, sir, my name is Mortice Rebello, at your service. Your name is Marty, correct?"

"Yes, it is, my friend. Will you be riding in one of the wagons?"

"The king gave me an excellent horse for my use. I will be riding her for the time being. The king has asked me to lead the rest of the troops he is sending as well."

"It looks like we have some very nice wagons," I said.

"Yes, they have sleeping quarters, storage for food, supplies, and, of course, a place for our horses to ride as we change them out."

Jack, Steve, a few of the girls, and a couple of our pets were standing there, and of course, all of them had not really looked inside of those wagons like Bailey had. So off they went to look around.

"I have been informed one of those new wagons belongs to your team now. Our workers took immense pride in what they created. The workmanship on these wagons is fit for royalty," he said.

All of us looked inside of the wagons that seemed to expand outward from the top of the sideboards. We had a view of the crown, which could be raised for more room as it had a cranking system to lift it. The floor area was raised up from the base of the wagon, and you could tell it was a storage area as there were compartment doors flush with the floor. Each side of the carriage was set up with fold-down bunk beds and pull-out couches, which would become beds for people to sleep on.

"You can get inside and raise the entire roof area another two feet, which gives you space for those top two beds to be used if need be," Mortice commented.

"I noticed this wagon in your garage or barn, whatever you wish to call it, and at first, it seemed like a regular wagon until I noticed the metal band all the way around," I said.

"Yes, the design is special as it allows for enormous amounts of storage and comfort," he said.

As we looked, we found storage areas along the inside walls as well. I walked up and opened a door, looked inside, shook my head, turned to all the rest, and said, "I guess you won't need a bush anymore, but you may have to contend with a line."

"What are you talking about, Marty?" Vanessa asked.

"I am talking about how Bailey yelled out about having a toilet. All of you need to look for yourselves."

As I was walking back out, others were walking in, passing me to see what I had been talking about. The pets were changing into people so they could have a good look. Some of them were saying, "They even have toilet paper and a sink to wash up."

I walked over to Mortice and said, "You will have to make sure we know more about how to take care of that."

As we viewed the outside, he pointed out long storage cabinets mounted under where the upper section bowed outward from the top of the wagon bed. From the back, the look of the wagon reminded me of a lightbulb. The lower part alone gave us plenty of room for storage space.

I said, "This is amazing."

"Yes, it is," Mortice agreed.

As we walked to the front, he showed us how the cab could be used for sleeping. There was more storage space on the top of the cab.

As we finished the tour, Mortice called his men over and asked them, "Have all the supplies been placed in the wagons?"

One of the guards spoke up and said, "All the wagons are stocked with supplies, tarps, long-lasting food, blankets, shovels, at least four canvas boats, and even heavy coats in case they are needed."

I asked, "Does it really get cold here?"

"It does from time to time, and when it does it can become life-threatening, it can be on us in no time flat," he replied.

I said, "That's like some of the weather in a few places back home."

The soldiers showed us the horse trailer loaded with hay, water, and food for the animals, and I was as surprised as the rest of the people at the amount of room in that wagon.

Mortice told me, "I will ride in front following the excavation wagons, and my men will be spaced out between the wagons and a couple in the back."

I got the feeling we would soon be in what I remember wagon trains to be from stories, TV shows, and photos in books. I must admit it was an exciting feeling, and everyone gathered around all of us, talking about how exhilarating this was.

"Okay, when we leave, we will need a driver for both wagons. Who is it going to be?" I asked.

Jack said, "I can take care of either one, but I am used to the one we have been traveling in so far. So how about if I take that one?"

"That's fine with me, but you will also need a rider."

As soon as I said that, Burdock said, "I can ride up front with Jack."

I looked at him and said, "I thought you were happy riding with your brother and Datilina."

He replied, "I have not had a bit of sleep since those two got back together, and I need a break. All they do is talk, talk, talk, and if that's not bad enough, when they are not talking, they are like two idiopids bouncing around."

Bailey said, "Now that is a new one on me. What the heck is that?"

Jack spoke up and said, "They look like small children, in a manner of speaking, but have the facial features of what Tabby is as a kitten, with big round eyes. Their bodies are covered in hair, just like Tabby, but have hands and feet that are similar to a person. Small animals, but they always look so sad."

"Yes, they look sad until they find a mate. Then they become happy and bounce around like one big furry ball," Burdock commented.

I said, "Well, Burdock, sounds like you might get more sleep over here with all of us."

Tasha spoke up and said, "I can handle the new one, and it seems we will be riding in real comfort."

Sophia asked, "Can I sit up front too?"

Bailey said, "That's fine with me as I will probably be riding in the old wagon on lots of new straw."

Of course, a few like Heather and Krystle, along with Sam and Snowball, said, "I want to ride in the new wagon."

I spoke up and commented, "Well, Bailey, if you're riding in the old wagon, I guess I can force myself to join you."

As she turned and gave me a blithe look, she replied, "Marty, you do what you must, but just be sure and understand I don't wish to force you to do anything. I can travel in that wagon without you as I will have Ziggy and the rest with me."

Ziggy, who was always at my side, was now standing next to Bailey, and she had a big grin on her face and said, "Yup, hotshot, you do what you feel is right. No one here wants to force you to do anything."

Steve looked at me, and we both looked at Ziggy, and I asked, "Did that really come out of your mouth?"

"Yup, it sure did. Steve taught me that."

As I turned and looked over at Steve, he turned away and was laughing and stomping his feet. Then it seemed we had a full group laughing.

CHAPTER 40

Bailey Spills the Beans

Bailey asked me, "Have you contacted your mom lately?"

"No. Why?"

"I think they are on their way over here."

Steve walked up and said, "Oh, nice job, Bailey, as my mom contacted me last night also and told me. But it was supposed to be a surprise for Marty."

"I thought they were getting in touch with him, too," Bailey said.

Tasha asked, "Is Meesha with them?"

"Yes, she is."

"How are they coming over here?"

"They said they left a few days ago by wagon and should be at Mike and Marilyn's today or tomorrow," Bailey commented.

"Well, that is several days from here," I said.

"You know we can change that," Steve said.

"What are you talking about, and how can we change that?"

"We have this little guy called Max, you know, my little buddy who can fly."

"That is true. But how do we make sure that more than one person can ride as he is flying? You do remember I have flown with him, and it was not that easy for me."

"Max and all the rest of us have been talking about that," Ziggy said.

"So, that is what all of you have been discussing that you didn't want me to hear about?"

"This is what we came up with." Steve walked to the wagon and pulled back a tarp.

I looked at it and asked, "What the heck is that?"

CHAPTER 41

A Seat to Fly In

"It's a special seat made for an eagle that will allow three people to sit comfortably, with a small case behind the seat for storage. We estimate it will take half the time for Max to fly up there and back than it took us by wagon. That means if Max leaves now, he can be there in a day, maybe a day and a half, and be back here within about three to three and a half days total," Jack replied.

"Who is taking care of the farm?" I asked.

Vanessa spoke up and said, "Mom and Dad are."

Bailey explained, "Our dads were over there as they wanted to see Jasmin and Sky. Then they returned home to button things up. They are traveling over tomorrow, with George picking them up at the stream in the morning."

"Wow! You guys have been planning all this and not telling me?"

Bailey said, "I am sorry I spoiled it all, Marty."

"It's okay. So how are we going to make this work?" I asked.

"Max!" Steve yelled.

Max walked over to us, looked at everyone, and asked, "Are we going to do it?"

I looked at all of them and gave them a look that probably portrayed, "What the heck?" Then I asked, "Are you sure it will be safe for everyone, including Max?"

"Yes, we believe so," Steve said.

"So, Max, are you ready for a long flight?" I asked.

"You bet. Let's get it done."

"Do all of you want to do this now? I asked.

"Marty, it's like you always love to tell me — 'I will never get an answer unless I ask.' Well, now what I am saying is 'Why put off till tomorrow what we can accomplish today?'" Steve replied.

Soon, all of us moved people back so we could make sure Max had room to grow into a new form of transport. Many people were asking, "What's going on?"

We were all gathered in the center of the field. Suddenly, Max, the young man, opened his arms as if to put on a show, and people all around us just stopped whatever they were doing or talking about and watched what was about to happen.

He waved his arms and told the people, "Stand back," and as soon as he said that, he changed into a small eagle.

The people could not believe what was taking place. People all over came to see what had just happened, and all we could hear were "*oohs*" and "*aahs*" and "Look at that." Some of them wanted to get closer to see what the neat little bird had become.

I spoke out in a voice that was loud enough to be heard on top of the cliffs, saying, "Please continue to watch but stand back."

Bailey said, "Look up on top of the mountain."

All of us turned our heads to see what she was pointing to, and we saw what looked like a thousand people all along that ridge watching what was happening down here. Even the people in those homes along the side of the mountain were on the walks. Many who were traveling up and down the road going to the top stopped just to view what was happening below. It was like people all standing around for a good old-fashioned Fourth of July fireworks display. Many of those people who had been outside of the gates were running in to see what was going on, and soon the crowds we had around us outside were around us here.

Everyone was watching that small eagle begin to grow. Soon, most of the townspeople who had gathered around us looking at Max were backing up to give him room. As he grew and grew, everyone seemed to get more excited because they had the chance to see something, they have never seen before. Some were saying, "I can't believe that a young man can become a beast, a kid, and now a bird that is growing so huge."

He finally reached a size that Steve thought was just about right. Then we placed the harness on him and secured it. Max was now the size of a small four-passenger plane, only this one had no window to block the cold air.

"How does that feel, Max?" Steve asked.

"I think it's just as we figured it would be, and it feels good. Now I need to grow a bit more to fit the harness better."

Steve, Bailey, and I walked around him and checked the straps and made sure everything was in place properly.

"Max, don't you take any chances. If you run into trouble, you dump this thing and just continue to the farm in a different manner. Do you understand me?" I said.

"I understand, Marty, but this will work. Rest assured, if I have problems, I will dump it."

"Okay, buddy. Be safe."

Tasha asked, "Is he headed back to the camp now?"

"Yes, he is," Steve replied.

"Why? Do you want to go back to the camp?" I asked.

"That would be great if I could as I know I can help back there, and I do miss Meesha."

"You won't be able to ride back, you know. At least, not at this time."

"That is fine with me if Meesha and I can be together."

"Okay, get what you need and climb on board. Then get ready to fly. You will need to make sure you're strapped in tight."

Bailey said, "In that basket are blankets because I am sure it may be cold flying."

Heather said, "Just a minute. You can't just leave without food and water for both of you."

"Good idea," Steve said.

242

Tasha ran and got a bag, which must have had some clothes and personal items. Then she climbed up in the seat and said, "I am ready anytime all of you are."

Heather came back with a basket of food, water, and her orange additive, set it in the seat next to Tasha, then she secured it in place.

Krystle came over with a blanket, handed that to Tasha, and said, "Use this one so you won't have to dig through that other basket. Just wrap up in it as I have found it to be really warm."

"Thank you both," Tasha spoke.

Soon, Max was rising to his feet, claws, or whatever you wish to call them, and he was stepping away from the crowds and flapping his wings. People in front of him were moving out of his path, creating a runway. Within a matter of minutes, he was in the air. People everywhere, from the top of the cliff to all the people around us, were cheering, yelling, and whistling, and we even heard a few horns blow around us and high up on the side of the mountain. Soon, they were circling around us, with Tasha waving to all below.

"Boy, I sure wish I had a camera," Steve said.

"You and me both, my friend," I said.

Everyone from the top of that mountain, the walkways around the face of the cliffs, and around us all looked like they were just staring at Max and Tasha in an unbelievable manner. Mortice, the young guard, was watching along with all the rest of the guards, and his mouth was wide open. His eyes were as large as they could get.

I walked up and said, "Now that is amazing, don't you think?" He turned and looked at me with his mouth still open, and I said, "You can close your mouth now."

He shook his head and lowered it a bit and then looked at me, and we both laughed.

He was still laughing as he turned to the others, seeing all of them looked about the same, then said, "I guess I am not alone."

"No, you're not alone, my friend."

Everyone was waving goodbye and whistling and yelling up a storm. No, there was no real storm. This is only a figure of speech telling you everyone was excited and happy.

BOOK FOUR
COMING SOON

LOOKING AHEAD...

As the people load up into the wagons and head out to the western region, everyone is excited to be traveling once again.

We have heard about large excavations in the old townsites of the giants, so we are looking forward to finding out more about those.

We have heard there are many dig sites heading west and after we reach the west-most area, we will find a mountain range where the giants built their empire. The three of us have been learning more about the powers we have, but I feel shortly we will all be learning a lot more.

This time, it seems we have more than invisible beings and creatures as dinosaurs have never been something all of us have expected to see or must deal with. However, this is not home, and I am sure pleased we have powers to confront what we are about to face.

The following is just a taste of the first Chapter of Book 4

CHAPTER 1

Heading To The Excavations

"Load them up, fall in line, and let's rock and roll," I yelled.

Then it dawned on me, Tasha would have been driving one of the wagons. I turned and looked at the sky one more time. I looked all around, and Bailey walked up to me, then asked, "Well, who is the person holding the reins of this new wagon?"

I looked at her with what must have been a very flushed, and stupid, expression. I shook my head and said, "Well, I guess, it's you and me." So, Bailey and I climbed up front, and she held Tabby in her lap. I gave Steve a mental thought and asked, *Where are you going to be riding?*

He replied, *Those who are not riding in our old wagon, are climbing into the back of this new coach. We are finding we have a lot of seats, so I will be riding next to Vanessa.*

I sent a thought to Ziggy asking, *Are you with Bailey and me in the cab of this new wagon?*

Ziggy replied, *You bet, just a minute.* Then she came running over and hopped up front, with Tabby and the two of us.

I noticed Jack and Sophia driving our old wagon with Max, Sam, Snowball and Agatha riding in the back. They pulled up behind the wagon for the excavation crew. Then both of those wagons started to move out.

As I was getting ready to move the wagon Steve sent me a mental message, *Can I please see your driver's license?*

I just laughed, and I whipped the reins as I had seen George and Tasha do, then suddenly, those horses just started to move.

Soon, we looked like one of those old wagon trains. From the wild, wild West, with a dozen well-armed soldiers and wagons filled with animals and people. We were all now leaving town. Mortice was riding in front of all of us, just behind the carriages of the excavation crew. Then it was our old wagon, then a few soldiers with us behind them. The rest of the coaches and guards were riding at different locations behind us. It looked like the guards had a good idea of how to protect every wagon and each person.

Many conversations were flowing up front and in the back of the wagon.

Vanessa said, "This is so roomy and comfortable with padded seats. This is luxury compared to the wagon my father built."

Steve said to Vanessa, "George is going to have to create some wagons like this."

She said, "I am going to have to tell him all about this one."

Bailey and I were talking about the comforts of the new wagon and Bailey said, "I am so impressed with the fact it even has a toilet in it."

I said, "Yes, yes. I think almost everyone knows you're impressed with that feature, but I need to find out how often it has to be emptied and what they use to keep the smell down."

Bailey asked, "What do you really think we will find out there where we are going?"

"I don't know, but I do know whatever it is will be facing a tremendous amount of power. What is weird, is I have no feelings of anything being destroyed in any direction around us."

"Maybe it's further away than you can feel," Bailey commented.

"Maybe. But my feelings have been covering longer ranges lately. I guess I will feel it when we get closer to the events."

We spent the entire day traveling, and Nomi stopped and walked back to tell us, "We will be at one of the digs soon."

"We are following all of you," I said.

As we continued to travel, we passed areas of rocks that looked like something was dropped into a water bucket. You know, how you get a splash and water shoots out in different directions. That is what this landscape looked like. It had vast mountains, many large trees, but not the size we viewed back near Etheral. All of the colors that seem to be painted on all of the mountainsides reminded me of photos I had seen of the Bad Lands back home.

Suddenly we heard a knock, knock, knock, and Bailey and I turned to look at each other expecting to see the other person doing the knocking. Then it came again, knock, knock, knock. As I was looking at her, both of us turned to see where the noise was coming from. Bailey reached up and flipped a latch, and a small panel moved to one side, and we were soon looking at a little face. Heather said, "This is so nice back here, and we even have a toilet with rolls of paper."

Everyone in the back laughed, and so did we. I said, "All of you seem to have a toilet fascination for some reason."

"Well, it is nice to know we have one in case we need it," Krystle replied.

Be sure to ride along with us in Book Four

THOSE TRAVELING TO ETHERAL

Marty
Steve
Bailey
Ziggy
Tabby
Max
Vanessa
Krystle
Heather
Sam
Snowball
Jack stargazer
Burdock
Tasha,
Datilina
Sophia Atherton

Who we meet as we travel
Emmitt Bastion — the birdman
Marta — owner of the laundry and bathhouse in Molumphy
Sophia Atherton — waitress at Bobbles Burrow
Bobbles Burrow – café in Molumphy
Tony Matthews and his wife, Becky — store owners in Molumphy
Dohadie — Burdock's brother and street vendor

Averell, Mincer, and Tangent — the elders of Etheral
Haskin and Natalie — the king and queen of Etheral
Nomi Tinder — excavation expert
Manna Day — the lady who spoke to travelers and said she could cook

Envoys from the King, Queen, and Elders
Mortice Rebello — captain of the guard for the king and queen
Philip Danassia — captain of the guard for the elders

At the Home Base
Mike and Marilyn – April Roberts, brother and sister-in-law
Ruther — carpenter
Oscar — engineer
Magic — cook
Mathew Gaspard — runs the sawmill
Winterish — protector of the camp

Traveling to the Farm
George and April Roberts
Meesha
Sky and Jasmin flying up above

At the Farm
Marie Daniels — Marty's mom
Wanda Rogers — Steve's mom
Catrina Anderson — Bailey's mom
Mary — Marty's grandmother

Monsters and Gods
Medina — goddess of the forest
Targus – a beast with it's head in his chest.
Anubis — keeper of the dead

Things of Interest

Raniango — looks as big as a horse but has horns, lots of hair, and red eyes and spits out juice that burns and melts people (oh, and it has a bad temper)

Scroll — tab or credit

Scriptable — money

Denarians — what we call dwarfs back home

Redbird — bursts into flame for protection and vanishes

Molumphy — a town south of the team's home base

Bobbles Burrow — a café in Molumphy

Charros — potatoes

Topo — corn

Hawkins — llamas

Primary race — the human race

Pew yews — skunks

Tempts — coins

Ledkin — first Denarian village over the falls

Cartful act — circus act

Tanners — bats

Bejeebies — scaring the hell out of someone

Mistress Emerson — said in place of foul words, so if someone were religious, they would not be offended by a four-letter word

Tootler — a whopper

Cardo — dynamite

Twirlers — short for cyclones, twisters, or tornadoes

Old Etheral — oldest Denarian townsite

Lower and Upper Etheral — Denarian towns

Horses pulling the king's and our team's new wagon — four strange-looking animals in harnesses pulling the large wagons. They are like horses, only more significant than the ones the guards are riding. All of them are bigger than regular horses. They almost look like a cross between a Brahma bull and a Clydesdale, and they are all white.

Idiopids — look like small children, in a manner of speaking, but have the facial features of a kitten with big round eyes. Their bodies are covered in hair, but they have hands and feet like a person. Small animals, but they always look so sad until they find a mate. Then they become happy and bounce around like one big furry ball.

Smackers — something that seems so great, it comes up and smacks you between the eyes

57301977R00161

Made in the USA
Middletown, DE
29 July 2019